ONLY ONE WAVE:
THE TSUNAMI EFFECT

An FBI & CDC Thriller–Book 3

JENIFER RUFF

COPYRIGHT

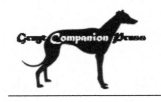

BOOKS BY JENIFER RUFF

The Agent Victoria Heslin Series
The Numbers Killer
Pretty Little Girls
When They Find Us
Ripple of Doubt
The Groom Went Missing

The FBI & CDC Thriller Series
Only Wrong Once
Only One Cure
Only One Wave: The Tsunami Effect

The Brooke Walton Series
Everett
Rothaker
The Intern

Suspense
Lauren's Secret

ACKNOWLEDGEMENTS

This book is dedicated to my younger brother. He knows just about everything there is to know about history, government, and national and global security. He is kind enough and patient enough to answer my questions and explain things while I scribble notes as fast as I can.

CHAPTER ONE

Saturday morning started like any other April day on Nalowale Island. Sunshine, a pleasant ocean breeze, and a pace a little slower than just about everywhere else.

Captain Craig Barstow marched down a path toward the ocean, appreciating the sweet-scented air. He would miss the island when his deployment ended. There were far worse jobs than guarding old bunkers in a peaceful, tropical setting.

With Barstow walked Colonel Tim Nelson, a former champion swimmer and the best boss Barstow ever had. Demanding but fair, the Colonel treated all the Airmen with respect.

As they headed south, toward the sound of waves crashing gently against the shore over the next hillside, an edgy feeling crept through Barstow's veins, as if he had consumed four cups of coffee rather than his usual two. He pulled a small container from his pocket. Snuff. It always helped calm his nerves. He pinched some between his thumb and forefinger, almost dropping it when one of the German Shepherds from the base galloped past. The dog was breathing hard and dripping wet.

"Tank is acting weird. Don't you think?" Barstow held the snuff under his nostril and inhaled. "Maybe he caught rabies."

Colonel Nelson's gaze followed the animal. "Our dogs can't get rabies. They get vaccinated for everything."

Tank came to an abrupt stop on the path ahead. Snorting and shaking his head, he dug into the ground with one paw, sending dirt flying out behind him.

"He's acting strange," Barstow said. "Like he's jacked up on something, pacing and running everywhere. He usually lies down every chance he gets. I haven't seen him be still all day."

Tank jerked his head up and tensed, his shoulders trembling.

A swamp rat darted out from the bushes and sprinted across the path.

Tank raced after it.

The rat slid under a tight thicket of brush and disappeared.

Without hesitating, Tank forced himself through the tangle of thick brush, ramming his body past the spiky branches that dug into his sides, tearing fur and flesh. From behind the wall of bloodied bushes, a frenzy of snarls mixed with dying squeals.

"What the—?" Barstow said. "See? Nothing normal about that. That had to hurt like hell. I told you, there's something wrong with that dog."

Above them, tropical birds screeched and flew off in a panic-stricken flock. A humming noise filled the air, growing louder. The ground vibrated.

Placing a hand on his weapon, the Colonel slowly turned in a tight circle.

The rolling, unsettling sensation underfoot grew stronger. Barstow instinctively widened his stance as fruit fell from nearby trees and hit the earth with soft plopping sounds.

2

The humming intensified to a roar, like an approaching freight train…except there were no trains on the island.

Barstow locked eyes with the Colonel. "What's happening?"

Corded muscles tightened in Colonel Nelson's neck as he continued to scan their surroundings. "Earthquake?"

▼▲▼

On the south side of Nalowale Island, near Market Street, Ben hoisted his ten-year-old body up a coconut tree. Two ropes circled the tree's trunk. One he'd wrapped around his waist, the ends of the other he gripped in his hands. Digging his bare feet into the bark, he shimmied his way higher. He was getting good at climbing, if he did say so himself. He aimed for the fruit at the top, but grabbing it was just an excuse to practice his skills and strengthen his muscles. His mother would be mad if she saw him up there. She said she loved him more than anything in the whole wide world and couldn't bear for him to get hurt. Whenever she found him in his favorite look-out tree, she stared up with fear in her eyes. He didn't want her to feel afraid. That's why he only climbed when she wasn't around to see him. Now was one of those times. She was in a store looking for a job. She'd recently been fired from the one at the fancy new vacation complex.

High enough to reach the coconuts, Ben punched one from its stem. The fruit plummeted down and hit the ground with a thump, landing near his phone and soccer ball. As Ben watched, thinking he might be imagining things, the ball suddenly moved on its own, like an invisible foot was nudging it from side to side.

Shouting came from the beach.

With a bird's-eye view, Ben squinted into the sun toward the sea. A peculiar white foam topped the blue water. And there was something else different out there. The beach seemed wider, which didn't really make sense, but he was seeing it with his own eyes. The tide was pulling away from the shore, farther and farther back, leaving a growing expanse of the sandy ocean floor exposed.

3

The usual chatter ceased. People stood still and gaped at the ocean. Two teens carrying surf boards jogged toward it. A woman grabbed her kids and ran in the opposite direction, leaving toys and a basket behind on their blanket.

A massive wave rose from the water and lurched forward.

The surfers changed directions and ran.

Along the row of stores, car alarms started wailing and honking.

Ben's heart hammered away in his chest.

The wave rose higher and higher, thundering toward the shore like a roaring monster.

Just when Ben thought it would never stop growing and it would reach the clouds, the colossal wave curled over, towering as if suspended by a powerful hand, then crashed down. An enormous wall of water swallowed the shore, snapping trees like toothpicks, snatching people up like ants blasted with a hose.

Frozen with fear, Ben clung to the tree. The wave hurtled past the beach toward Market Street. Water engulfed the road, lifting cars and buses, sweeping them along with it, barreling straight toward him. He screamed and gripped his ropes, hanging on as the wave smashed the tree and sent him spiraling around its trunk. The water ravaged past, exploding the Pharmacy's glass walls, devouring the bakery, the Police Station, the mayor's office, the Fresh Mart, the Dollar Store, and the Island Mercantile. But Ben's tree remained standing. A loud rush of air clogged his ears and yet he heard the shattering and flattening occurring at break-neck speed around him. He watched it all in mystified horror. In slow motion, the tree toppled into the roiling water with Ben still attached.

Up and down, the tree tossed and turned in the ferocious brown swirl. Ben kept his death grip on the rope. Where the tree went, he would go, as long as he could hold on. Careening. Reeling. Sputtering. Suffocating. He gasped and choked, gulped a breath before getting yanked back under. Unseen objects attacked him. Jabbing. Pulling. Something big. Something hard. Something small. Something sharp. Another quick breath. Back under. On and on. Again and again.

And then, when he wasn't sure he was alive anymore, or if he wanted to be, he was above the water. He sucked in the deepest breath he could manage, preparing to get jerked under. It didn't happen. He retched and vomited salty water. The sea calmed. He floated on the tree, his cheek pressed against the trunk. Exhausted and battered. The sun beat down on his back, and he shivered.

Eventually, Ben opened his eyes, blinking in the strong sunlight. Every part of him throbbed or ached or stung. The skin around his right eye burned. So did his hands. Still gripping his ropes, he lifted his head, and looked around.

Where there had once been stores and streets, a brown lake strewn with garbage surrounded him. Boards. Shards. Giant sheets of metal. Layers of ugliness and destruction thrown together. Looking for something familiar, anything to anchor him, he spotted the bright red roof of The Fresh Mart sticking out from under water. Everything else—the storefronts, buildings, and signs that formed the south side of his island—crushed, mangled, and smashed into unrecognizable forms. Or gone.

A body floated past, face down. And then another.

Ben squeezed his eyes shut again and prayed his mother was safe.

5

CHAPTER TWO

Dr. Madeline Hamilton, Director of Special Projects with the Centers for Disease Control, studied the disturbing before and after satellite images of Nalowale Island. She couldn't reconcile the difference between the photos. In the first set, the south shore was calming shades of turquoise meeting white sands then bright emerald-green vegetation. In the subsequent images, a ravaged brown mess replaced the vibrant colors. The pictures humbled her. The power of nature could make anyone feel small and helpless. Setting the photos aside, she adjusted her focus, concentrating on what her boss had to say about her new assignment.

Sitting behind his desk, Patrick Wallen crossed his arms. "Nalowale is an unincorporated U.S. territory approximately twenty square miles. About the same size as Bermuda. There's an Air Force base with fewer than two hundred military personnel and a civilian population of around ten thousand people. Two days ago, a magnitude seven-point-zero earthquake occurred along the ocean floor, seventy miles south of the island, causing the tsunami. A NASA satellite caught an image of a wave. Six meters high. The world has certainly experienced larger, but Nalowale is a small island. The wave hit the south side hard."

Madeline's gaze returned to the images beside her. "As soon as I get there, I'll do an outbreak assessment and set up a surveillance system to deal with the natural disaster. I need an estimate of the impacted population to determine the size of my team."

Wallen settled back in his chair. "Actually, you'll be going alone. The Secretary of Health and Human Services has already imposed travel restrictions."

"Alone?" Madeline scrunched her forehead, thinking she might have misheard.

"You'll be guiding the medical staff who are already on the island."

"What specifically am I guiding them toward?"

"On how to prevent an isolated public health crisis from becoming an epidemic."

Madeline remained silent for a few seconds, her hands resting in her lap, thinking about what her boss had just told her, and what he *wasn't* telling her. And that was a lot. "We're not talking about the type of outbreak illnesses that typically follow a tsunami, are we?"

Wallen shook his head. "The island is experiencing a wave of symptoms characterized by hyperactivity and violent behavior. They're not sure what it's about. The outbreak has already led to military and civilian deaths."

Madeline frowned. "That doesn't sound like anything a natural disaster would cause."

"No. It doesn't." Her boss turned away and stared out the window. Madeline followed his gaze. Flowering crab apple trees and azalea bushes filled the view.

"Unfortunately, we have very little information," Wallen said. "The tsunami took out cell towers and communications are limited. In some ways, that's a good thing. After everything that happened with Covid-19, no one wants to chance this outbreak spreading. Nor do they want word of it getting out. Not until we know what we're dealing with. Our economy can't afford to take another hit."

"Interesting. Well, you know I can keep quiet if necessary. *And* if warranted."

"Yes. Thanks to your commendable work with the outbreak in D.C., people trust you to be discreet. And when I say people, I mean the most powerful people in the country. President Moreland or one of her cabinet members specifically requested you make this trip."

"Should I be honored or disappointed?" Madeline offered a weak smile. "Because I'm not sure what to think."

"It's an honor, Madeline, although…it might not feel like one when you get there."

"Great, Patrick." She offered a slight smile. "Sure you don't want to come with me?"

"We arranged for you to leave tomorrow." Wallen slid a black bag across his desk toward her. "There's a satellite phone and laptop inside. Those will be your only means of communication with us—with anyone—while you're there."

"Guess I better get packing."

Wallen pushed his chair back and got up. "Be careful, Madeline."

CHAPTER THREE

Madeline grabbed her toiletry travel bag from under the bathroom cabinet. An unopened pregnancy test kit rested on top of her curling iron. Where she was going, she would not need either item. She had packed comfortable, casual clothing. Nothing fancy. Her baggage mostly comprised diagnostic tools. Experiences, her own and years witnessing her parents' missionary work in Nicaragua, El Salvador, and Haiti, made her confident she could bear any accompanying personal discomfort.

A tsunami, like all natural disasters, would heighten any inherent weaknesses in a community, testing the limits of infrastructure and individuals on every level. The opportunity to help solve an epidemiological mystery made Madeline eager to get to Nalowale sooner rather than later, before the situation worsened and more people died.

Placing two large tubes of sunscreen in a Ziploc bag, a wave of sentimentality washed over her—a premature sense of nostalgia. This assignment was bittersweet. Thinking about what lay ahead in her personal future, the plans she hoped, God-willing, would come to fruition…her work on Nalowale might be her last trip of a high-risk nature, at least for a long while.

Madeline's phone rang as she rolled her packed suitcase into the corner of her bedroom. She grabbed the device off her nightstand, glanced at Quinn's name on the screen, and smiled as she answered the call.

"Hello," her fiancé said. "Are you home?"

"Yes. I left work early because the dishwasher got delivered. All the new appliances are in the garage now, except for the refrigerator. And Fred dropped by. He needed to get more measurements and run a few things by me."

"Again? Jeez. I know your friend recommended Fred, and he does good work, but he's a little high maintenance."

In front of the mirror, Madeline let her shoulder-length chestnut hair down. "He is. I think he wants us to approve every detail so we can't complain about anything later. Anyway, he was available and can work within our budget, that's why we hired him. He said he'll be ready to gut the kitchen in a few days."

"He said he *will*? Or he said *he'll be ready to*? Didn't he say that two weeks ago?"

Madeline laughed as she freshened her lip color. "This time, I think he means it."

"That's good, except at the rate he's moving, I'm not looking forward to a few weeks, or months, without a kitchen."

A pang of guilt struck her. Since she was leaving, Quinn would have to handle the kitchen ordeal alone.

A horn blasted on Quinn's end of the phone. Atlanta traffic. "I'm about an hour away," he said. "Moving at a snail's pace but I'm moving."

"Be safe. I'm going to make dinner for us now. I'll see you soon." She would save the bad news for later. The timing wasn't great. Quinn had been away for two weeks and now that he was home…she was about to head out. One of them was almost always out of town. It had been that way ever since she accepted his engagement proposal, without the slightest reservation, four months ago in Washington, D.C., in front of the U.S. President and several cabinet members. So tonight, while they were in the same place, Madeline intended to make the most of the evening.

She left the bedroom to get dinner started. She and Quinn had gotten everything ready for the remodel and their vision of a gleaming white kitchen. The cabinets were nearly emptied. Only a few dishes remained inside. She'd recently packed everything else—including a shocking amount of kitchen "things" they probably didn't need—and lugged the boxes into the dining room. She wouldn't miss the dark cabinets or the cracking tile floor. White quartz with wispy gray lines, looking remarkably like marble, would replace the black countertops.

After feeding Maddie, their mixed-breed dog, named by Quinn before he and Madeline were officially a couple, she put together a meal that would be ready by the time he got home. She'd almost finished cooking when the loud, mechanical grind of the garage door signaled his arrival. As Maddie jumped from her dog bed and rushed to the back door, Madeline grabbed the notepad off the counter. She ran her finger down the long list of things that still needed repair in their new fixer-upper house. Laundry room. Redo porch screens. Shower doors. Replace back porch steps. Her finger stopped about halfway down the paper. Garage door was already on the list, written in Quinn's neat handwriting.

The back door opened and creaked shut. Quinn's voice resonated from the hallway. "Hey, Maddie! Who's a good girl?"

Maddie's collar jingled as she jumped around her favorite person. Madeline heard the rustle of Quinn's coat coming off and the thumping of his shoes hitting the floor. He came around the corner and walked straight to where she stood in front of the old stove. They lingered in a kiss that made her want to postpone dinner.

"It's so nice to see you," he said, nuzzling her neck.

"It is." She didn't want to ruin it yet by telling him she had to leave.

"Something smells great. What can I do to help?"

"The table is set. I put out candles and a bottle of wine. Dinner is almost ready. All you have to do is sit down and be charming."

"I'll do my best. Be right back," he said as he left the kitchen.

Madeline had just placed the roasted chicken on the table, next to a green salad and rice, when Quinn returned.

"There's something you have to see," he said. He pulled a chair out, sat, and handed over his phone.

Madeline took her seat and read the headline on his phone screen. *Harvard Fellow: Terrorists Could Engineer The Next Pandemic.*

Quinn snorted. "I just thought that was funny. Like this Harvard fellow's idea is new and revolutionary."

"Not everyone deals with terrorists for a living." She raised her brows and grinned. "Maybe you could invite him to shadow you for a week."

With a relaxed smile, Quinn opened the bottle of wine and poured two glasses. "I sat through intelligence meetings almost the entire day. How about you? Anything noteworthy happen at work?"

"Yes." She had to tell him now. "Patrick called me into his office just before I left."

Quinn tilted his head as if he knew what was coming.

"Someone high in the chain of command is sending me to Nalowale Island in the Pacific. A tsunami hit the southern coast a few days ago. Now there's an outbreak. I'm leaving first thing tomorrow."

Quinn set the bottle down on the table. His expression turned serious. "What sort of outbreak?"

"Unexplained, irrational behavior." She shrugged and rotated her glass in her hand. "It's escalating into violence."

"They're sending the CDC to assess the cause of violent behavior? Sounds like something the FBI should get involved with."

Madeline spooned some rice onto her plate. "It does, but they must have reason to believe it's an epidemiological or medical issue. I won't know for sure until I get there."

"Hmm. If there is a natural cause, what could it be? Something in the water?"

"I've been thinking about it, and that was my first thought. Water contamination from sewage or chemicals is a big concern after a tsunami. But a bacterial outbreak, like cholera, takes around five days to emerge, and wouldn't cause violent behavior. Viral encephalitis or meningitis can cause confusion and irrational behavior, but the medical staff would have tested for those. This is something atypical."

Quinn stared at Madeline as he picked up his glass. "You know, governments have sunk tons of chemical weapons into the Pacific Ocean over the years. Every so often, a fishing trawler dredges something up in a net, something bad, forcing the crew to quarantine. It's the stuff of nightmares. Radioactive chemicals and nerve agents leaking from ancient containers. Entire crews stuck on board waiting to see how bad things will get and if they'll ever get off alive. What if an earthquake or the tsunami washed something toxic to shore?"

"Let's hope it isn't anything like that," she said, taking her first bite of salad.

Quinn set his wine down. "I'll go with you."

After a few seconds, when he didn't laugh, she knew he meant it. "I love that you offered." She reached for his hand across the table. "And I would love to have you with me. But I can't expect you to leave your work behind. I don't know how long I'll be there. It could be weeks."

"All the more reason for me to go with you. I'll go for the first few days. I'd like to see what you're dealing with."

"You can't be leaving your work behind every time you're worried about me."

"This is just one time. Look, I know you don't need an escort, but you wouldn't mind if I came along, would you?"

"Of course not. Except...this outbreak...we don't know what it is. And with the tsunami...I expect things to be chaotic. There's always a risk. I don't want to put you in harm's way."

"If there's that much of a risk, then maybe you shouldn't go either."

Madeline grinned. "Touché."

"If there are outbursts of violence, it wouldn't hurt to have someone from the FBI look into them. Unofficially, that is."

"If you can get away...great. And maybe the timing isn't so bad. If we get lucky, Fred might have the kitchen finished by the time we return."

"See? Perfect."

"After dinner, I'll make a few calls to get you clearance. I don't want you going all the way there unless it's cleared."

"Why wouldn't it be?"

"Patrick said there are travel restrictions. I can tell it won't be a typical assignment."

"When do you ever have a typical assignment? Tell them it makes sense for me to run a parallel evaluation of the situation."

"I will. They know what you're capable of doing."

After they finished eating, Quinn cleaned up while Madeline called her boss and requested clearance for Quinn. To her surprise, Wallen called back after a short time. He said getting the approval was easy, almost as if someone had anticipated the request.

14

"We're all set," Madeline told Quinn. "They'll be expecting both of us."

"Good." He took a seat at his desk and opened his laptop. "I need to clear my schedule. Then I want to find out just how bad things are on this island."

Madeline put an out-of-office message on her own work email and voicemail, then called her parents.

"Where are you going?" her mother asked.

"Nalowale Island."

"Tim! Tim, can you hear me?" Madeline's mother shouted to her husband. "Madeline's going to Nalowale Island tomorrow. Look it up."

"Quinn is going with me," Madeline said.

"He is? That's wonderful. A sort of pre-honeymoon. Maybe you'll want to honeymoon there."

"I don't think it's that sort of place," Madeline said. "There was a tsunami."

"Oh. Then don't drink the water while you're there." Madeline's mother couldn't seem to help herself from offering comments of that sort, even though her daughter was a medical doctor who specialized in infectious diseases and had a PhD in epidemiology. "Pack sunscreen," she added.

"I did." Madeline prepared to hear a list of items sure to follow.

"And insect repellant."

"Got it," Madeline interjected before the list could go on. "Can you and Dad watch Maddie for a week? Could be two. Or three."

"We'll come get her tonight so I can see what you've done with your kitchen."

15

"Nothing yet. It's the same, but there should be some significant progress while we're gone. Thanks so much, Mom, for watching Maddie."

"We're proud of you, Madeline."

After the call, Madeline pulled a chair up beside Quinn at his desk.

"This is odd," he said, staring at his computer screen. "There's not much about the damage caused by the tsunami, but I did find this. Check out the video of this guy." Quinn clicked the play button as Madeline scooted her chair forward to watch.

Palm trees and a backdrop of lush foliage flanked a man in a crisp, white shirt and khakis. Perfectly centered behind him, a grand archway bore the words *Azure Cove*.

"I think that's where we're staying, compliments of the government. Azure Cove wasn't affected by the tsunami." Madeline stopped talking as the man on the video began.

"Hello. I'm Devon Wheeler." His voice was unmistakably American. "As you may have heard, a tsunami recently hit Nalowale Island. Our thoughts and prayers are with those who lost their lives, and those with damaged homes and businesses. But this island is strong. The people of Nalowale are resilient. We will get through this and emerge more united than before. The tsunami will not delay the grand opening of the Azure Cove luxury living resort."

The camera swept to cliffs with a view of turquoise water, white sand, and graceful palm trees swaying in what Madeline could only imagine was a lovely breeze. "Wow. It's beautiful there. Nothing like the pictures of devastation that Patrick showed me in his office."

"Doesn't sound like there's an impending health crisis either," Quinn said.

16

"Maybe it won't be bad." Madeline wrapped her arm around her fiancé. "This could be really nice for us. There are certainly worse places to get sent for work."

CHAPTER FOUR

Madeline yawned as she peered out the plane's window into the darkness. She and Quinn had been traveling all day and most of the night. First, a commercial flight from Atlanta to Hawaii with a layover in Los Angeles. Now, another long flight, the last leg of the journey, to Nalowale Island. A young woman wearing a sage green Air Force uniform piloted their small plane.

"Did you know Nalowale means missing in Hawaiian?" Quinn asked, speaking through his headset. "I looked it up in the airport. Polynesian colonists settled there in the 1600s after shipwrecking on reefs that surround the island. They found tools, artifacts, and giant stone monoliths. But no people. They had vanished without leaving a record of where they had gone or why. No one knows what happened to them."

The pilot gripped her earpiece. "I'm guessing they all got sick and died, or someone massacred them. Just my theories. The island has a museum with the artifacts and a historical society of people and some professor types who are still trying to make sense of it."

"Are you stationed on Nalowale?" Madeline asked her.

"No. I've only visited during supply runs. The island is a little boring, but absolutely beautiful. It was before the tsunami, anyway."

"What else can you tell us about it?" Quinn asked.

"There are three principal areas. The south coast is busiest. It's where the permanent residents live and work. It's got shops, restaurants, and homes. That area was hardest hit by the tsunami. The Air Force base occupies the west side of the island."

"Did the tsunami damage the base?" Madeline asked.

"Floodwaters reached the southern parts but didn't do much damage. The base is scheduled to close in a few weeks. Only a skeleton crew was living there when the tsunami hit. Mostly Airmen guarding old bunkers."

"What about the hospital?" Madeline asked. "Was it affected?"

"No. It's farther inland. Although it's not a hospital like what we'd think of in the states. It's smaller. Built by the military, even though it's not on the base. I don't know why that is, but the locals use it too."

"Madeline has worked on health crises all over the world." Quinn said, his admiration obvious. "She's seen it all."

Madeline nodded, thinking of the months she spent in field hospitals in Sierra Leone with the most basic equipment and simple accommodations inside tents. "What about the rest of the island?"

"The northern part is especially beautiful. It's above sea level and it has these cliffs that descend to a gorgeous shore. It's got forests with hidden waterfalls, and lagoons, just like something out of a movie. Investors purchased most of the area recently. The primary investor is that American millionaire or billionaire, whatever he is. Wheeler. He's building Azure Cove, a 'boldly conceived'—that's his catch phrase—resort with hotel rooms and condos. *Exclusive luxury meets unparalleled beauty*, or something like that. It's all for the super-rich. And just so you know, not everyone on the island is happy about it."

"We saw one of Wheeler's videos," Quinn said. "Who sold him the land?"

19

The pilot adjusted her controls before responding. "The island's governing council. The U.S. basically took Nalowale. No pleasant way to say it. That's how it went down. Eighty years ago, we stole it from the original residents—who weren't really the first ones here, but like you said, no one knows what happened to them. The base is closing soon, so the U.S. gave the island back. The island's council members voted to sell part of it to developers."

"I was told there are about ten thousand permanent residents on the island," Madeline said.

"Sounds about right. Another hundred or more contractors were working on the new development. But most weren't there when the tsunami hit. They left the island for an extended weekend. It was super last minute. They were excited to get the time off. Rumor has it—well, not rumor, more like fact because several workers have told me—Wheeler works his crews in continuous long shifts, twenty-four hours a day, seven days a week, which is a little much if you ask me. He's offering nice bonuses if the jobs get done on schedule. Anyway, they finally got a break, and it couldn't have happened at a better time."

"Have you been to the south shore, where the damage is?" Quinn asked.

"I haven't. And now I only have clearance to land and then get back in the air. We received orders not to allow anyone on or off the island. No one except you two. You're the last."

Madeline tightened her grip on Quinn's hand as they exchanged a look.

"We're rounding the western side of the island now," the pilot said. "Almost there."

Madeline slid her arm through Quinn's and whispered, "No matter what awaits us, I'm so glad you came with me."

They exited the plane and descended stairs onto the deserted tarmac with only the sound of screeching frogs and chirping insects to greet them. As they set their bags on the pavement, headlights appeared from one end of the airstrip. A white van approached and parked near them. A man wearing an Air Force short sleeve uniform got out, leaving the van running.

"I'm Airman First-Class Nate McDonald," he said, still striding toward them. Up close, he looked to be in his early twenties. His eyes strayed to the gun in Quinn's holster. "Welcome. I hope you had a safe trip here."

"We did, thank you," Madeline answered. "Long but safe."

"I'll be taking you to Azure Cove," he said, grabbing two of Madeline's bags and carrying them to the van. "Excuse my appearance. I've been working search and rescue and recovery all day." Nate shook his head. There was something strange about the motion, more of a nervous tic. His clothes were clean; his body was not. In the light from the vehicle, smudges of dirt covered the dark skin on his arms and the side of his neck. Trickles of sweat ran from his hairline down his temples, despite the cool evening air. His eyes were bloodshot.

He opened the back of the van and effortlessly swung Madeline's heaviest suitcase inside. When all the bags were in, they took seats inside the vehicle. Madeline secured her seatbelt and opened her window to let the cool air inside. She signaled Quinn to open his window as well. Nate put the car in gear and headed away from the airstrip.

"How long have you been on the island?" Quinn asked from the passenger seat.

"Six months, sir. Only a few weeks left. Never expected something like the tsunami would happen. Everything on Nalowale used to be calm, like not much could ever go wrong here."

"Lots of damage?" Quinn asked.

21

Nate made a fist and bounced it up and down against the steering wheel. "So much. Right now, it seems impossible for things to get back to normal." His fist kept tapping. "Everyone from the base is trying to help. The islanders need all the muscle power they can get. Every able body has been working non-stop. I think adrenaline has kept me going." Nate idled the van beside a gatehouse with a satellite dish on top. He saluted the Airmen inside, who wore masks, and one of them opened the gate. He waved as he drove through, and in the light from the gatehouse, his clenched jaw shifted as if he was grinding his teeth.

"Then thanks for taking a break to drive us here," Madeline said.

"What?" Nate jerked his head to the side.

"Thank you for driving us," Madeline repeated, puzzled by his odd reaction.

"Oh, right," he said, looking at her in the rearview mirror. "It's really good you're here, that they allowed you to come. This illness is bad. A lot of people have it now. Once they start acting real sick, they get taken away."

"Taken away?" Madeline asked. The phrase sounded wrong.

"You know, to the hospital," Nate answered. "I think."

The van's lights cut through inky blackness as they traveled up winding hills through a tropical jungle thick enough to hide anything. Branches drooped into view from all sides.

Ned took a turn faster than Madeline thought wise. She gripped the door handle and held on. In the back of the van, luggage and equipment slid against the wall. No other cars passed them, but the possibility of barreling off the road and into who knew what—it was too dark to see—seemed very real.

"You want to slow down some," Quinn said as the dark-shadowed scenery whirred by on either side of them. His tone made clear it was not a question.

22

"Oh, sure," Nate answered. "Sorry." He let up on the gas.

"Is it always this dark on the roads at night?" Madeline asked.

"Here—yes," Nate said. "But everywhere—not usually. Downed power lines electrocuted two people. Electricity is off everywhere until it's safe. We've got generators on the base. But uh—" Something to the left of the vehicle was distracting him. "Azure Cove has generators too, so you'll, uh—"

The car screeched to a stop. Madeline and Quinn lurched forward.

With a wide-eyed look, Nate pressed his hand over his heart and stared at the bushes to his left.

"What happened?" Madeline squinted into the darkness. She saw nothing to cause Nate to slam on the brakes.

Nate rubbed his eyes. "I uh…I thought I saw—never mind."

"What was it you thought you saw?" Quinn asked.

"Uh, it's…no. It's nothing. Sorry about the abrupt stop." Nate drove forward, now swinging his head from side to side, as if something might suddenly plunge out of the trees at them. "We're almost there; it's not much farther."

Thank goodness. "When was the last time you slept?" Madeline asked.

Nate wiped his hand over his forehead. "I guess it's been a few days."

"Maybe it's time you took a break," she said. "You have to care for yourself if you want to continue helping."

"I know," Nate said. "I will."

Around the next corner, lights illuminated the tree-lined road. Tucked into the greenery to their right, a vibrant mural of a smiling mermaid and a dolphin caught Madeline's attention.

Painted on a two-story wall, lights illuminated it from below and spotlights from above. Farther down, on the opposite side of the road, two giant stone monoliths towered above ground in an area cleared to showcase their strange magnificence.

The Azure Cove archway loomed in the distance. Surrounded by thick jungle, it reminded Madeline of Jurassic Park. A tall fence stretched out from each side. Blockades prevented vehicles from driving onto the property. If that wasn't enough of a deterrent, two men carrying rifles stood guard behind the barriers. They could have been NFL linemen or bouncers at a rowdy club, the sort of men no one in their right mind would mess with.

Nate stopped the van at the arch. Under bright lights, the hefty guards lumbered over to the vehicle and peered in at Quinn and Madeline. One guard had a dark beard. The other had blond hair, dyed from the looks of his dark roots, and a gleam in his eyes that instantly made Madeline uneasy.

"I've got Dr. Hamilton and Quinn Traynor," Nate said. "They just landed at the base."

The blond guard nodded and stepped back, eyeing the vehicle as the bearded one pushed the roadblocks aside.

Nate sped up. He failed to slow for an unfinished section of driveway, causing the van to rattle in and out of the depression.

A grand building with balconies appeared around the next curve. Smaller, separate dwellings, each with the same distinctive architectural flair—contemporary and luxurious, made of travertine stone—stretched out on either side. Heavy machinery, scaffolding, and palettes of material were everywhere.

Nate parked in front of the central building and jumped out. While he unloaded their bags, Madeline inhaled the lush air and took it all in.

"I'll be back at first light to take you to the hospital," Nate said.

"Thanks." Quinn lifted a small suitcase on top of a larger one. "I hope you get some rest before then."

As soon as Nate got back in the vehicle, Quinn raised his brows at Madeline. "What was that about?"

Madeline swung her backpack over her shoulder and grabbed a suitcase. "I think he's exhausted. I hope that's all it is."

To their left, a backhoe started up under spotlights. The treads slowly rotated, rumbling beneath the machine. The crane creaked as the metal scoop bent inward to gouge the earth.

"The pilot wasn't exaggerating about late shifts working at all hours," Quinn said.

A man approached from the front entrance and came toward them with long, purposeful strides. Madeline recognized him. He stopped walking and stood several yards away, looking just as he had in the video. Tan skin. White teeth. Custom shirt. Hair slicked back and not a strand out of place. Wheeler wasn't overweight, but there was a softness to his face, his chest, and his belly. Just the opposite of Quinn.

"Welcome to Azure Cove. I'm Devon Wheeler. I've been expecting you."

"I'm Madeline Hamilton from the CDC."

Quinn set his bags down. "Quinn Traynor." Quinn didn't elaborate on his working title, nor did he mention being her fiancé. He wasn't on official business, but Madeline was a bit surprised that he didn't introduce himself as a special agent in charge in the FBI's counterterrorism unit. Or an agent at the very least.

Wheeler didn't seem to notice or care. He focused on Madeline. "Most of my crews left the island before the tsunami hit. Wouldn't you know, the one weekend where I grant everyone time off, well, almost everyone—this happens. First my crews couldn't come back because of the tsunami. Now, this mysterious plague is screwing with my timeline. The minute the government got wind of the outbreak, they imposed travel restrictions. No one is

25

officially calling it a quarantine, but that's what it is. That *must* change so I can get back on track here. I've lost several days. Somebody needs to give the go ahead. Are you that someone, Dr. Hamilton?"

The U.S. Government would likely follow Madeline's recommendation to extend or cancel a quarantine, as it would come from the CDC, but she immediately sensed her job there would be easier if Wheeler didn't know that. "I'm here to gather data and make an assessment. I understand the tsunami damage is on the south side of the island. How bad is it?"

"I hear it's a mess. But that's not why you came." Wheeler gestured into the air with one arm. "I know you're among the best at what you do. I have friends with influence in the government. As soon as I learned about the outbreak, I pulled some strings to get you here. I want an update from you as soon as you understand what's happening. I'm trusting you can quickly make a diagnosis and give people what they need to recover." He crossed his arms. "Without bringing the problem up here."

Less than a minute talking to this guy and already Madeline didn't like him. "We'll be heading to the hospital in a few hours," she said, thinking the less time she spent with Wheeler, the better. Quinn's expression remained neutral, but she knew Wheeler's attitude would put him off in a big way.

Wheeler smoothed his hand over the surface of his hair, flashing a silver watch. "You'll wear masks and protective gear while you're at the hospital? So you won't get sick when you're there?"

"Yes, of course, if necessary. I brought a supply of hazmat and personal protection gear," Madeline said, feeling more annoyed by the second. Tiredness from the long trip might have been part of it...or not.

"Okay." He studied her for a few seconds. "You practically have the entire complex to yourselves, but don't get too comfortable. You aren't here on vacation. You'll be staying in the

26

staff accommodations. That's where everyone who works here will live. There are plenty of rooms and there's electricity in the main building, something you won't find right now on the rest of the island. The dormitory kitchen is stocked with enough food for both of you. Not the type of food we will eventually serve here, but I'm sure you've gotten by with worse. I understand you're not a stranger to roughing it." Wheeler turned and began walking away from the main building, back toward the road they came in on. "The tsunami had no direct impact up here, so the water is fine to drink straight from the tap. One of the first systems I established was a reverse osmosis purification system."

In the distance, the excavation machine shut off, leaving the complex eerily quiet.

"You said most of the contractors left," Madeline said. "Where are the others?"

"Only ten or so stayed behind at my complex. Most went to help on the south side. They wanted to. But enough is enough. I already have only a fraction of the people necessary to get the resort opened on time. I needed all my crews back here yesterday. Provided they're healthy, that is. Now that they've left the property and gone to other parts of the island…they've put those of us who stayed here at risk." Wheeler ducked onto a narrow gravel path almost concealed amidst trees. "This way," he said, keeping several yards between himself and his visitors.

Lit by small solar lights, the path wound deeper into the woods, taking them away from the main resort. It emerged in a clearing with several small, box-shaped buildings and one large, rather bland building.

Wheeler pointed to the largest structure. "There's the dormitory. You'll find the front door unlocked. Pick any unoccupied room or rooms, whatever suits your needs." There was something lascivious and suggestive in his statement and the way he looked from Madeline to Quinn. "Just remember why you're here."

27

"Thank you and goodnight," Madeline said, eager to go inside and get away from Wheeler.

Without another word, Wheeler pivoted around and disappeared down the path.

▲▼▲

A long list of anticipated to-do items circled Madeline's mind, preventing her from sleeping. Priority one—do a scientific, data-driven study to determine the causes and risk factors and control the health problem. The list kept expanding, and soon it had little to do with epidemiology or the island and included personal items and things that needed to be fixed at their new house. Feeling frustrated, she pulled the sheet up to her chest in the double bed and nudged her shoulder against Quinn's.

"You still awake?" he murmured.

"Yes. I can't stop thinking about things. As soon as we get back, I'll start planning the wedding."

"That's what you're thinking about right now? Weddings?"

"Not weddings. *Our* wedding. We should have set a date by now, shouldn't we?"

Quinn turned toward her, resting on his side. "Planning a wedding is time-consuming, and we already have a lot going on. Renovating the kitchen. Our careers. Trying to stay in shape. Why not hire a wedding planner? We tell her our budget, what we want and don't want. She does the rest. That's how it works. Otherwise, this wedding might not get off the ground."

She sometimes forgot her fiancé had already planned one wedding—with his first wife. Quinn talked little about Holly, but Madeline knew things hadn't been perfect between them. Holly was a partier who stretched the limits of the law and sometimes Quinn's patience, while Quinn played by all the rules. Quinn wanted children. Holly had not. In that respect, and many others, Madeline and Holly could not have been more different from each other.

Madeline rolled onto her side to face him. "Do you even want a wedding?"

"What are you saying?"

She trailed her finger from his bare shoulder down his arm. "I'm not asking if you want to get married. Just if you want the wedding part of it."

"I do if you do. Or if it's important to your family. I'm also okay with skipping a big ceremony if that's what we decide."

She smiled. "That's not much of an answer."

He touched her cheek. "If you want the truth…"

"I do."

"I'd like to be your husband sooner rather than later."

"And more than anything…I want to be your wife." She stared into his eyes, her hand resting on his side, her fingers grazing the rough texture of a scar. "That's all that matters."

"Then it's settled. Let's forget about planning a big event. We'll do a small ceremony with your parents and a few friends and then treat everyone to a nice celebration dinner."

It made sense. Why go through all the work to plan a big wedding if the result meant the most important part of it—their official commitment—got pushed off? Putting so much energy and savings—what remained after buying and renovating the house— into a wedding made little sense. She smiled. "I love that idea. Let's do it. As soon as we get back—an intimate celebration."

He kissed her forehead, letting his lips linger on her skin. "Do you think skipping a traditional wedding will disappoint your parents?"

"No. I'm not in my twenties anymore. And especially not if it means we give them grandchildren sooner."

He grinned. "I'm all for that. I can't wait to have children together. But we better get some sleep now. Long day ahead for you."

Madeline rolled over, facing away from Quinn. In the small bed, they were touching from their shoulders to their toes. She closed her eyes and her stomach stirred, a familiar sign of anticipation. Soon enough, they would find out what the island was dealing with.

▲▼▲

Under the bright light of the Azure Cove entrance, Lucas passed time thinking about his future. He would make more money working for Wheeler this month than his father made in a good year in the fruit orchards. His recent economic good fortune was mostly because of his imposing size and athleticism. He was two hundred and sixty pounds of solid muscle. Everyone told him that if he lived in America, he could have been a pro football player. Lucas didn't think so. He wasn't much for hurting anyone or anything, even though he had the power to do it. Besides his menacing frame, another quality made him an appealing prospect for his position: Lucas had a certain reserve. He knew how to be quiet. He only spoke when spoken to or if he had something important to say. That made people respect him. Someone had recommended him to Wheeler Properties, and he was now the only local on the new security team. His jet-black beard and dark brooding eyes made him look older than his twenty-four years.

Working for Wheeler was a great opportunity. After a few years at Azure Cove, Lucas might get moved to another resort. Eventually he could be head of security. With a job like that, he could continue helping his family *and* start a family of his own. All he had to do was impress his boss and Wheeler by proving he was capable, dependable, and loyal.

But staying loyal to Wheeler had become a challenge in ways Lucas hadn't expected. Why had he imagined someone like Wheeler, with loads of money and power, would be a decent person? He knew why. *To whom much is given, much is expected.* Wheeler didn't seem familiar with that saying.

Lucas didn't trust Wheeler. Right before the tsunami, he'd sent away everyone working at the complex, except the security team and the excavators from Blythe Enterprises. Wheeler said they deserved a break, but Lucas wasn't buying that. Did the hurried sendoff have something to do with the new violent syndrome affecting people on the island? Thinking about the bizarre illness made him worry about his sister. She was at the hospital and at constant risk of being exposed.

As Lucas moved farther away from his post so he could have some privacy, he had a gnawing feeling he would someday regret protecting Azure Cove and its secrets.

"Where are you going?" Ronnie asked.

"Taking a piss," Lucas said.

As big as Lucas was, he should fear no one. But Ronnie creeped him out.

When he was far enough away, he stepped into the jungle and turned on his high-powered radio, the one Wheeler gave him when the cell towers stopped functioning. Funny that Lucas was using it now to contact his sister. They used to play with two-way radios when they were kids. Not that his current experience was anything like that. There was no sense of fun. Nothing about his life at Azure Cove felt like playing around anymore.

He pressed the talk button. "It's me, sis. Are you still there?" It was late, but that didn't matter. Not now. He waited a few minutes for a response that never came. Lucas pressed the talk button again, anyway. "The disease specialist is here now. Please be careful."

CHAPTER FIVE

Nalowale was fourteen hours ahead of Atlanta, and instant coffee from the dorm's cafeteria-style kitchen had done little to help Madeline feel less jetlagged. A dull headache lingered behind her eyes. But once she stepped outside, the tropical breeze was invigorating, just as she'd imagined it would be when they watched Wheeler's video from her home.

Wearing light-weight pants and long-sleeved shirts to protect against insects, she and Quinn walked the path from the staff dormitories to the central building on the resort where they would meet Nate. They carried backpacks and bags with protective gear and portable lab equipment.

Eventually, the resort would be incredibly beautiful, but now...it was most notably unfinished. Daylight revealed just how much work still needed to be done. Construction and development had decimated much of the land. Mounds of blackish-gray dirt and muddy holes pock-marked the area, along with piles of paving stones, construction cones, machinery, and a giant orange dumpster. Despite the early hour, men were already on the job. Near a giant crater, four of them were standing around, smoking cigarettes around a bulldozer and a backhoe. They wore forest-green shirts, all with the same white lettering and insignia—indecipherable from the distance. The men spotted her staring in their direction, so she waved.

Multiple trenches, each approximately six feet wide, branched out from a central crater-like hole and meandered across the property. "Looks like an asteroid hit," Madeline said to Quinn. "I wonder what that's going to be."

"No idea," Quinn said. "Let's check out the beach before Nate gets here."

They left their bags near the front of the hotel and walked through its gaping center, a contemporary take on a Grecian-style courtyard with large palm trees and a mosaic-tiled pool. The pass through brought them to the top of the cliffs and stunning views of the ocean. Staircases with several landings led down to a picture-perfect cove with white sand and crystal-blue water. A priceless gift of nature.

The tsunami had spared the north side of the island. It hadn't reached the cliffs, and the cove didn't appear damaged. The water was clear near the shore, evolving into shades of turquoise, intensifying in color as it met the horizon under the rising sun.

Madeline stood still, letting the breeze lift her hair and listening to the small waves—gentle whooshes of sound that grew silent as they gently died on the shore. She wanted to go down the stairs, take her shoes off, and push her toes into the sand. "It's so beautiful. It almost takes my breath away."

A car's engine broke her reverie. A white van appeared on the other side of the courtyard. "Our ride is here," she said, with a bit of reluctance. It would have been so nice to linger a few more minutes.

Quinn took one last look at the breathtaking scenery, then reached for her hand. "I hope we'll have time to come back here later."

"We'll make the time," she said.

It wasn't Nate waiting for them on the other side of the courtyard. A different man stood by the white van. He wore an Air Force uniform. A mask covered his mouth and nose.

As Quinn introduced himself to their driver, Madeline admired her fiancé—the way he carried himself, his lean strength, his shirt clinging to his waist when he turned, hinting at the washboard abs underneath. Aside from tiny lines etched around his eyes, he looked the same as when he was the quarterback at West Point. Madeline didn't know him then, but after their move, she helped unpack some of his boxes and fawned over old pictures and video clips. She felt a stir of gratitude and desire then, and now. He was all hers.

After loading their gear into the van, they climbed inside. As they drove away from the complex, the driver tilted his head toward the group of men in the green shirts. "Those are the guys who got stuck here. All from the same excavation company. Wheeler sent the rest of the contractors away just in time."

"Sent away?" Quinn asked. "We heard he gave them the weekend off."

"I mean, yeah, I guess. But it was real sudden. They got paid to leave, same as if they stayed and worked. I heard from one of the pilots who flew them out. It's just weird, right? Almost like Wheeler knew the tsunami was coming."

"Yeah. It is weird," Quinn said.

They went through the arches and traveled the same road they'd taken yesterday. With her window wide open, Madeline admired the stunning green hills, a plunging waterfall, and trees laden with tropical fruit. Wild orchids and plumeria—yellows, whites, and pinks—blossomed in the lush vegetation. The gorgeous flowers, valued in many countries for their medicinal properties, scented the air with a rich fragrance.

Their driver pointed to a narrow dirt road cutting through a grove of trees. "That road goes to another part of Azure Cove's property. Fruit orchards. The fruit here is amazing. Papayas, bananas, coconuts, mangoes, and guavas. They taste totally different than on the mainland. And somewhere out there are fields and fields of tobacco. The tsunami didn't come up this far, obviously. The groves are all fine. But the devastation on the south side is unbelievable. Some people lost everything, including their

34

lives. There's so much emotion… you know? And now this sickness. There are too many in the hospital already with crushed bones and other injuries. They definitely need more doctors."

She heeded the Airman's words, steeling herself for what lay ahead. She'd seen the pictures in Wallen's office. The alluring serenity of the landscape at higher elevations, and the business-as-usual attitude at Azure Cove were not representative of the suffering on Nalowale Island.

After a few more miles, they took the second exit on a roundabout, joining a slow-moving line of cars and trucks heading in the same direction.

"Almost there," the driver said, inching along in the traffic.

They passed a large stone etched with an American flag. Another turn, and there was the hospital. The rectangular concrete structure was larger and more industrial than Madeline imagined. But it wasn't the building that captured her attention. It was the people. They were everywhere. The trampled grass of the front lawn looked like a refugee camp. Dozens of small tents cluttered one side. An enormous tent, the type used for outdoor parties and events, took up most of the other side.

"You should get out here," the driver said as they idled in the vehicle-crammed driveway. "Will be faster if you walk the rest of the way."

"We will. Thanks for the ride," Madeline said, finally looking away from the people and tents to grab her gear and step out of the van.

Just a few yards away, two men unloaded a body from the back of a pickup truck. Long black hair trailed from the corpse, which they carried toward the building and placed on the ground in a row of others concealed by sheets.

She and Quinn were silent as they walked across the lawn toward the buildings, passing close by the large tent. After Patrick showed her the images of the devastated island, this—the sure

35

signs of death and displacement—is exactly what she expected to find. And yet the surrounding scene was still overwhelming and difficult to process.

The large tent was noisy and packed with beach chairs, benches, cots with thin mattresses, and sleeping bags. Children, ranging from infants and toddlers to elementary-school-aged, milled around inside. The youngest ones played with toys in groups or alone. Some were clean, and some were visibly dirty. All had words written on their arms with a black sharpie.

Near the tent's entrance, Madeline stared at two whiteboards covered with names and photos of people.

"Are you looking for someone?" a woman with short black hair and nose piercings asked from behind a card table.

"No. Sorry," Madeline answered.

"Then, consider yourself lucky." The woman turned to a child nearby who bounced her weight from one leg to the other.

A dark-haired boy perched on the edge of a cot had captured Quinn's attention. The boy's shoulders slumped forward. He clutched a thick, dirty rope and rolled it against his bare legs. Bruises marred his neck. A patch of black stitches crossed his forearm, and another patch was dangerously close to an eye. He was at least ten years old. Old enough to understand everything had changed.

Madeline felt a lump form in her throat. She felt sad and also guilty. She wasn't sure why. Probably just from seeing the child and all the other children, imagining their loss and pain, and then walking past.

"Hey, big guy!" someone shouted from behind them.

Madeline turned around first. One of the men who had been carrying the corpse was looking at them.

"I think he's talking to you," she said to Quinn.

"Give us a hand?" the man asked. "We could use some fresh blood."

"Sure thing," Quinn answered.

"Hold on." Madeline lowered her voice. "Be careful. Very careful." Quinn would know exactly what she meant. She pulled gloves and masks from her bag and tossed them to him. "I'm going to find Dr. Wilcox. I'll catch up with you later."

"Okay. Good luck," Quinn said before walking toward the stranger.

Madeline watched them exchange words for a few seconds before she walked the rest of the way to the hospital and went in. She had just enough time to register the packed hallways, warm air, and flickering fluorescent ceiling lights when shouts erupted from the far end of a corridor. The disturbance came from a tall, broad-shouldered military man with a body like an Olympic swimmer. He was shouting and threatening a woman in a physician's coat.

As Madeline tried to make sense of the scene, an unshaven man with a crewcut ran past her, toward the commotion, pushing an empty wheelchair. His shirt sleeve bore a medic's insignia. "Colonel Nelson, stop!" he yelled.

Unable to look away from the escalating conflict, Madeline hurried toward it.

A bloody bandage surrounded the Colonel's leg. Drops of blood spattered the floor. Filth coated his shirt. He wore boxer shorts and no pants. "Get the iguanas out of here!" he hollered, closing in on the woman. "Get them out before I tear this place to shreds!"

The medic reached them. He let go of the wheelchair and plunged a needle into a vial.

The woman in the physician's coat stumbled backward, holding her hands up in front of her masked face. She was running out of space before she would hit the wall. "Please, go back to

37

your room, Colonel," she pleaded. She wasn't freaking out. She was trying to be calm and reassuring, but fear resonated from her shaking voice.

The Colonel raised his arm overhead, and Madeline felt her heart do a little flip.

Just in time, the medic grabbed the Colonel's arm and plunged the needle into his shoulder.

The Colonel spun around. His eyes were wild, manic. Muscles bulged from his neck. He yanked away from the medic's grip and swung at him, connecting with a punch square in the jaw. The medic fell backward, tripping over the wheelchair. The Colonel pivoted back to the woman and took a wild swing. She jumped back, but not fast enough. His fist grazed her cheek, yanking off her mask, and making her gasp.

Swaying slightly, the Colonel lunged toward her again.

Madeline launched herself at him, shoving his muscular body with all her weight.

He staggered sideways and slumped against the wall. "Not putting me in there with all the iguanas. Not...down...there." His words slowed, their volume deflated, as the contents of the syringe took effect.

"I'm sorry, sir," the medic said, lowering the Colonel into the wheelchair. "I'm so sorry."

The woman still had her hand pressed against her cheek. She appeared to be in a daze, momentarily captivated by the trail of blood on the linoleum. Her mask dangled off one ear.

Dr. Grace Wilcox, the physician Madeline was told to find, was only thirty years old and three years out of her residency. The attractive but disheveled woman standing in front of Madeline appeared even younger. She had lovely, defined bone structure and skin several shades lighter than anyone else Madeline had seen so far on the island. She also had dark circles under her eyes, errant strands of reddish-blonde hair escaping a ponytail and going every which way, and an overall air of complete exhaustion. Slowly, she lifted her head and turned to Madeline, as if she just realized there was someone else with them.

"I'm Dr. Madeline Hamilton. From the CDC. Are you Dr. Wilcox?"

"Yes. Call me Grace, please. I'm glad you're here." The doctor's raspy voice reminded Madeline of college friends after non-stop cheering at close-call football games. "We're overwhelmed, as you can see. And what you just witnessed—it was no isolated incident. We're going through sedatives like water." Grace's hand trembled as she pulled her mask the rest of the way off. She looked back at the sedated colonel. His lips moved soundlessly as his head lolled to one side.

"I've got this," the medic said, pushing the Colonel away in the wheelchair.

"Thank you, Matthew." Grace returned her focus to Madeline. "Let's go outside and talk. I could use some fresh air."

"Sure." Madeline kept stride with Grace toward the front door.

On the way, a young woman backed out of a room marked laundry, pulling a cart of clean linens. Without making eye contact, she smiled at them.

"Maria, you are the sole semblance of normality here," Grace said. "Thank you for keeping up with everything."

Maria nodded and looked down, her face flushing with color. She continued past them with the linen cart.

"I know I'm a fright," Grace said when they reached the front entrance. "I haven't slept in over forty-eight hours, and the hospital is in complete disorder. We don't know what happened to our Medical Director or anyone else who was off duty when the tsunami struck. It's just been myself, two nurses, and Matthew, the man who rescued me back there. He's a medic with the Air Force; he's been with me since the wave hit. We're the only ones treating patients and it's been one thing after another. At first it was all triage, then dealing with internal injuries and broken bones. We were doing minor surgeries, stitching up wounds, handing out antibiotics. We've all had to do things we aren't qualified to do. Now we're seeing injuries from the floodwater. It's not letting up. We have so many patients who need follow up care. More people are sick or injured than well. At least that's what it seems like. And on top of all that…this outbreak. Unexplained, uncontrolled behaviors."

"You can only help one person at a time," Madeline said. "I'm here to study the outbreak, but let me pitch in." Having worked in challenging conditions with a shortage of personnel and supplies, she related to Grace's frustration. Regardless of why the CDC sent Madeline—or whoever sent her, she really didn't know—she felt compelled to lend a hand if the immediate needs of the tsunami's victims were so pressing.

"Thank you," Grace said. They exited the building into the cooler air, heading toward the row of bodies covered with sheets. "What we really need is to get people off the island to a better equipped facility or bring in more physicians and surgeons. But apparently that can't happen until we understand more about this surge of aggressive behavior—if it's contagious, or if we have an epidemic on our hands. Of course we requested help, lots of it, and I'm assuming that's why you came. How many are with you?"

"It's just me."

Grace looked stunned. "Oh. It's just…I imagined more people. I hope they're coming soon. Anyway…I am grateful you're here."

Listening to Dr. Wilcox, Madeline could not understand why the rest of the world hadn't sent health care workers. Doctors without Borders for example. If she was the first one to arrive, that was the equivalent of putting a Band-Aid on a massive wound. While it hardly seemed adequate, it also made her presence and contribution more pressing and reinforced her need to get started.

"Please, tell me more about the outbreak," she said as they walked on a path toward the side of the buildings.

"People are exhibiting states of hyper-alertness, aggression, and insomnia. Heavy sedation is the only thing keeping them under control. It's mostly been Air Force personnel, but also a few others who don't live or work on the base." At the row of covered corpses, Grace crouched down by the first body. She lifted the sheet, took a quick glance at the figure underneath, then put the sheet back down.

"Have you tested for known waterborne diseases?" Madeline asked. "Cholera? Typhoid? Hepatitis? Shigellosis? Dysentery?"

"I ordered tests for all known bacteria and diseases. I don't have any results yet. I know that sounds absurd or pathetic, whatever you want to call it, but no one has worked in the lab since the rogue wave. We prepared specimens to go to the mainland but received no confirmation they even went out. I don't know what happened to them. Now, we're hearing they're not allowing anyone or anything off the island."

"Nothing? Surely we can get specimens out for analysis."

"I hope so, but I don't know." Without missing a beat, Grace moved on to the next body, lifted the sheet, then put it back down. "Even without the test results, what these patients are experiencing doesn't fit with the typical symptoms or timeline for illnesses related to water contamination or bacterial infections. Everyone on the island knows to boil water or use bottled. We're boiling and chlorinating the supply here, at the hospital, but the symptoms keep getting worse for those infected. So far, they haven't responded to any of the medications we've given."

"What have you tried?"

"Antibiotics, in case it's a bacterial meningitis, even though I'm certain it's not. Antifungals. Antivirals. Corticosteroids."

"When did you start noticing symptoms?" Madeline asked.

41

"Soon after the tsunami. At first, we thought people were reacting to the horror of the situation, experiencing shock and trauma."

"That makes sense," Madeline said.

"Especially since several of the patients worked day and night on rescue and retrieval efforts. But when given the chance, they still couldn't sleep. Or focus. Or calm down. And at least some of them have no pain threshold." Grace continued to move along the row of bodies, crouching down and briefly lifting the sheets away from the faces.

"What made you conclude they aren't experiencing pain?" Madeline asked.

"The man you saw in the hallway is Tim Nelson, the base colonel. His men brought him in, against his will. He had a large, open wound in his thigh. Lacerated and exposed hamstrings. Would you agree he shouldn't have been able to move without being in excruciating pain?"

"Yes."

"Yet he didn't seem to be aware of the injury at all. He has a massive infection. I managed to administer IV antibiotics and wanted to monitor him, but his behavior made it impossible to keep him on one of the upper floors with other patients. We're short on space and don't know if the condition is contagious."

"He was shouting about iguanas," Madeline said. "What was that about?"

"He was hallucinating. Which can happen from post-traumatic stress, dehydration, or not getting enough sleep...and all of those things apply here to just about everyone. But believe me...it's more than that." Grace walked past two large bodies, then crouched and lifted the sheet off a smaller corpse.

Madeline softened her voice. "Are you looking for someone?"

When Grace looked up, the pain in her face was unmistakable.

"Doctor! We need you!" someone shouted.

Before Grace could answer Madeline's question, a man rushed toward them, carrying a teenaged boy in his arms. The boy's head hung to one side. His limbs flopped lifelessly.

Grace sprang to her feet.

"Something bit him," the man said. "His leg swelled up. He passed out."

"Where is the bite?" Grace asked. She grasped the boy's ankle and located the site on the back of his foot. "It's a snake bite. Did you see what the snake looked like? The pattern on its body?"

"No," the man said, his eyes pleading. "We were wading through floodwater. No one saw it."

"Let's get him inside. Hurry." As Grace jogged toward the hospital, she yelled over her shoulder to Madeline. "Find Matthew. He can tell you more."

▼▲▼

On the second floor of the hospital, moans and cries echoed through the hallways. Cots lined the walls, all of them occupied. People sprawled over blankets on the floor. An elderly woman held a plastic cup to the lips of a barely conscious man slumped in a chair. Some patients wore masks.

Madeline spotted Matthew and followed him into a room. The beds held two patients, heads at opposite ends like the bedridden grandparents in Willy Wonka. Heart rate monitors chimed softly.

Matthew greeted a patient and lifted her chart from where it hung on the end of a cot. The medic was compact, muscular, and on the short side, reminding Madeline of a male gymnast. She caught his attention when he put the chart back down.

43

"You're a medical doctor?" he asked. His piercing blue eyes were rimmed in red.

"Yes. Madeline Hamilton."

"Glad you're here. We've triaged all the patients on this floor and color coded their charts. You can start with the patients in the room across the hall," Matthew said, moving to the next patient, a frail woman with bandages around her head and casts on her arm and leg.

"The CDC sent me here to research the recent outbreak. Please fill me in on the illness."

"Oh." He closed his eyes for a second. "The symptoms are hyper-aggression—as you saw earlier with the Colonel—agitation, insomnia, hallucinations."

"When did it start?"

"Right after the tsunami." Matthew lowered his voice to just above a whisper. "Some Airmen were acting hyper-active and irritable. Almost like they'd gotten hold of LSD or crystal meth. That's what I remember thinking. But with so many dead and injured, we couldn't worry too much about drug use right then." Matthew stepped away from the beds and leaned against the wall where they had less chance of being overheard. "But those symptoms were mild compared to how they're currently presenting, and initially, some of them got over it. Now—they aren't. They're only getting worse. They're experiencing increased heart rate and blood pressure. Tremors. Their symptoms are intensifying."

"Are they febrile?" Madeline asked.

"Slightly. Though I believe their fevers are worsening."

"What tests have you done?"

"I collected blood and urine samples and nose swabs for analysis. I sent them to the base with an Airman, to get flown to another lab. With all that's going on here, I can't be sure they even went out. Anyway, I've lost track of how many with symptoms are down there now."

"Down where?"

"In the containment area. It's in the basement." Still keeping his voice quiet, Matthew cleared his throat. "It's not ideal. Someone started rounding them up and bringing them here."

"Who?"

Matthew shook his head. "I don't even know. Anyway, we really didn't have any other options for them…with all that's happening. There are others out there with the symptoms. Maybe a lot of others. The afflicted don't seem to realize they're sick until they lose it completely. They feel invincible until they're totally out of control." Matthew pressed his fingers against the side of his head and massaged his temple. Just like Grace, his work over the past several days had taken a heavy toll on him. At this rate, Madeline wondered how much more he could take before he collapsed.

A young man on a cot curled into a fetal position and moaned.

"I need to get back to these patients," Matthew said. "A few have waited long enough."

"Okay. I'll find the containment area." Madeline began walking from the room.

"Doctor," Matthew called after her.

She walked back to him so he wouldn't have to raise his voice.

"Thank God you're here," he whispered. "Grace needs a break. Although, not having a moment to herself might be the only thing keeping her personal grief at bay."

"She lost someone?" Madeline asked.

Matthew nodded. "She hasn't seen her fiancé since the wave hit."

CHAPTER SIX

Madeline headed to the basement, wondering what the term *containment area* meant. She hadn't taken more than a few steps down the second-floor hall when a woman tapped her arm. "Excuse me, are you a nurse? Please, can you look at my daughter? There's something wrong with her." The woman held a girl about thirteen years old close to her side. The girl's eyes were puffy from crying. Dirt streaked her pink shirt.

Madeline crouched to eye-level with the girl. "Hi. I'm Dr. Hamilton. What's your name?"

"Dominique,"

"What doesn't feel right, Dominique?"

"She has a bad headache and trouble breathing," the mother answered.

"You're experiencing shortness of breath?" Madeline asked the girl.

Dominique nodded. "And it sort of feels like I'm going to throw up."

"We used a kerosene heater, not inside the house, but on a covered porch," the mother said, her face scrunched like she was about to cry. "We aren't using it anymore."

"Are others in your household experiencing similar symptoms?" Madeline asked as she examined Dominique's pupils and checked her pulse.

The woman nodded. "But Dominique especially. She was on the porch the longest."

"Any chest pain?" Madeline asked.

Dominique shook her head.

"Loss of consciousness? Did you faint?"

"No," the girl answered.

"Vomiting? Confusion?"

Dominique shook her head again. "I kind of feel like I might vomit, but I haven't."

"Well, it's a good thing you're here so we can get you checked." Madeline stood and faced Dominique's mother. "Her symptoms are consistent with mild carbon monoxide poisoning. Let me find her an oxygen mask. Stay for a few hours and let her breathe pure oxygen. It will replace the carbon monoxide in her system. If that doesn't help her feel better, we'll do some tests. But the most important thing is that you eliminated the exposure."

"I know," the mother said. "I know that now. It was a mistake."

Madeline looked around the crowded hallway. She wasn't sure where to tell Dominique or her mother to wait. And she didn't know where to find the oxygen. "Wait here, please. I'll be back as soon as I can." She walked down the hallway, searching for a medical supply room. Something swatted her leg. The elderly woman sitting on the floor looked up at her. "Do you know when they're going to check on my husband again?"

"The medical staff are doing rounds right now. Dr. Wilcox or Matthew, or a nurse will be with you as soon as possible." She realized she didn't know Matthew's last name, and she didn't know the nurses' names.

Faced with so many injured and in need of medical attention, Madeline understood how Matthew and Dr. Wilcox were stretched and unable to focus on the outbreak. The island had more than enough medical issues to handle without an illness that turned its victims into menacing threats.

Madeline was opening random doors when Maria came down the hallway, again pushing a linen cart.

"Can you tell me where the medical supplies are?" Madeline asked her.

"Follow me," Maria said, silently leading Madeline to an unlabeled door. It was unlocked.

"Thank you, you're a lifesaver. I don't know where anything is," Madeline said. "Oh, and I never introduced myself. I'm Dr. Hamilton. Madeline. I'm here from the Center for Disease Control in Atlanta, about the outbreak here, the violent behavior."

Maria nodded, again lowering her gaze.

"Thanks again," Madeline said as Maria went back the way she'd come.

Although shy, Maria appeared to be a tireless and dedicated staff member. Perhaps she was grieving for lost ones and losing herself in her work was her way of coping. Madeline had little time to think more about it as she located what she needed inside the small storage space, behind an injured couple sleeping on the floor. She hurried back to Dominique and her mother and set up the treatment in what looked like the last remaining patch of open hallway space. After providing instructions, she resumed her walk to the basement, vowing to stay focused and get there sooner rather than later.

She reached a stairwell and descended two levels in near darkness, gripping the railing to avoid falling. As expected, the facility was prioritizing the generator's electricity for critical functions. At the bottom landing, she had to stand just inches from a sign in order to read it.

Laboratory. Morgue. Containment.

She opened the door. A frightening cacophony of shouts and cackles greeted her. The sounds came from behind a set of blood-red doors at the end of the hallway.

She made her way toward the noise. The only light came from small rectangular windows in the hallway near the ceiling. Two men sat in chairs by the red doors. They rose as she approached. One wore an Air Force T-shirt and boots. He had a ginger-haired crewcut. The other resembled a surfer with long hair and a goatee. He was dark-skinned and on the short side, where the military man was fair-skinned and tall. Standing together, both wearing face masks, they made an oddly matched team.

Madeline put on her own mask as she got closer, noting bully sticks and face shields lay on the ground near the men. "I'm Dr. Madeline Hamilton from the Centers for Disease Control. I'm looking for the containment area."

"Oh, good. Thank God," the military man said. "I'm Captain Craig Barstow." He gestured to the red doors. "This is the containment area. Sixteen of my fellow Airmen are in there and our Colonel was just brought in. They need help and they need it fast."

The civilian pushed aside the hair hanging in his eyes. "I'm Brian. My brother is in there. I wouldn't have let them take him here if I knew it was going to be like this, but he can't go back to his family acting the way he is. Can you help him?"

"I'm going to do my best," she said, glancing at a list taped to the wall beside the doors. Over thirty names. From behind the doors, anguished voices blended together. Was the entire area full of people who were behaving like Colonel Nelson?

"They're getting worse," Barstow said. "We're about to sedate them again."

Madeline took out her notepad. "Have you seen anything to suggest their symptoms are contagious?"

Barstow lifted one shoulder in a shrug. "I've been with the Colonel since before he started having symptoms and I'm fine."

"You've experienced no unusual symptoms?" Madeline wrote *mode of transmission* on her paper and put a question mark after it.

"I don't think so. Maybe I was a little wired earlier. But nothing like them." Barstow looked toward the double doors. "I might have imagined it, like a hypochondriac type of thing. We were all jacked up and emotional because of what happened. And if I *was* feeling a little weird, I'm fine now. They aren't."

"Do you know where the Colonel was and what he was doing prior to showing symptoms?" Madeline asked.

"Yes." Captain Barstow gazed up at the concrete ceiling and his lips curled in. Pain flashed over his eyes before he looked away. "We've done two deployments together. He's the best person to work under. Everyone will tell you that. It's killing me to see him locked up in there." Barstow swallowed hard, then turned back to her. "We were on base when the tsunami hit. We proceeded directly to the south shore, where the flooding was the worst. We worked nonstop. Like I said, we've been together since the tsunami. I brought him here yesterday, against his will, because anyone could see his leg was bad and he needed medical attention."

Madeline addressed Brian. "And your brother—do you know where he's been?"

"He's worked at the Azure Cove complex for most of the month, barely left the place. After the tsunami came ashore, he sped down to the south beach area, where the stores are…what is left of them…and started rescuing people. By the time he got home…he was sick."

At the end of the hallway, the stairwell doors opened inward. Two men walked through carrying a full body bag and walked in the opposite direction of the containment area, toward the morgue. The doors opened again, and Maria entered. She

51

dropped a stack of clean and folded blankets on a table. "Shall I get the soiled linens?" she asked, her voice so soft Madeline could barely hear her.

"We'll bring them out for you," Madeline said, imagining a disaster in the making if Maria went into the containment area, became infected (if that were possible), and then went into every room of the hospital dropping off linens. "Thank you so much, Maria." Madeline gestured to the clean stack of blankets. "This is important. It makes a difference. But please protect yourself when you touch the dirty linens. Wear gloves, a mask, and a gown if you have one. Precautions are critical until we know for sure what we're dealing with."

Maria nodded. "I will." She left two large laundry bags behind for the used linens. "I'll come back for these later." With her head down, she hurried away and exited through the stairwell doors.

"There's something else you should know," Captain Barstow told Madeline. "Tank—he's a German Shepherd—he was acting kind of strange *before* the tsunami. Restless. Unusually aggressive. Maybe he got sick first?" Barstow explained how Tank had plowed through the bushes, seemingly without feeling pain.

"Where is the dog now?" Madeline asked.

"I haven't seen him in days. If he's still alive, he has to be hurt pretty bad."

Madeline wondered if Matthew or Grace knew about the German Shepherd and if they'd considered a zoonotic transmission, from animals to humans. Rabies in humans started with flu-like symptoms and anxiety. It progressed to neurological problems and cerebral dysfunction, which included hallucinations, agitation, and aggression. It sounded very much like what these patients were experiencing. But surely one of the afflicted persons, if not all of them, would have mentioned being bitten by an animal. Perhaps, with the ensuing chaos, no one had asked. Or maybe the transmission was airborne. Bracing herself, she glanced at the red doors and said, "I need to see the patients."

"We better go in there with you." Barstow scooped one of the face shields from the floor.

Madeline put her notepad back in her bag and put on gloves and a gown. Barstow handed her a face shield, and she accepted it.

"I'm going to wait out here," Brian said. "Let me know if you need me."

When her gear was in place, Barstow opened the doors. The tortured voices escalated in intensity.

Shivering in the doorway, Madeline squinted as her eyes adjusted to the dim light coming from a single fluorescent tube overhead.

"Oh, no," she murmured. She recalled the pilot saying the military built the hospital, so what she was seeing made sense, but it still horrified her. The containment area looked like it was or had once been a prison. Cells with concrete walls lined both sides of the long passageway. The doors consisted of steel bars running from floor to ceiling. Each cell was about half the size of her freshman year dorm room, which had barely fit her twin bed, dresser, and desk. The whole place smelled like sickness.

"Are they locked in?" she whispered.

Barstow's expression was grim. "They have to be. None of them would stay in here if they had a choice."

Under normal circumstances, she would insist they move the patients out of the basement and into beds where they could more humanely restrain them. But she had already seen the overcrowded hospital rooms and hallways.

"There's a new doctor here to help everyone," Barstow announced. His breath fogged up his face shield as he shouted to be heard over the noise.

Standing between the rows of cells, Madeline acknowledged the patients one at a time, introducing herself, though she doubted anyone heard her over all the racket. The collective noise from their muttering and shouting brought bizarre and frightening to a whole new level.

Several of the cell blocks held two or more patients. Others contained a single occupant. Most were young, in their twenties and thirties, and male. In the first enclosure, the Colonel sat on a bench with his back against the wall. Matthew or someone else must have helped him into surgical scrubs. Fresh blood seeped through his bandages and into the green material around his thigh. He held an object in his hand and squeezed his fist around it while settling his steely glare on Madeline.

Like the Colonel, even those who appeared heavily sedated had their eyes open, watching her. They must have been afraid—not knowing what was happening or what would come next—but the dominant emotions permeating the room were anger, desperation, and paranoia. Disturbing sounds of muttering, shouting, and swearing rose around her, bouncing off the walls and sending a cold chill down her spine.

A woman's voice: "I can't take this anymore!"

A man's raging command: "Shut up! Shut up! Shut up! God have mercy and shut up!"

Another patient shouted as he faced the back wall of his cell. "Noises in my head. Trapped. Ghosts and monsters telling me to go do it. Go do it! I can't because I can't stop and get things cleared with them in the way. All in my way. That's why I went. Why they took me. They took me. They took me! I can't. You gotta help me."

Someone cackled. "Oh, we're having fun now, aren't we? All of us in this together!" He broke into song. "Three blind mice. Three blind mice. See how they run. They're watching us. They're watching us every hour and minute and second. Then the time runs out. And when the time runs out, we all die."

Madeline had firsthand experiences with SARS, smallpox, Ebola, and E-Coryza-1, a deadly and weaponized cross between the common cold and a hemorrhagic fever. In contrast, the containment area patients weren't bleeding out, exhibiting disturbing rashes, or spewing phlegm. Yet their anguish unsettled her more than any of the other outbreaks she'd previously encountered.

She paused in front of a cell with three women inside. They appeared insane, as if she'd entered a ward of deeply disturbed patients in a psychiatric facility. One of them sat on the ground with her arms wrapped around her knees. Rocking forward and back, she shook her head in jerky movements as tears streamed from her eyes. Across from her, a petite woman twisted a sheet and muttered with a murderous look in her eyes. "Make it stop. Make it stop. Make it stop."

The youngest of the women gripped the bars of the cell and snarled.

"I'm so sorry about what you're experiencing," Madeline said. An enormous understatement. "I'm going to check your temperature." She held the thermometer close to the woman's forehead. It beeped and Madeline pulled it away just before the woman snatched it.

One hundred and two degrees. Above normal.

She moved to the next cell. A man crouched in the front corner, gnawing on his fingernails. His eyes locked with his cellmate's in some sort of bizarre staring contest, and Madeline wondered if it was safe to have more than one person in a cell. She lowered the thermometer to his forehead and registered another elevated temperature. The next two people she checked also had high temperatures.

Fever was usually the first sign of an infection from a virus or bacteria, though there were other causes. She preferred not to treat a fever if it didn't exceed one hundred and three degrees.

Allowing it to run its course was often a patient's best natural defense.

Barstow stood outside the Colonel's cell. "You need to eat and drink something. Take this," he said, offering the Colonel a plastic cup of liquid.

"You think I trust you now?" Reaching through the bars, the Colonel smashed the drink from the Airman's hand. Liquid splashed over the floor, some of it hitting Madeline.

"What are you giving him?" she asked as droplets rolled off her gown.

"Water. He won't drink it. None of them will."

"Where did the water come from?"

"I poured it out of a gallon container. Bottled water."

"Good. Keep encouraging them to drink. They need to stay hydrated or they'll have a new set of problems." She couldn't imagine how they would administer IV fluids to these patients with the limited space and staff in the hospital, but they might soon have to. "I'm going to need your help to collect fluid samples," she told Barstow, who nodded from behind his fogged shield. She was eager to get started. She planned to check the patients for lumps and bites, listen to their hearts and lungs, and find out if they had other medical conditions predisposing them to the outbreak.

The containment area doors swung open. Matthew burst in, out of breath. His eyes met Madeline's. "Doctor, have you ever dealt with flail chest before? Or done a cricothyrotomy?"

"I—I'm certainly not a surgeon, but I've seen those, yes," Madeline said.

"Would you mind helping? Right now. There's no one else to ask."

Feeling torn, she glanced back at the patients inside the containment area.

"Make it stop. Make it stop. Make it stop."

"Three blind mice. No! Three blind mice. No! Nooo!"

The woman twisting the sheet let out an ear-shattering, primal scream.

The patients in containment needed help.

And so did others.

Madeline turned to Barstow. "While I'm gone, while you're administering the sedatives, can you get blood and urine samples and label them for as many patients as possible?" The request wouldn't be easy. And as far as she knew, Barstow had no medical background and was only stepping in to help because there was no one else.

Barstow stood as if at attention. "I will."

"Thank you." Madeline turned away and strode toward Matthew, trying to recall everything she could about the condition and the procedure he mentioned. "I'm coming."

CHAPTER SEVEN

Wondering what he was about to get himself into, Quinn joined the stranger who requested his help.

"I'm Mitch," the man said, clopping along in tall rubber boots, a muddy shirt, and jeans. He had deeply tanned skin, an unruly mop of brown hair under a cowboy hat, and thick eyebrows. Small wrinkles lined his face, but his muscles were taut, leaving his age a mystery.

"Quinn Traynor."

"You from the base, Quinn?"

"No. I just arrived on the island last night."

Mitch stopped walking, crossed his arms, and gave Quinn a hard stare. "I heard no one could land or leave here."

"I heard that too. *After* I arrived." Quinn shrugged, not wanting to get into something he didn't fully understand yet. "My fiancé is an infectious disease expert. She's helping at the hospital."

Mitch eyed the weapon in Quinn's holster. "What's the gun for?"

"I'm an FBI agent. I always carry. But I'm here in an unofficial capacity."

Mitch nodded and resumed walking, although he kept studying Quinn. "Right now, none of us can be picky soliciting help. An FBI agent will do."

"Just tell me what you need," Quinn said, unsure of how to interpret Mitch's comment.

"I need a hand moving a body."

The corpse lay in the back of Mitch's truck, a Ford F150 with a University of Hawaii sticker on the back window. Mitch pulled the large body forward and cradled the head, leaving Quinn to support bare feet. The solemn task sobered him further. The tsunami hadn't seemed real when they were at Azure Cove, but it did now. People were dead. Children had lost parents. Family and loved ones were missing. As he trudged backward, carrying the dead man across the hospital's lawn, Quinn wondered who was going to miss the man the most. He stared down at thick calluses and a raised, zigzagging scar over one leg. He wondered about the scar, if the man was a farmer who had a run-in with his machinery, or a motorcyclist who'd crashed his bike years ago. "Do you know who this person is?" Quinn asked.

"I don't," Mitch answered. "But someone will. Once he's identified, a family member will have him buried or cremated. Ceremonies and funerals will come later. If no one identifies him, someone will move him into the morgue tonight. Technically, it's full, but we keep stacking them every which way and finding more space."

As they moved closer to the decomposing bodies, the smell of death hit him.

They set the corpse down.

A woman with an old Polaroid camera took a photo of the body.

Mitch looked off at the woods bordering the hospital. "It may not seem like it, but we're trying to do this in as dignified a manner as possible. We're giving families the best chance of identifying their own, so they know what happened. So they have closure." He turned to face Quinn. "We could use all the help we can get. Can you come with me to the shore?"

59

As the woman taped the photo on a board, Quinn glanced toward the hospital, wishing for cell service so he could send Madeline a quick message in case she needed him. "Sure," he said, never one to refuse someone's request for help. He walked back to the truck with Mitch and climbed in the passenger side.

Static crackled from a CB radio in the center of the truck's console as Mitch drove away from the hospital. A woman's voice came on. "This is Shayna. There's someone trapped in the back of the Fresh Mart. He's still alive. Can anyone get over there now?"

"That's good news," Mitch said, picking up the transmitter. "Not much rescuing happening anymore. Mostly recovery." He pushed the talk button. "It's Mitch. Heading to the Fresh Mart. ETA twenty minutes."

"You part of an official rescue crew?" Quinn asked.

"Everyone who is physically able is part of the rescue crew. And then we'll all be part of the rebuilding crew. That's how it works around here. The mayor and the police are gone, as far as we know. Their offices were on Market Street. Which is where we're going now." Mitch was silent for a few seconds. "I am on the island's governing council. And the volunteer police department. Five generations of my family have lived on this island. I left for college and came back ten years later."

"What do you do for a living, Mitch?"

"I'm a broker. Do most of my work remotely. How about you? What's your background?"

"I was in the army. Now I'm in the FBI's terrorism division."

"You prevent terrorist attacks, huh?"

"Yeah." Most of the time, Quinn's work meant hours and hours of sifting through intelligence combined with navigating layers of political bureaucracy and completing mounds of administrative work. Then there were the other times...the cases that made his life the stuff of Tom Clancy novels and left him exhilarated, exhausted, and convinced he was doing what he could, playing a small but significant part in making the world a more peaceful place. Those life-changing experiences kept him motivated through the other drudgery. And though he wasn't on Nalowale Island at the FBI's request, after seeing the crowded hospital lawn and the tent filled with children, he had a feeling the trip might be one he would remember forever. Where there was a need, there was an opportunity to make a difference, even if only for a few people. It was like his mother always said: never underestimate the large importance of little things.

"Do you have a place to stay on the island?" Mitch asked.

"Azure Cove."

Mitch snorted.

Quinn kept quiet, waiting for Mitch to elaborate. It didn't take long.

"Don't get me wrong. I told you I was on the island's governing council. I voted along with the others to sell Wheeler Properties all that land. I hate that they got the monoliths. We're proud of those. But it's not like they can be moved. Anyway, there's revenue that's sure to come from tourists and vacation homeowners. We're going to use the money to make improvements. A modern school, new businesses, water system enhancements. The sad thing is that because of the tsunami damage, now we'll need all of that money and then some just to rebuild what we already had."

"Shame," Quinn said.

"Yeah. There's still a lot of opportunity for everyone who lives here when the resort opens. It's hiring housekeepers, servers, maintenance, and landscaping crews. I just don't want Nalowale to meet the fate of other small islands—overrun by commercialism and tourists. We need to preserve what makes this place special."

Quinn nodded.

"And while I'm complaining to you—" Mitch snorted again "—that's not all I have issue with. There's something suspicious going on up there at Azure Cove."

"What?"

"I don't know. A close friend of mine, name is Eve, she's the head of our historic committee. She worked at Azure Cove until she was let go recently."

"Why was she let go, if Azure Cove is hiring?"

"That I don't know," Mitch said. "Eve had something to tell me. We were supposed to meet Saturday afternoon. Instead, the tsunami hit. I haven't seen her since." He let out a long exhale before continuing. "Whatever Wheeler has going on there, he just might get away with it."

"What do you think he has going on? Something illegal?"

"Yeah. I doubt Wheeler plays by the rules unless they're his own. He has plans to build mega resorts on other secluded islands. The funding is, of course, dependent on the successful opening of Azure Cove. There's a lot at stake here for Devon Wheeler."

"I met him last night."

Mitch glanced at Quinn. "And what did you think?"

"Not sure yet," Quinn said, adhering to a rule from elementary school. First grade with Mrs. Hancock. *If you have nothing nice to say, don't say anything.* That didn't apply when in pursuit of terrorists, but as far as Quinn knew, Devon was just a pompous ass.

"Well, I don't trust the guy." Mitch hung a right onto a road marred with potholes. "He has several men who work for him. Bodyguards. One of them is a local. The rest came from who knows where. I heard Wheeler has them standing guard at the entrance to his complex now. Is it true?"

"Yeah, it's true. I thought it was to protect himself from the outbreak."

"Like I said, I think he's hiding something. But you're right too. He wouldn't take any chances with his own precious self, I'm sure of that. You won't see him lending a hand down here. Least he could do is lend his equipment."

"Did you ask?"

"Not me. Someone did. Couldn't ask him directly, but sent a message through his guards. I haven't seen any of those machines yet." After a few more miles, Mitch pulled off the road onto a grassy field and parked next to two military vehicles. "This is as far as we can drive. The rest of the way is underwater."

Quinn opened his door and turned sideways in his seat. He removed watertight boots from his backpack and put them on.

"You came prepared," Mitch said.

"I did. My fiancé knows what she's doing." He grabbed the bug spray from his bag. Not the environmentally friendly kind, but a powerful DEET spray. "She also insists I use this." He sprayed the repellant around his upper body and handed the can to Mitch.

Mitch raised his palm. "Thanks, man, but I'll be fine. I don't use that stuff."

They left the vehicle and tramped across a field to the edge of a steep ridge. Quinn's mouth fell open as he got his first look at the tsunami's aftermath. Flattened buildings and snapped trees littered the valley below, their remains floating with trash in the invasive dark water.

"This was Market Street," Mitch said. "Nalowale's shopping and social center. You should have seen it before you got here. It was worse."

With the streets concealed underwater, Quinn had no sense of layout or order. The area looked like a shallow lake, with trash and broken buildings emerging from the water. He was speechless

63

as he shielded his eyes from the sun and followed Mitch down the hillside toward the destruction.

At the bottom, the floodwater reached their shins. Rubble rose from the muck in every direction. Quinn set each foot down gently, wary of sharp objects lurking underneath the murky surface. They passed a mound of boards, then a jumbled pile of trees and trash swept against a washed-out delivery truck. A car door drifted past.

"That pile of rubble over there was the police station," Mitch said. "The mayor had an office in the same building."

In a line of damaged buildings that were still somewhat standing, the first store had shattered glass windows. A sign with RX and a mortar and pestle hung diagonally from the top corner.

They waded past the pharmacy to a two-story structure with a red roof. The front doors had blown off their hinges. One wall angled like the Leaning Tower of Pisa. "That's the Fresh Mart," Mitch said.

Two men stood in front of the store, speaking in raised voices. As Mitch and Quinn got closer, the slender one with a protruding Adam's apple shoved his hands onto his sides. "If we pull that slab away, the remaining space gets crushed," he said. "We have to bolster the wall."

The larger man with the rounded belly shouted back. "You an engineer now? If the water rises, he won't last in there. He's already been down there for days!"

The smaller man got in the other man's face. "I'd rather give him a chance than kill him on the spot. We have to bolster the wall."

"Bolster it? With what, Eddie? What are we supposed to use?"

Some people dealt with stress by lashing out at others. That was normal. The islanders had already endured so much, and tensions were high. But to Quinn, it sure looked like these men were itching to get in a fight. They reminded him of his ex-wife's friends—high on one of their drug binges. And the rival high-school football player who came after Quinn in a steroid-induced rage after losing a big game. As those vivid memories flashed through his mind, and he swatted at a mosquito undeterred by the repellant, he wondered if the island had a drug-use problem.

Arms held out wide, Mitch pushed his way between the men. "Everyone needs to take a step back and calm down," he shouted, sounding just as loud and upset as the other two.

The larger man didn't budge. His face was mere inches from Mitch's. "Get out of the way. We're getting him out of there. Now."

"Not if I can help it." The man named Eddie picked up a board floating nearby. He gulped, his Adam's apple retracting and bulging again like a giant bullfrog.

Quinn let out a loud whistle.

They turned to face him.

"Who the hell are you?" the large man asked.

"I'm here to save a life, just like you. So let's stop arguing and get to it. I want to see what we're dealing with."

They trudged through the flooded building, past toppled shelves, water-logged boxes, stinking perishables, and walls tilting at odd angles. As they got deeper inside, Quinn's uneasy feeling grew. The structure looked like it could collapse at any moment.

In the back of the store, in what might have been a storage area, two interior walls had fallen. One caved toward the other, creating a coffin-sized space underneath.

Mitch crouched and peered in through a head-sized crack. He pulled away and let out a string of expletives. "It's Alex. Rita's boy. Just a damn teenager." He crouched again, shouting into the space. "Alex! Can you hear us?"

No answer.

Mitch backed up, wringing his hands and swearing. "We gotta get him out of there."

Quinn peered inside. He saw a mop of dark hair above a face almost too pale and grayish blue to be human. Water reached his shoulders. Quinn could see the precarious challenge they faced, and why Eddie warned them about moving the wall. Shifting any of the parts might collapse the others or cause the water to rise. And yet they had to do something. "We need a truck with a winch. And something to prop up and stabilize a wall," he said, wondering if any of the machines at Azure Cove were small enough to maneuver into the constricted confines of the damaged store.

A soft moan came from the space below them.

"He's alive! Alex! Hang in there," Mitch yelled into the opening. "We're going to get you out."

A squelching, scraping sound came from beneath the water.

"Hurry!" The large man gripped a slab of concrete he had no chance of lifting alone. He tugged anyway, his face reddening and his muscles bulging. "Help me with this!"

"Stop moving!" Quinn said, studying the surrounding walls. The top wall slid, just barely, then faster, with a shuddering grind, garbled by the water. Quinn watched in horror as wall above the trapped boy slammed into the water and the coffin-sized space disappeared.

"Alex!" Mitch screamed.

The sound of tearing metal came from above, then a rumbling erupted round them.

"We have to get out of here," Quinn shouted. "Go! Go!" He pushed the men ahead of him. The creaks and moans intensified. Chunks of ceiling sliced into the water like giant balls of hail and one grazed Quinn's head. A cloud of plaster dust filled his throat and stuck to his wet skin.

They made it out, stumbling and choking on dust. Quinn turned to look back on the building as the remains of the red roof gave way, toppling down and smothering everything below. Including the boy.

The other men stood nearby, mouths agape, gasping. Mitch gripped the sides of his head. Tears streamed down his face, making dirty rivulets of wet dust.

Quinn took his bottled water from his pack, gulped some down to clear his throat, then splashed it over his irritated eyes. A sense of loss and helplessness tore at his insides. A teenager, someone's child, had just lost his life while four grown men were figuring out what to do. Still shocked, with his hand over his chest, he said a silent prayer for Alex and asked for strength. How many more would survive against all odds and then die?

So much for making a difference.

▼▲▼

Quinn excelled as a student athlete at West Point, served two tours in Afghanistan, and gone countless stretches without sleep as an FBI agent, yet this one day on the island's south shore had left him more emotionally and physically drained. It was dark when he and Mitch returned to the hospital. They were filthy and soaked with sweat as they delivered two more bodies to the growing row of corpses outside.

Mitch wiped his hands on his pants. After taking his keys from his pocket, he tossed them from one hand to the other. "We're done for the day. We risk doing more harm than good out there now that it's dark."

It made sense to stop, and Quinn was eager to catch up with Madeline. Throughout the day, Mitch had worked like the Energizer Bunny—moving debris, assessing damage, salvaging what they could salvage. He'd shown no signs of slowing or tiring. Quinn assumed it had something to do with their failure that morning.

67

"I've got people I need to check on," Mitch said. "Can you meet early morning?"

"Depends on when my ride comes."

Mitch scratched his head. "You know, my brother's truck is sitting at his house, and I think it still works. He won't need it."

"You sure about that?"

"I'm sure. My brother was the mayor." Mitch closed his eyes and made the sign of the cross on his forehead. "Come on. I'll take you there. You can drive it back. Air conditioning doesn't work, but otherwise it got him from point A to point B every day."

▼▲▼

With the keys to the borrowed truck in his pocket, Quinn slung his backpack over his shoulder and headed across the lawn toward the hospital. Flames rose from barrels surrounding the large tent, illuminating the profiles of the children seated around the edges. The boy with the ropes was still there, staring out into the night. A striking sense of aloneness and stoicism emanated from the child and pulled at Quinn's heartstrings. Drawn by a powerful feeling he didn't quite understand, Quinn walked over, kneeled down, and said, "Hey. What's your name?"

The boy lifted his arm. Someone had scrawled his name across his skin in black permanent marker.

"Ben Misawaki?" Quinn asked.

"The lady spelled it wrong." Ben shrugged. "It's Misowski. My father's last name. He's dead."

"I'm sorry." Quinn wondered if one of the bodies he'd retrieved might be Ben's father.

"Happened before I was born. I never knew him. He was military."

"Oh. So, you live with your mother?"

68

Ben hesitated before answering. "Yeah. I'm waiting for her. Even if cell phones were working, she can't call me to say where she is because I lost my phone. Are you from the Air Force base?"

"No. I'm just visiting the island. My friend is a doctor. She's helping inside the hospital."

Ben glanced toward the building behind them but said nothing.

"I live in Georgia, in the United States of America," Quinn said. "You know where that is?"

"I know America. I'm part American. My dad was from Minnesota. I've never been. This is the only place I've lived." Still holding the rope, he tucked his hands under his legs and scooted to the edge of the cot. "And I've visited Hawaii."

"I've been to the airport in Hawaii. It was night. I couldn't see much. If it's anything like Nalowale, I'd sure like to go back and visit again someday." He gestured toward the stitches over Ben's eye. "Did that happen in the tsunami?"

"Yeah. Stuff was flying at me from everywhere." At first, he sounded like he was trying to be tough. His voice changed, sounding more his age, as he added, "It was scary. Really scary."

"I bet it was." Quinn waited a few more seconds to see if Ben had anything else to say, if he wanted to talk. The ensuing silence lengthened. "Well, I better go inside and see what I can do to help. Good night, Ben. It was nice to meet you. Hang in there."

"Yeah." Ben lowered his gaze to the ropes. "Night."

Quinn walked around the tent. The woman with the nose piercings still sat near the entrance.

"Excuse me," he said. "That boy over there, Ben Misowski, he said he's waiting for his mother to come back. Do you know anything more about that?"

69

The woman gave Quinn a strange look. "They're all waiting for someone. If anyone is looking, this is the best place to be found. A few are here because their parents are hospitalized."

"What about Ben's mother? Is she inside?"

Her face softened. "I don't think so."

CHAPTER EIGHT

Clouds covered the moon, shrouding the road in darkness. After the unexplained episode where Nate slammed on his breaks, Madeline half expected a creature or madman to come charging out from the dense vegetation. Those same worries might have been ridiculous at home, but here? She flinched as a compact car whizzed past, dangerously close to their own.

"Mitch told me the refrigeration units are full." Quinn scratched at a large welt on his wrist and spoke without taking his eyes off the road. "Are you concerned about dead bodies decomposing outside the hospital?"

Madeline put her elbow on top of the door and leaned her head against her hand, partly outside the open window in the fresh air. "No. It's true that disease often follows natural disasters, but not because of exposure to dead bodies. Not so far, anyway. It's almost always related to sanitation failures. Death eliminates most diseases."

Covering her mouth, she yawned, and rested her head back against the worn seat. Her thoughts swirled with questions related to the outbreak. What was causing it? Bacteria? A fungus? A virus? A chemical exposure? A zoonotic infection? How was it being transmitted? How could they best treat it? Sharing her thoughts helped her identify missing pieces and challenged her to fill them with workable possibilities. But right then, she was too tired to speak.

Before she knew it, they had passed the mural and were approaching Azure Cove's archway. She'd completely lost track of time.

They kept the car running while they waited for the guards.

"Identification." The dyed-blond guard held out his meaty hand, staring blatantly and unapologetically at Madeline's breasts.

Madeline and Quinn handed over their passports.

The guard took Quinn's temperature, then walked around the car to take Madeline's. After a few more questions, the guards huddled together like two hulking bears and exchanged words Madeline couldn't hear. Then one spoke into a handheld radio while the other moved the roadblocks and waved the truck through.

As Madeline and Quinn reached the buildings at the end of the long drive, Wheeler came out, waving his arms above his head. He halted yards away from the driver's side of the truck and lowered his arms. "Have you figured out what's going on?"

"No." Madeline answered. "I'm gathering data."

"When can my crews return?"

"I don't know that either," she said.

Wheeler crossed his arms. "When will you know?"

"It depends on when I can get testing done and determine the nature of the outbreak."

Wheeler's frown deepened. "I thought that's what you went to the hospital to do. What *did* you do all day?"

Madeline wanted to ignore him. Instead, she took a deep breath before answering. "It takes time. The hospital is understaffed. I helped with some emergency situations."

"Is that why the CDC sent you here?" His tone made clear he thought otherwise. "Because that's not my understanding."

Quinn cleared his throat. "Look, we've only been here a day, and it's clear the island is suffering. If you came down to the south shore, you'll see you're in a position to help."

"I'm not sure what you're implying." Wheeler glared at Quinn. "The island's council is flush with money, thanks to me. I'm the one who chose this location. And almost immediately after that wave came ashore, I began sending gallons of fresh water around the island for those who need it. I also sent food and towels. And I decided I'm going to set aside a percentage of the resort's initial profits for an island relief fund. Provided my crews can ever come back and the complex can open as planned. Otherwise, there will be no profits. Only loss. Colossal loss."

"That's wonderful, about the fund, and what you're doing, but there are other ways you could help right now," Madeline said. "Adults and children lost their homes. They're sleeping in tents outside while there are empty rooms in the hotel and the dormitory. Those people could be inside rather than outside. They're exhausted and the mosquito population will soon exponentially expand."

"You're suggesting they come here?"

"Yes," she said. "I'm asking."

Wheeler snorted. "Absolutely not. I won't allow it. I won't turn this property into a makeshift hospital for the sick and violent, especially when you don't even know what's wrong with them. Imagine what that would do for marketing efforts. No one would want to step foot on this resort."

Madeline blinked back her frustration. "Not those with the outbreak symptoms, then. Just some of the injured and those who are in tents right now. They can move into the empty staff accommodations."

Wheeler stared without answering.

"Do you have any idea the extent of the damage and loss of lives?" Quinn snapped.

73

"I have enough to worry about over here. Investors, including myself, are going to lose billions if this complex doesn't open as planned. Do you understand that?" Wheeler huffed. "No, of course you don't. You couldn't conceive of it. The staggering costs associated with such an ambitious effort…just getting the necessary equipment here. And don't be asking me about that either. It stays. Without it…nothing gets finished. The two of you have some nerve."

"Anyone who has billions to lose has nothing to complain about." With a final look of disgust for Wheeler, Quinn put the car in gear and hit the gas.

Madeline was in shock from the conversation. She wasn't sure if she should laugh or cry. "That did not go so well."

"Unbelievable," Quinn said. "I needed to get away from him before I did something I might regret. He's a pompous ass."

"He is." She bit down on her upper lip. "But we need his cooperation and access to his resources here. If only he would leave the resort and see what's happening elsewhere on the island. That would change things for him. I think he'd feel differently and want to help."

They left the truck and followed the path to the dormitory buildings. In their room, Quinn plopped into a corner chair. Madeline sat on the bed and turned on her satellite phone.

Director Wallen answered her call on the third ring. "Madeline, good to hear from you. How is it going there?"

"I'm off to a slow start with the assessment. The outbreak patients are practically incoherent. I did some observing and gathered some data, enough to know there definitely *is* something unusual going on here and it's deadly. I expect there's an explanation that will make sense of it all, but I don't know what it is yet. I'm going to need more time."

"What does the lab work tell you?"

"Nothing yet. I can do some basic testing tomorrow with the equipment I brought and what little they have at that hospital, but I'll need to send samples back as soon as possible. I just have to figure out who to give them to."

"Couldn't the hospital staff tell you that?"

"They haven't had luck sending their own samples out. It's a mess here. If help is coming, it's not coming fast enough. The hospital needs more supplies and health care workers. FEMA. Is the quarantine preventing them from arriving?"

"Let me look into it," Patrick said. "I have a call with the Secretary of Health and Human Service later. She's worried about the outbreak."

When the call ended, Madeline checked the rest of her work messages but wasn't able to access her personal voicemail. After a few tries, she gave up.

"I'm going to shower." Quinn pushed himself up from his chair.

"We're lucky we can take a shower tonight. Too many others here can't." For the second time that day, Madeline felt guilty. She was going to sleep in a clean bed in a dry room. She felt even worse when she thought about their place in Atlanta, and the dated but fully functioning kitchen they were gutting. "I doubt the water in this area was compromised, but don't drink any of it."

He leaned against the bathroom doorframe. "Wasn't planning to."

"Along those lines," Madeline said, "I need to know what's going on with the water supply. Where it comes from and if anyone has tested it yet for contamination. And I need to know if the sewage system ran over. Could you help me get those answers while I'm at the hospital tomorrow?"

"I can look into it. Mitch can point me in the right direction."

75

"Thank you. Oh, and one more thing. An Airman looking after the outbreak patients mentioned a dog named Tank. He was sick on the base before the tsunami hit. Any chance you could locate the dog?"

"What do I do if I find him?"

"Good question." Madeline undid the buttons on her blouse. "I'd like a blood and stool sample. Ask his handler or someone who knows the animal to get them. I don't want you getting bit."

"Great." Quinn chuckled. "See, this is how I know you're one in a million. I think most women visiting an island with their fiancé would ask for a piece of art or jewelry—something special to take home with them. But you want me to check out the sewage system and find a sick dog."

She let out a soft laugh. "So glad you appreciate me. We're definitely not on vacation, but I love the idea of taking something special home with us to represent everyplace we go together, even if the trip is work related. Something small like an ornament to hang on our Christmas tree or a local craft to support the islanders. If anything like that survived the tsunami."

Quinn smiled as he stripped out of his clothes. "Anything else I can do for you?"

Madeline grinned. "Let me join you in the shower?"

"I thought you were tired."

"Oh, I am." She pushed her shirt off her shoulders and let it fall to the floor. "I'm beyond tired. This must be my second wind."

"I think I can accommodate your shower request. It's a little sexier than your last one."

Naked, Madeline waltzed past Quinn and into the small bathroom, pushing away the stress and grief of the day, if only for a few hours.

Madeline's call with her boss, followed by his call with the Secretary of Health and Human Services, caused a chain reaction. Within a few hours, the CIA Directorate of Operations sent out an urgent communication to the Electronic Warfare Group in the Pacific.

IMMEDIATELY INITIATE EYAM PROTOCOL

COORDINATES 18°27'12.9" N 155°25'09.5" E – RADIUS 3.0

TERMINATE ALL LAND/SEA/AIR COMMUNICATION
FREQUENCIES

CHAPTER NINE

Clouds hung low in the morning sky over the hospital and a row of bodies awaited identification on the lawn. Quinn wondered if they were all new arrivals, or some of the same ones from yesterday.

"Be careful out there," Madeline said.

"You, too." He kissed her forehead. "I'm proud of you."

"The feeling is mutual, Quinn." She rose onto her toes to kiss his lips.

Her hips swayed in a smooth rhythm as she moved away from him. When she was about halfway to the entrance, she turned and waved. Once the hospital's doors slid closed behind her, Quinn made his way across the lawn. He smelled meat cooking on barbecue grills set up between the tents, reminding him of the time a tornado took out electricity at their new house. It happened the day after he'd gone to Costco and stocked the extra freezer with meat. He and Madeline had invited all their new neighbors to a cookout feast. Their dog thought she'd died and gone to heaven eating pure sirloin. Using all the meat at once disappointed him, but he'd enjoyed meeting their new neighbors, and they knew it was only a short matter of time before their electricity returned and they could restock their fridge. Not the case on Nalowale. Some things on the island would never be the same.

An old man ducked out from inside one of the small tents.

"Good morning," Quinn said, his tone absent any lightness.

The man grunted, looked around at other people trudging across the lawn, and went back inside his shelter.

Inside the large tent, the middle-aged woman with the nose piercings squatted on her heels in front of a line of children. She handed a juice box and a brown bag to a little girl. The child moved away from the line and another child stepped forward to take her spot.

"You're still here," Quinn said to the woman, stating the obvious. He intended his comment to show he noticed and appreciated her dedication.

"Where else would I go?" She wiped something from the child's chin. "My home is uninhabitable."

"I'm sorry," he said. A woefully inadequate response. He waited until the woman stood up before posing his question. "Think I can borrow one of these kids for the day? Ben Misowski. If he'll come with me?"

The woman looked him over, her gaze settling on his gun. "I don't know. Are you the police? American police?"

"FBI. I can sign him out or something. I'll be with Mitch…um…he's on the island's governing council. And I'll put my name and cell number on your board there, in case someone comes looking for Ben. Does that work?"

"There's no phone service."

"Well, when it comes back, you'll have my number."

She shook her head as if she meant no, but what came out of her mouth was, "Okay." With that, she squatted back down, giving her attention to the next child in line.

The ease of obtaining permission made Quinn incredibly sad. He walked around the outside of the tent, unable to imagine how the next days, weeks, months and years would roll out to be anything but sad for all but the youngest children. Then he spotted

Ben. He wore the same clothes as yesterday and was tying the shoelaces of a younger child. His ropes hung from his belt loops.

"Morning, Ben." Quinn wasn't sure exactly what to say next. He didn't want to make the child uncomfortable. He forged ahead with, "I have to check out some things on the island. I'm going with a man named Mitch."

"My mom has a friend named Mitch."

"Maybe it's the same guy. Anyway, I was thinking, in case Mitch gets busy with something else, I could really use help from someone who knows the layout of the land. Would you be willing to show me around?"

"You have a car?"

"I do. So, you want to help me? Maybe we can look for your mom while we're out."

"Yes!" Ben jumped up. "Let's go now."

Ben's immediate enthusiasm surprised Quinn. "Great. I'm going to write my info on the board over here, next to yours. Then...if your mother comes while we're gone, she'll know who you're with and that you'll be back later."

"Okay, good. Do that."

After updating the board, they headed toward the borrowed truck. Quinn tried to lead Ben away from the row of dead bodies, but a man sobbed as he carried a small figure away from the others. It was impossible not to notice. Quinn wondered if someone was checking the corpses for Ben's mother.

A woman rushed over to Quinn and held a photograph to his face. "Have you seen my sister? Her name is Mary."

Quinn studied the picture, although he was certain he had not seen the woman anywhere. "No, I'm sorry. I'll keep an eye out for her."

"Thank you," the woman mumbled. Her posture sagged. She lowered her hands and stumbled away, leaving Quinn feeling terrible for her and so many others like her.

"Maybe we should wait in the truck," Quinn said. "This is my ride." He motioned for Ben to get in the passenger side.

"Where's Mitch?" Ben asked, opening the door.

"He should be here soon. He'll find the truck." Quinn suddenly felt uncomfortable. If Mitch didn't show, Ben might think he'd concocted his story for a sinister purpose. Or maybe that wouldn't occur to the child. Perhaps that sort of suspicious attitude came with age and experience. Maybe it was uniquely American to assume people were up to no good.

Ben sat on the front edge of the seat, his shoulder against the door, studying Quinn. "Why do you have a gun?"

"I'm an FBI agent." Quinn touched the holster at his hip. "Sort of like the police."

"I know FBI. I've watched Criminal Minds. Don't tell my mom. It's not for kids."

"Right." Quinn smiled, then looked out the window for any sign of Mitch. The seconds seem to pass slowly. "Have you had breakfast yet?"

"Nah." Ben shook his head.

"I brought some to share." Quinn lifted a bag off the seat, holding it between them. "See if there's anything in there you like."

Ben removed a single-serving box of cheerios and tore open the package. "I like these. Thanks."

"You're welcome. Listen, since I've never met your mom. How would you describe her? Is there anything unique or unusual about her I might recognize?"

81

Ben poured cereal into his hand. Quinn noticed the thick burn marks across the child's palms.

"I made her a friendship bracelet out of rainbow colors," Ben said. "It's her good luck charm. She always wears it. And she's got a sea goddess tattoo on her shoulder."

"A sea goddess?"

"You know…a mermaid. You can see it when she wears a tank top."

"What's her first name?"

"Eve."

Quinn didn't think he knew an Eve, and yet there was something familiar about the name. He continued to watch for Mitch while Ben finished two boxes of cereal and a banana, eating mostly in silence. After ten minutes, and still no sign of Mitch, Quinn grabbed the CB radio. He pressed the talk button and asked for Mitch but got no response. "He must have gotten held up," he said, putting the radio back on its holder. "I don't want to wait here all day. We can get going and come back to meet Mitch later."

"Okay." Ben clutched the empty boxes and banana peel in his hands, and Quinn held the brown bag out for the trash. "Where do you have to go first?" Ben asked.

"The Air Force base." Quinn twisted the key in the ignition. The vehicle let out a metallic squawk and then rumbled in protest before starting. "I have a general idea of how to get there, but I might need your help. The GPS on my phone isn't working."

Ben pulled his seatbelt across his chest. "Why are we going to the base?"

"I need to check water sources and search for a German Shepherd named Tank," Quinn said, pulling away from the hospital.

"We need to find a dog?"

82

"Yes."

"I love dogs. I've always wanted one. A big one, like a lab. Or a little one, like a Chihuahua who can go with me anywhere I go."

"I've got a rescue dog," Quinn said. "Her name is Maddie."

"Did you bring her?"

"No. Madeline, that's my fiancé, the woman I'm going to marry—her parents are looking after our dog in Atlanta."

"What's she like?"

"Madeline?"

"Your dog."

"Oh. She's a mut—a mix of lab and terrier and who knows what else. She enjoys chasing balls more than anything on the planet, besides me. And food. She's very friendly. She loves everyone. Especially kids. She likes car rides, too."

After a few miles, Ben leaned forward and looked out the window on Quinn's side. "See that sign?"

A large sign featured a gleaming rendition of Azure Cove, the finished product in all its glory. *Azure Cove Luxury Complex, the global debut and signature resort for Wheeler Properties, is now hiring.*

"That means we're near my house. Down there is where I live." Ben pointed to a flooded road. Large yellow roadblocks rose out of the brown water, clearly marked: *Danger. Downed Power Line. Do not Cross.*

"We aren't allowed through," Ben said, still staring out the window. "And the people who were at home can't drive out. I walked all the way here from Market Street. I was standing right over there—," he pointed, "—the signs and stuff weren't up yet. I saw that power line hanging down. I was going to go around it. That's when the survivor truck came."

"What's a survivor truck?"

"It's a big green truck with tall sides on the back. It goes around and picks up kids. Makes them get in. And it catches anyone with the sickness. Guys with guns are driving it, but they're not military. They made me and another kid get in the back. They put us on one side, and the sick people on the other. And they weren't sick from the tsunami. It was something else. They were angry. They didn't want to get in. The men from the truck stuck needles into them to make them calm down. Then they took us to the hospital. The kids had to go to the tent. They said our parents would meet us there. I don't know where the sick people went."

Quinn thought of Madeline. Unless someone had pulled her into helping elsewhere again, she was working directly with those sick people. "Do you have family besides your mother on the island?" he asked. "Grandparents? Aunts or uncles?"

"Nah. It's just me and my mom ever since my grandfather died."

"Where was your mother when the tsunami came ashore?"

"In a store on Market Street."

A heavy weight formed on Quinn's chest. He'd seen the area. "And where were you?"

"Attached to a tree." Ben lifted the ropes tied to his pants. "These saved me." He held up his hands. "That's how I got these." Turning to the window, he ducked his head and peered into the side-view mirror. He touched the stitches around his eye and winced.

"If you want to talk about what happened, I'm a good listener." Quinn decided to leave it at that rather than asking more questions. Ben had to be traumatized, though it didn't show. The child was exceptionally brave and stoic, but maybe he was in denial, and the possibility of his mother's death hadn't fully hit him yet.

"Where did *you* sleep last night?" Ben asked.

"I'm staying at the new resort that's being built on the north side of the island." Quinn felt a twinge of anger. So many empty rooms there. So many who could use them.

"Azure Cove?"

"Yeah. You know it from that sign near your neighborhood?"

"My mom used to work there. She got fired because she wouldn't mess around with the owner."

Quinn had to suppress a bark of laughter. Ben's comment wasn't funny, but it caught him by surprise, coming in such a matter-of-fact manner from a child. "That's what she told you?"

"I heard her telling Joyce. Her best friend. I don't know what that means, but she was angry." Ben's expression remained serious. "I think you have to turn here."

"The owner you mentioned, do you know his name?"

"Yeah. Mr. Wheeler."

Exactly the name Quinn expected to hear. His dislike for Wheeler intensified.

"Why do you need to look at where the water comes from anyway?" Ben asked.

"Most of the fresh water on your island comes from rainfall," Quinn said, relaying information Mitch had shared with him yesterday. "It's contained in a reservoir on the base. And with a natural disaster, like the tsunami, water systems are pretty vulnerable. They can get contaminated."

Ben made a face. "Huh?"

"Polluted. And if the water isn't clean like it should be, people can get sick."

85

"People are already sick. I told you. The ones on the survivor truck. And I heard adults talking about it around the tent. There are lots more. Acting crazy and dangerous."

"They are. And we don't know why yet. That's what you and I are going to help find out, so people can get better and no one else gets sick."

Ben settled his head against his seat, resting his hands in his lap. "My dad lived on the base before I was born. And I've been there before. Two times. I had a friend in school whose dad worked there. I went with them."

Quinn knew they were close when they came to an American flag flapping at the top of a pole. Farther down the road, a tall chain-link fence secured the base. The words *Welcome to Nalowale Island Air Force Base* arched over the checkpoint's gate. It was like Azure Cove's archway, except far smaller and much less elaborate. He hadn't noticed it when they arrived on the island.

Quinn pulled up to the check point with the satellite dish on top. He shut off the truck's engine.

"Good morning," said an Airman wearing an Air Force Security Forces armband. "Can I help you, sir?"

"Hi. I'm Special Agent Quinn Traynor with the FBI's counter terrorism unit. And this is Ben Misowski. He's helping me navigate the island."

"My dad used to live on this base," Ben said with a certain measure of pride.

Quinn showed his personal identification verification card, his FBI credentials, and the certificate the CDC obtained for Madeline, which allowed them to land on the island. "I'm here because of the outbreak the military and islanders are experiencing. I need to have a look around the base."

"Right," the Airman answered. "We were told you were on the island. I can have Airman Williams escort you."

"I'm also looking for a German Shepherd named Tank," Quinn said. "Know where I can find the dog?"

"Haven't seen the dog or his handler, but you can ask around the base. Just a few steps to take first. New protocol." The Airman took their temperatures. "Are you experiencing any signs of unusual aggression?"

"No," Quinn answered.

"Any hallucinations?" the Airman asked.

"No."

"What's a hallucination?" Ben asked.

"It means you're seeing things that aren't really there," Quinn told him.

"I'm not." Ben shook his head. "I'm not sick."

Airman Williams arrived wearing a mask. He got into the truck with Quinn and Ben to guide them around the base, starting with the reservoir.

The base covered over three miles, and its beauty surprised Quinn. Natural green spaces with palms between barracks and buildings looked more like a college campus in a tropical setting than a military base.

"There's no one around," Ben said. "When I was here before, there were a lot of soldiers. Men and women."

"The base is closing soon," Williams said. "Most who are still on the island are out helping to clean up after the tsunami. Some are sick. Some are missing."

Heading to the reservoir took them west, away from the airstrips and hangars. He parked under the shade of trees so the truck wouldn't feel like a sauna later, got out, and walked around to the back. The truck bed contained a hodgepodge of tools, a large flashlight, empty thermoses, and a cooler. Quinn grabbed a crowbar.

"Why are you taking that?" Ben asked.

"Tank might be dangerous if he isn't feeling well. That's what happens with animals. They can't help themselves."

"Just like the people on the survivor truck who had to get shots to calm down," Ben said as they walked to the reservoir with Williams a few steps behind them. "But you've got your gun."

"I know. But if the dog is acting aggressively, I'd rather scare him away with the crowbar than shoot him."

The water supply was contained in a picturesque valley surrounded by grassy hillsides. From a lookout tower, an Airman watched them approach. He nodded and waved, giving Quinn the impression the Airman at the entrance had radioed who they were and why they were there.

With Ben skipping ahead of him, Quinn walked to the concrete platform surrounding one end of the reservoir.

"We're over a mile from the ocean," Williams said. "The floodwater didn't come this far."

"If this is where my water comes from, how does it get all the way to my house?" Ben asked.

"Through underground pipes," Williams answered.

Quinn studied the structure surrounding the water. The concrete showed cracks and signs of aging. The pipes would also be old and might have problems with corrosion and leakage underground. But even if that was the case, could leaking pipes have anything to do with the outbreak?

"Come on, let's find Tank," Quinn said to Ben. "And remember, if we find him, we don't touch him. We'll get someone who knows him to help us."

"Haven't seen Tank since the tsunami," Williams said. "Heard he was sick. Shame. He was a good dog. Might have crawled off to die quietly in the bushes or something. Animals do that. And depending on where he was when the wave hit, he might have gotten—"

"Yeah, okay," Quinn said, cutting the Airman off to spare Ben any gory details.

"Tank! Come, Tank! Where are you, Tank?" Ben stuck a finger on each side of his mouth and spit out air. Quinn watched him do it again before he realized Ben was trying to whistle.

"Let me show you how I learned that." Quinn demonstrated with a loud whistle. "Lick your lips first. Then pucker your mouth. And when you blow, try to lift your tongue up a little, get it out of the way."

Ben tried several times and finally got it.

"Good job, little man," Williams said.

Ben's eyes lit up. The corners of his mouth rose, forming dimples in his cheeks.

"Can't whistle and smile at the same time," Quinn said, glad the child had a little something to feel good about.

They walked southeast on a trail toward the ocean, continuing to call the dog's name. Ben whistled so many times his mouth must have been sore. As they descended a hillside, Quinn noticed small pools of water filling nooks and depressions. "The floodwater came up here. See how it flattened the grass and covered it with silt?" As he pointed to the ground, a brown creature that looked like a beaver scurried across their path. "What was that?" Quinn asked.

"A swamp rat," Williams said. "Those things are trouble. They eat the wires under cars. You don't want them around."

"Hey, see that?" Ben pointed to a bunker, most of it concealed into the hillside. "The Hobbit Hole. Like from Lord of the Rings."

Williams laughed. "That's a bunker. A hardened storage facility."

On the front of the bunker, a large metal door sat flush with the ground. A steel plate covered a large padlock, preventing someone from cutting the lock with a torch or hitting it with a hammer to gain entry. Moss, grasses, and wildflowers covered the top and lent the structure a cozy, secretive look.

"My friend calls them Hobbit Holes," Ben said. "Would a bunker have been safe during the tsunami?"

"Probably," Williams said. "They're good protection for tornadoes and out here in the Pacific Ocean—typhoons. They built these during World War II."

Ben looked up at Quinn. "Were you alive then?"

Williams laughed again as Quinn answered. "Ah, no. I'm not quite that old, Ben. That was in the 1940s. Your great, great, grandparents would have been about my age then."

Ben kicked at the ground, pushing dirt into a horse-shoe shaped mound around his sneaker. "Were you in any wars?"

"I was in Afghanistan."

"Were you the good guys or the bad guys?"

"The good guys."

"Did you win?"

"It's sort of hard to say. It was the longest war in the history of the United States."

"Wow. What were you fighting about?"

Quinn gazed up at the horizon, wondering how to condense years of politics, strategy, and history into a response that would make sense to an inquisitive child.

"What's inside the bunkers, anyway?" Ben asked while Quinn was still forming an answer for the last question.

"I don't know. I'm sure Airman Williams can tell us."

"Obsolete munitions," Williams said. "They're on many bases. Bombs the U.S. no longer needs because they're technically outdated or deteriorating – but just as dangerous. One of our jobs here is to guard them until disposal."

"Who wants to steal them?" Ben asked.

"Terrorist groups. Criminals. Rednecks who think they'll make a good fireworks display." Williams chuckled. "That's why we guard them on an isolated island."

"Have Explosive Ordinance Disposal inspected them yet?" Quinn asked. "Since the tsunami?"

"Our EOD man is missing," Williams said. "These aren't nuclear or chemical munitions, if that's what you're thinking. They're conventional bombs. And all munitions stored in bunkers are inert until they are loaded onto aircraft and armed, for safety reasons."

Movement came from the earth, as if a large truck was rumbling past. Ben gasped. He crouched down, then quickly stood and grabbed Quinn's arm. The shaking ceased as suddenly as it began.

"Just an after-shock," Quinn said. "It's nothing for us to worry about."

Ben let go of Quinn.

They were back on the path and walking through trees when Quinn noticed the first black vulture. As they got closer, he heard the buzz of flies. "Wait here, Ben. I'm going to check on something."

Ben did what he was told.

Quinn unzipped his backpack and put on a mask. He and Williams walked toward the area directly under the vulture. Quinn used the crowbar to push the bushes back, sending a swarm of blowflies up from a mass of black and tan fur. Definitely a German Shepherd. Quinn was glad Ben wasn't there to see the dead animal.

Quinn smacked an insect away from his neck and took what he needed from his bag—gloves and the sample collection equipment. He got the sample and swab and moved to an open area. There, he put the samples in his bag and pulled off his mask and gloves before returning to Ben.

"We'll give Tank a proper burial," Williams told Ben.

Quinn nodded. Would the dog's death provide a clue to the outbreak?

CHAPTER TEN

Matthew and Captain Barstow were outside the containment area when Madeline arrived. Dozens of brown paper bags filled large bins on the floor. Another bin held syringes.

"Good morning," she said, scanning the list of patients' names. There were more. "How did they get down here?"

"Someone is rounding them up, sedating them, and bringing them in," Matthew answered.

"Who?"

"I don't know. Civilians. It's more for the safety of others than anything else. I can't say any of them are getting better in here."

The thought of sick and violent patients freely roaming the island unsettled her. How many others were out there? Were new infections occurring every day, or had there been one wave of the disease?

"You hand them the food," Matthew said to Barstow. "When they take it—if they do—I'm going to jab them with the sedative anywhere I can, as fast as I can."

"Do you have tranquilizer guns here?" Barstow asked. "That's what we need."

"Unless there are some on the base I don't know about, we'd have to get them from a vet. And the only vet was on Market Street."

"Wait," Madeline said. "I want to examine everyone and ask them some questions. It's critical we find out how and where they got sick. Can you hold off on the sedative until I've done that?"

"Yeah. Sure," Matthew said. "But don't expect to get much from them. They're barely making sense. The guys who were monitoring them last night don't think any of them slept. Not at all."

After putting on masks, gloves, and gowns, Matthew entered the containment area first. Shouts rose above the moans and delirious, non-sensible mutterings. The stench of sweat had grown stronger.

"Dr. Hamilton!" A sharp voice startled Madeline. She spun around to face a man who gripped the bars of his cell and pressed his head against them, staring at her with an insane intensity. A sheen of sweat glistened on his flushed skin. Something about him was at once frightening…and familiar. After a few seconds, Madeline knew why. Goosebumps rose on her skin.

"Nate," she whispered. Only two days ago, she and Quinn had shared a confined space with the Airman for almost half an hour on the drive to Azure Cove. She prayed the illness wasn't airborne. Nate's condition made her question the source of her current unease—the tightening in her chest, the edgy churning sensation in her stomach. Was she already infected? Did those symptoms represent the first signs of the illness? Or were they simply her body's autonomic response to the pandemonium spiraling around her? She pressed her lips together, forcing herself to dismiss her rising panic—it served no purpose—and focus on her goals for the day. *Collect the data. Analyze the results. Determine treatment and prevention protocols.*

Nate rocked on his feet, hitting his head against the steel bars with each forward movement. "Open the damn door now or so help me, you will be one sorry bitch when I get out of here."

Madeline moved closer. "Nate, what happened?"

"They're taking over our brains. That's why we can't use our phones. They're using the radio waves to control us." Nate glared at her. "And I think you know that, doctor. That's why you're here." His voice became even more agitated. "You're the ringleader. You're the instigator."

"Nate, I'm not...I'm here to help you."

"Like hell you are!" Nate spit at her and retreated to the back of his cell as thick fluid dripped down the front of her shield.

She looked from Matthew to Barstow. "Can one of you stay with me? Help me examine each person?" Even sedated, the patients' behavior was unpredictable. She'd prefer help from Matthew *and* Barstow, which made her think of Quinn. She wondered what he was doing. He was strong, trained to handle dangerous men, and wouldn't hesitate to help wherever needed, especially if she was the one asking. But she didn't want him down here. She wouldn't put him at risk. Not if she could help it.

"I'm all yours," Barstow said. "I was planning on staying most of the day to look after the Colonel and the others. Just tell me what to do."

"I planned to spend the morning down here, too," Matthew said. "Let's start the exams with Martina. She was one of the first brought here."

Matthew and Captain Barstow opened Martina's cell and guided the petite woman to the windowless exam room in the back of the containment area. Hair matted, face pinched into a grimace, Martina pressed a trembling hand over her heart and said, "So fast...so fast...so fast."

"We're going to give you some blood pressure meds to help you with that," Madeline said. "But first, we need you to answer some questions."

They lifted her onto the exam table. She couldn't have weighed more than a hundred pounds, if that. Barstow kept his grip on Martina's arm, but Matthew let go to get her chart. With her eyes squeezed shut, she shrugged her shoulders to her ears and held them there. She might not feel pain, but her mental anguish was apparent.

"Can you please tell us when your symptoms first started," Madeline said.

Martina's hair fell across her face as she scratched at her arm. "Things are crawling under my skin." Her voice rose with each word. She dug deeper, drawing blood as she raked her nails across her arms. "There's something in there! They're going up my arm!" She looked at Barstow with panic in her eyes. "You're putting more in! No! No!" With no warning, her hand shot forward and clawed down his cheek.

Barstow grabbed her arms and wrestled them behind her back. She screeched and flailed against him. "Give her more sedative already," Barstow said. "I'm not real comfortable using brute force against a woman here." He was much bigger and stronger, but she struggled like a feisty wild animal caught in a death trap.

"I've got her." Matthew dropped Martina's chart and helped Barstow hold her still. Martina thrashed between the two men, jerking her shoulders and hips, throwing her head every which way.

Madeline cringed at the scene playing out before her, it was unlikely Martina would answer her questions, but she had to know how the patients got sick. "Martina, this is important. Do you remember if you drank tap water after the tsunami? Or if you swallowed floodwater?"

Martina snarled. In one quick movement, she sunk her teeth into the exposed skin between Barstow's gown and gloves.

To his credit, Barstow maintained his hold on Martina and didn't wrench away. "Sedative!" he shouted.

Matthew grabbed a syringe, poked it into the woman's arm, and expelled half the contents. Martina made one last attempt at pulling free before her shoulders dropped and her head lolled forward.

Rotating Barstow's wrist, Matthew examined the bite. "Oh, crap. You don't need stitches, but it broke the skin. I'm giving you an antibiotic, just in case."

Barstow's chest rose and fell with quick breaths as he stared at the angry red welts on his wrist. "I guess we'll find out soon enough if it's contagious."

Barstow was right. The bite would now prove to be an experiment of sorts.

Martina was finally quiet.

"Do you remember where you were when your symptoms began?" Madeline asked again, though she no longer expected to get a reliable answer.

Martina didn't answer. Her eyes remained open, but she went into a semi-catatonic state, staring ahead at nothing while she slowly twisted her fingers, methodically switching from one to the next. Madeline wished she knew what was going on behind Martina's cold eyes. Her sudden silence was more frightening than her shouting.

Madeline helped Martina lie down, took her vital signs, then checked for insect and animal bites, wounds, and any outward sign of infection. A few raised lumps dotted Martina's arms and legs. Possibly mosquito bites. She also had minor cuts, which may have been self-inflicted from scratching her skin.

"Has she received a broad-spectrum antibiotic yet?" Madeline asked.

Matthew checked Martina's chart. "Yes. We gave her ampicillin when she arrived. Doesn't seem to be helping."

"Let's try ciprofloxacin." Madeline studied Martina's face. There might have been a yellowish cast to her eyes and skin. "Do you think she looks a little jaundiced?"

Matthew narrowed his eyes, studying Martina. "Maybe."

"I'm wondering about hepatitis or cirrhosis. Do you have her medical history?" She felt terrible talking about Martina as if the woman wasn't present, but Martina was in no condition to give coherent answers and there were still so many more patients to see.

"Not that I'm aware of," Matthew answered. "But the guy who was here yesterday with Barstow knew her. He said she had no known health concerns. I don't know Martina, but I've seen her before. She works in the pharmacy. She was there when the tsunami hit. She's lucky to have gotten out alive."

When it came time to draw blood, Madeline had trouble finding a vein. She pressed her finger into Martina's skin. "Minimal elasticity. She's really dehydrated. We need to give her IV fluids."

"I brought some down," Matthew said. "In that drawer."

Barstow encouraged Martina to sip some water. She wouldn't open her mouth.

"Let me try to find a vein." Matthew wrapped a tourniquet above Martina's elbow and tapped her skin. When that didn't work, he removed the tourniquet and rotated her arm, attempting to insert the venipuncture needle into the veins on the back of her hand. "Got it," he said after a few tries. He drew a blood sample, then began hydrating her with an IV line. Finally, they walked her back to the cell and helped her lie down on the cot.

Madeline returned to the exam room. She disposed of her gloves and wiped the back of her hand over her forehead, pressing errant wisps of hair away from her head. At least it was cool in the basement.

"Can you examine Colonel Nelson next?" Barstow directed his question to Matthew. "He is our boss."

"Which is why you need to let me out of here," Colonel Nelson shouted. He had heavy bags under his bloodshot eyes. "I don't need help. Let me out or both of you will find yourselves with a dishonorable discharge."

"I need to get a good look at his leg wound," Matthew said. "There's no way we can examine him without sedating him first."

Barstow agreed and whispered, "I hate seeing him like this. I hate that we're about to stick him with a needle."

They unlocked his cell door, went in, and immediately administered the sedative. Holding Colonel Nelson on either side, they kept him from attacking them.

The Colonel became more manageable as the sedative took effect, but it was still a struggle to get him from the cell to the exam room. Once there, Matthew maintained a grip on his arm.

Catching his breath, Barstow took a seat in the room's corner. He removed a container from his pocket and pinched some snuff.

"Let me have some of that," the Colonel mumbled.

Barstow's forehead scrunched, forming wavy lines across his brow. "I thought you hated this stuff."

"Give it to me."

Barstow looked at Matthew. "That okay?"

99

"Fine by me," Matthew said. "I'd rather he ate and drank something, but give him whatever he wants, if it helps him feel better."

After Barstow gave Colonel Nelson a generous portion of snuff, Matthew treated the Colonel's wounded leg while Madeline checked his vitals and took fluid samples. From exiting his cell to getting him back inside it, the process took over twenty minutes.

Between patients, Madeline was changing her gloves in the exam room when Matthew shouted, "Oh, no! She's seizing."

Madeline rushed from the exam room in time to see the last rhythmic contractions of Martina's seizure on the concrete floor. Matthew yanked a pillow from the nearest cot and shoved it under her head, then rolled her onto one side. Her body stilled. A puddle of urine spread around her.

"Martina?" Matthew shook her arm, then jostled her. When she didn't respond, he shouted, "Can you hear me?" He made a fist and rotated his knuckles over her sternum.

Still no response.

"She's out," Matthew said. "Unresponsive to painful stimuli. But she has a pulse, and she's breathing."

"We have to get her upstairs and into a bed where someone can monitor her," Madeline said. "I'll get on her blood work. We need a CT scan. Maybe a lumbar puncture."

"We'll have to figure out how to run the tests ourselves or send them off the island," Matthew said.

"Good luck with that." Barstow frowned. "They quarantined the island. Nothing on or off."

"I heard. Do you know who made that call?" Madeline asked.

"I don't know," Barstow said. "Those are the orders the base got. And the Air Force planes are the only way things can fly out of here."

"I'll have to clear a bed. I'll be back." Matthew tore off his gloves as he jogged from the room.

Madeline cleaned Martina up as best she could and changed her into clean scrubs. She watched her breathing and made sure Martina still had a pulse. There was no further seizure activity or posturing to indicate brain swelling.

When Matthew returned, he was breathing hard, as if he'd run all the way there. Beads of sweat rolled down his temples. "I had to take care of something else. Grace needed my help. But I found a bed for her. Made one is more like it."

"She's still unconscious. No pain response. Her pupils aren't reacting. I think she's in a coma."

Matthew scooped Martina into his arms and carried her out of the cell.

"Don't you want to put her on a gurney—," Madeline didn't finish as she remembered the elevators to the second floor weren't operating.

"I'm needed upstairs," Matthew said, trudging through the containment area toward the doors. "Grace and Lydia are all alone. Find me later. Or I'll find you."

"I will," Madeline said. "Things will get better soon, Matthew. Hang in there."

▼▲▼

"I'm going outside for a few minutes," Madeline said, once she and Barstow had administered meds to all the patients. She clasped her hands and reached her arms forward to stretch. "Then I'll be in the lab."

She left the hospital through the back doors, stepping out into the fresh air. While she was in the basement, the sun had disappeared behind thick clouds. In the distance, a waterspout shot down from the sky in the distance. No one else paid attention to it, so apparently it wasn't a threat.

Now that she was alone, away from her patients, and had a few seconds to think about herself, her worries returned. She lifted a hand in front of her face and studied it. It was a little shaky. Simply from the stress of the morning? Or because she hadn't eaten lunch? Or something else...

Woods bordered the back and sides of the buildings. She walked to the edge of them and plopped onto the ground beside a tree. With her legs curled underneath her body, she read over her handwritten notes. Thirty-two patients in the containment area. Each showed some combination of the following symptoms:

- confusion
- loss of pain
- accelerated pulse and heartbeat
- hallucinations
- hyper-aggression
- hyper-activity
- insomnia
- loss of appetite
- dehydration
- increased sweating
- tremors
- dilated pupils

She clicked her pen and added seizures and coma to the list.

The patients weren't getting better. They were getting worse.

What did it all mean?

Her list of questions was long. The answers remained elusive. Getting lab work done was critical. They needed the information days ago. She could only hope those results would tell them more.

CHAPTER ELEVEN

The sky darkened in the distance over the north side of the island. Above Azure Cove.

"Look!" Ben pointed out the front windshield. "A waterspout. See it?" A rotating column of water shot down from the thick clouds. A tornado over water.

Quinn took glances at the anomaly as he drove. "You see those often?"

"Yeah. Can we drive by my street again?" Ben asked. "On the way back to the hospital?"

"Sure." Still focusing on the road ahead, Quinn reached into his bag. He handed Ben a bottle of water and grabbed another for himself. "Just give me directions."

"We're close. Turn when you get to the sign for Azure Cove."

When they reached Ben's neighborhood, the power lines remained draped precariously into the road. "Can you park so I can get out?" Ben asked. "Just for a few minutes? I have to see something."

Quinn parked in a wet, grassy area on the side of the road. Ben jumped out and Quinn followed him as he clopped up a muddy hill to one of the tallest trees. Its trunk was two or three times the size of a phone pole. Knotted branches reached in every direction. There were two giant stones nearby. Quinn leaned against one as Ben wrapped his ropes around the tree trunk.

"What are you doing?" Quinn asked.

Ben's eyes brightened. "Getting up high so I can see." Putting the ropes to work, he shimmied up the tree faster than Quinn thought possible, removing and adjusting the ropes as he ascended over branches.

"Wow. You're pretty good at that, aren't you?" Quinn's unease grew as Ben kept climbing. "Ben, that's far enough."

"Don't worry," Ben said. "Come up here with me. You'll see."

"Nope. I'm not a fan of heights." He had an irrational fear, though he'd dealt with it time and time again. But there was nothing irrational about his current reaction. A fall from Ben's height would shatter bones.

"I do this all the time. Sometimes I just hang out at the top and watch stuff happening on the ground. I can see my street from here."

"It's not a good idea," Quinn said. "I don't want you to fall."

"You sound like my mom now." Ben laughed. A wonderful, welcome sound, since there had been little to none of it on the island. "I don't want to fall either. That's why I'm not going to." He stopped climbing near the top and looked out across the neighborhood. "I don't see my mom. I don't see anyone."

"All right. Come on down," Quinn said. "We can come back tomorrow."

Ben scrambled down. Once he was safely on the ground again, Quinn felt a release of tension and could switch his focus to the neighborhood. Rows of quaint bungalow homes. Shutters popping with vibrant shades of turquoise, magenta, coral, and green. Surrounded by muddy water and debris, it would be a long time before the homes, the first floors at least, were inhabitable again.

"We better get back with the samples we got," Quinn said.

Ben took one last look at his neighborhood, then returned to the truck. He was quiet as they headed back to the hospital, allowing Quinn time to ponder why he'd taken a child along with him. Not just any child, but this child. Was it an odd thing that he'd done? It didn't feel that way. Having Ben in the passenger seat seemed natural. Quinn hoped he'd taken Ben's mind off the horrors of the situation, at least for a few hours, and helped the day pass a little quicker than it would have if he'd stayed in the tent.

A few miles from Ben's neighborhood, Quinn spotted a Ford truck with a University of Hawaii sticker parked alongside a narrow road. The driver's side door hung open. Quinn slowed and eased around the vehicle. "I think that's Mitch's truck. But I don't see Mitch. Maybe he had car trouble."

"Maybe a swamp rat ate through his gas line," Ben said. "But why would he leave his door open like that?"

Farther down the road, a man in a cowboy hat walked on the edge of the road with a long, purposeful stride, pumping his arms. He carried a rifle in one hand.

"There he is," Quinn said.

Mitch looked over his shoulder and scowled at the oncoming car.

"That's my mom's friend," Ben said. "I know him."

"He probably needs a ride." Quinn waved at Mitch.

Mitch didn't return the greeting. He kept walking, eyes straight ahead.

Quinn had to drive past Mitch to find a place to pull over, an alcove allowing just enough room for other cars to pass. "Wait here, okay?" he said to Ben.

"Okay."

Quinn got out and walked down the edge of the road toward Mitch. "Hey. Everything all right?"

"What do you want?" Mitch hollered. "You coming after me now? You want to cut off my tusks?"

"What?" Quinn almost laughed at the preposterous comment. Then he froze. Mitch had a crazed look in his eyes. He wasn't joking.

"You a poacher now? That what this is?" Mitch held his gun horizontally across his body. His finger wasn't on the trigger, but that could change in the blink of an eye. He was sweating and shaking.

Quinn held up his hands.

Mitch's gaze swung to the pickup truck. Ben leaned out the window.

"That's my brother's truck, you know?" Mitch shouted at the child. "And he's gone. Drowned or broke his neck. I'm never going to know which happened first while he was getting yanked around like a rag doll. Isn't that enough for you? My brother. His truck. And now you want my tusks, too?" Mitch's voice rose until he was screaming. He redirected his anger at Quinn. "Hell, no! Enough is enough!"

Taking slow steps with his arms up, Quinn moved farther away from the truck, wanting to put distance between Mitch and Ben. "Look, you're not in your right mind, Mitch. You need to be somewhere where you can get some rest and where you won't hurt anyone."

"How do you know, Mr. Big Man? You don't know me! You don't know the first thing about me! You think you can come to my home and tell me what to do?"

"I saw your truck on the side of the road and stopped to see if you needed help, Mitch. That's all. You and I planned to meet this morning, remember?"

Bushes rustled not far behind them. Mitch jerked his head toward the noise.

Two Airmen emerged from the tropical forest wearing gas masks and holding weapons. One had dark hair, the other light. Their eyes moved from Quinn, who still had his arms raised, to Mitch. They focused on Mitch. "You need to come with us," dark hair said. "You can't be charging around the island with a gun, man."

"You want to slice off my tusks and leave me to bleed out! Oh, that's nice! Real nice!" Mitch shouted, an angry, disturbed edge to his tone. "Not today, boys! Not today!"

Mitch seemed to grow taller. He puffed his chest, set his jaw, and strode toward the military men in a way that made Quinn worried sick about what would happen next.

"Stop! Drop your weapon!" the light-haired Airman yelled.

Mitch kept moving toward them. No fear. No hesitation. No common sense. He gripped his gun, though he wasn't aiming it at them, and shouted, "Over my dead body!"

"Mitch, stop!" Quinn pleaded from behind him. "Listen to me! You're sick. Stop moving! Drop your weapon!"

Mitch ignored him.

"Stop, man! Stop!" the Airmen shouted.

Mitch wasn't leaving them any options.

Hands shaking, the young Airman with the dark hair fired his gun. His bullet caught Mitch in the arm. A perfect shot. Just where Quinn would have aimed to stop Mitch without killing him.

But Mitch didn't slow.

"Don't come any closer, dude! Don't! Don't!" The light-haired Airman's voice rang out with fear as he fired, striking Mitch in the abdomen.

Mitch lunged toward them like a crazed animal.

Two more shots exploded into his chest.

His eyes glazed over. He dropped his weapon. His arms hung by his sides as blood spread across his shirt. Finally, he collapsed.

No one could survive those wounds.

Quinn rushed to Mitch's side, and the Airmen swung their guns toward him. He raised his arms overhead. "I'm not sick. I was just trying to help him." He kept his voice as calm as he could muster.

"Leave!" dark hair shouted.

"Okay. I'm going back to that truck behind me." He glanced over his shoulder as he walked backward. Ben stared out the window, wide-eyed. "You can calm down and lower your weapons. Everything is okay."

They kept their weapons trained on him until he was back in the truck.

"That was my mom's friend," Ben said, his voice shaking. "Mitch was my mom's friend."

"I'm really sorry. Mitch was a good man."

Tears streamed down the boy's face. "They told him to stop. Why didn't he stop? Why was he yelling about tusks?"

"He was sick. He wasn't himself." Quinn pulled Ben close and wrapped his arm around him. "I'm really sorry you had to see that."

Ben sniffled. "I'm sorry you had to see it, too."

Mitch's violent death had left Quinn thoroughly shaken; he couldn't imagine what Ben was feeling. *I've got to do better. This boy has already seen enough suffering. I'm trying to give him a break, not give him more nightmares.*

They sat there for a few minutes, Quinn holding Ben while the boy whimpered. Then Ben straightened, swiped his hand under his eyes, and scooted a few inches away on the seat. "We better get back to the hospital and give Madeline the stuff you got from Tank."

"Right," Quinn said.

On the drive back, Ben tied and untied knots in his ropes. All Quinn could think about was that there was no way he was going to drop Ben off in that tent and leave him alone to process what they'd just seen.

▼▲▼

The tent area around the hospital was bustling with activity when Quinn and Ben returned. People were standing outside in the drizzling rain. A green truck rumbled past, driving around them on the grass and right up to the hospital entrance, sending pedestrians scattering out of its path.

"That's the survivor truck," Ben whispered.

Before quickly escorting Ben away, Quinn glimpsed armed men unloading people from the back of the truck, manhandling them as if they were prisoners. Prisoners who staggered as they walked.

The woman with the nose piercings was still in the large tent and Ben went straight to her. Ben had obviously been crying. What would she think about his tear-streaked face?

"Has my mom come looking for me yet?" he asked, pointing to his name on the board. The name below his had been erased, leaving a row of smudged white space behind.

"No," the woman answered. "Not yet."

"Okay." Ben dropped his head for a few seconds, then looked around.

Two girls, younger than Ben, were curled on their sides on the cot he'd previously occupied. Ben stuffed his hands in the pockets of his shorts, as if he wasn't sure what to do next.

"Hold on," Quinn said to him. "Let me see about something."

Quinn showed the woman his ID. In case she forgot, he pointed to his name and phone number on the board. "My fiancé and I are staying at the Azure Cove complex. She's a physician working at the hospital. If Ben would like to stay with us, would that be okay? We'll be back in the morning." Quinn had no right to ask. For all she knew, he might have been a child molester, a trafficker, a kidnapper. But he wasn't any of those things. If he could help make a slight difference for one person, he wanted to. And not only out of a sense of duty. He simply could not bear to leave Ben alone when it didn't have to be that way. He hoped the woman could tell his intentions were good and his heart was in the right place.

"I don't know what to do in this situation," she said, turning toward Ben. "Would you like to go with this man tonight rather than stay here?"

"With me and my fiancé," Quinn was quick to add. "He'll have his own room."

"Yes." Ben nodded. "I should go with him." He lowered his voice to a whisper, but Quinn heard him say, "He needs my help."

▼▲▼

Quinn looked around inside the hospital's front doors. "Excuse me," he said to an emaciated-looking woman carrying a blood pressure cuff. "I'm looking for Dr. Madeline Hamilton."

The woman pivoted on her feet but kept moving, walking backward to answer him. "Last I heard, she was in the lab. Downstairs."

110

"Now we need to find the lab," Quinn said to Ben. He hoped Madeline was still there and they could find the lab without incident. There was obvious suffering in the overcrowded hospital, and Quinn was wary about what Ben might see. After witnessing Mitch getting gunned down, he had more reason to shield the child, rather than follow up one horror with a host of others.

They made it to the basement level with no unfortunate encounters and found the room labeled medical laboratory. Small rectangular windows lined the upper portion of the room, but with the dark skies, there wasn't much light. Madeline was alone inside, reaching into a lower cabinet.

"There she is," Quinn said, entering with Ben.

At the sound of Quinn's voice, Madeline straightened. Her eyes met his, then moved to the child at his side.

"Ben, this is Dr. Madeline Hamilton. And Madeline, this is Ben. He helped me out today."

Madeline smiled. "Nice to meet you, Ben."

Quinn placed his hand on Ben's shoulder. "He's going to stay with us tonight."

"Good," Madeline said without missing a beat. "There's plenty of room where we're staying. It's okay with—?"

"Yeah. It's okay." Quinn was grateful for Madeline's instantaneous graciousness. If she wasn't as accepting as she appeared to be, she certainly pretended well. Either way, it made his heart feel full.

"We found the dog," Quinn said. "I don't know if he succumbed to injuries or illness…but I've got specimens."

"Great," Madeline said. "Thank you."

He set the specimen containers near her on the counter. "What are you working on?"

"I'm taking stock of the diagnostic tools—analyzers, incubators, microscopes. It's all pretty basic and old, but I can use some to supplement what we brought."

"It's dark in here," Ben said.

Quinn flicked a switch by the door. Nothing happened.

"The generators only function for critical patient areas, to preserve power," Madeline told them. "Apparently, the lab is not an essential area."

"How can we help?" Quinn asked, eyeing a stand with vials and containers.

Madeline rummaged through a box of wrapped cartridges. "I need to incubate samples and run tox screens. I found boxes of test kits and step-by-step instructions to do tests with reagents. But I can't use them in the dark." She lifted a package encased in plastic. "I'm going to take a box of these back to our hotel...er, dorm. I have to get the rest of the specimens to the CDC's lab. I've got them all packaged up. I just need to find someone who can take them to the base for transport. If you don't mind waiting here, I'll be right back."

▼▲▼

Madeline went down the hallway to the containment area, hoping to find Barstow. The civilian with the surfer-look—his name was Brian, and someone she hadn't seen before were keeping an eye on the patients. Barstow wasn't with them. She walked up and down the hospital corridors searching for Matthew and couldn't find him either. Perhaps they had already left and returned to the base. She would have to drive the samples there herself. She hurried back to the lab. "Can you take me to the base?" she asked Quinn.

"Absolutely."

"You guys can help me carry this stuff, if you don't mind."

Ben stepped right up with his arms open. "What can I carry?"

Madeline filled Ben's arms with a box of the test cartridges. She and Quinn carried the patient specimens, already packaged and labeled as biohazardous and infectious materials. They walked back upstairs and outside. A steady rain fell as they set the supplies in the truck bed. Ben got in and sat between Madeline and Quinn. On their way to the base, Madeline cradled the patients' samples in her lap.

Quinn drove up to the entrance. An Airman came out of the guard station. Rivulets of rain streamed over his jacket.

Madeline leaned forward to speak to him. "I have specimens that need to get to the CDC lab. They're packaged and ready to go. Can you take them for me?"

"I can't let you bring anything in or drop anything off here until it's cleared first," the Airman said.

"Who do I clear it with?" she asked.

The Airman shook his head. "Sorry. I don't really know who you have to ask, I just know I'm not allowed to take anything from you."

"What about planes? Are they taking off and landing?"

"The last communication this base received—no one can take off or land on the island until further notice—still stands."

"I have samples that need to be analyzed. The results are critical to combatting this illness."

"I'll make sure the commanding officers know. But there's nothing they can do about it at this time. The orders were clear. We can't violate them."

"Who gave those orders?" Madeline's frustration was rising.

"That's not something I know."

113

Madeline sighed and tried again. "This is pretty urgent."

He eyed the package on her lap, the yellow biohazard label. "I'm sorry, ma'am. I'm following orders."

"Okay, hold on. Let me make a call." She took out her satellite phone and turned it on. "I'm calling Patrick," she said to Quinn. "See if he knows how I can get these flown back."

Her call connected but it was full of static. "Patrick?" she said. "Patrick?" She cut off the call and tried again. She could hear Patrick on the other end, but his voice was garbled. She couldn't understand a word he said.

"Shoot." She disconnected the call. "It's not working."

The Airman gestured to the satellite disc on top of the guard station. "Must be the storm," he said. "Ours isn't working either."

Madeline pressed her hand against her forehead. "The simplest tasks are proving to be so difficult here."

"He's only following orders," Quinn said. "We'll sort things out tomorrow."

"Okay, but I really needed the results yesterday."

Quinn circled the truck around and they headed back to Azure Cove. On the secluded road to the complex, a streak of lightning lit up the sky and the surrounding forest. Fat drops of rain splattered the windshield and challenged the truck's old wipers to clear the glass. "The last thing they need on the south side of the island is more rain," Quinn said, driving slowly around each dark bend.

They were heading down the long entrance to Azure Cove, passing the mural, when Ben said, "My mom did that. She painted it."

The mermaid smiled at them through the slashing rain.

"It's beautiful. We noticed it when we first got here. Your mother is a very talented artist." Madeline made a point to say *is*, rather than *was*.

Ben beamed. "I know. She can do lots of things really well."

At the archway, Quinn rolled the window down a few inches. Rain pelted inside the truck.

Wearing large rain slickers, the beefy guards looked like massive yellow blobs. The one with the close-cropped beard came to Quinn's side and the blond one went around to the passenger side window. Madeline grabbed a dirty towel from the truck's floor and used it to conceal the biohazardous package.

"There are only supposed to be two of you," the blond said.

"This is Ben Misowski," Quinn said. "He lives on the island. He's ten. He's staying with us while he's waiting for his mother. He's helping me navigate the island."

The dark-haired guard nodded and offered Ben a smile before he beckoned to his coworker. They moved aside to speak. A minute later, the bearded guard returned. "Are you experiencing any signs of unusual aggression?" He looked to Quinn, then Madeline, then Ben.

"No," they answered.

"Any hallucinations?"

They all answered, "no."

"One more test," the blond guard said, walking to Quinn's side of the vehicle. "Hold out your arm."

Quinn rolled his window down further and stuck his arm out.

The man jabbed him with a metal point. "Did you feel that?"

"Yeah, I felt it," Quinn said, frowning. "I also saw it happen."

"Okay." The guard stepped away. "You can go through."

"Why did he do that?" Ben asked.

"The outbreak patients have no pain threshold," Madeline said. "But that wasn't a great way to test for it. That proved nothing."

"I think I've seen that man before." Ben pointed to the blond guard moving the roadblocks. Most of the guard's face was shielded by his hooded raincoat. "I can't remember from where."

Quinn steered through the arches and toward the complex, parking as close to the dormitory path as possible. A gust of wind hit as they exited the truck, driving the rain harder against them. Heads down, they hurried along the path to the dormitory, then burst inside, dripping water onto the foyer floor.

The kitchen was as bland as the rest of the staff dormitory and as they walked past a myriad of simple tables and chairs to the counter area, everything appeared just as they'd left it. There was no evidence anyone else had been in there during the day. Madeline slid her package onto an empty refrigerator shelf. She draped several dish towels around it, concealing the contents and labels so as not to alarm anyone else. "Let's get our wet clothes off and find something to eat," she said. "And I'd like to get a close look at your stitches, Ben. And those burns on your hands, too."

"What's wrong with the stitches?" Quinn asked, leaning in to get a closer look at Ben's face. The stitched area was a little redder than the rest of Ben's skin.

"I just want to make sure they're staying clean, that's all." Madeline turned to Ben. "When your face got stitched up, did they give you any medicine to take afterward? An antibiotic?"

"They made my face numb before the stitches, but they didn't give me any medicine."

"That's okay. I'll get something for you tomorrow. Just to be super safe and to give your skin the best chance of healing well." She smiled at the boy. He was polite and confident, easy to like, even after all he'd been through. "There's an empty room next to ours where you can sleep and take a shower. Use the soap on your stitches, I know they're sore, so just be gentle and then let the warm water run over them."

"I don't have any other clothes to change into," Ben said.

"I saw a washer and dryer in our hallway. We can do a wash." Quinn pinched his grimy shirt away from his chest, then let it drop back down. "I think we all could use some fresh clothes. Come on, Ben. I'll help you find a room."

CHAPTER TWELVE

Rummaging through the kitchen cabinets in search of three meals, Madeline reflected on the growing attachment between Quinn and Ben. She understood why. Quinn was like a superhero come to life—handsome, strong, and exceptionally kind and patient. What boy wouldn't look up to him? But what really touched her was Quinn's concern for the child.

She pulled a sleeve of crackers from a shelf and opened it. Going through most of the day without food had left her stomach empty and her brain less than sharp. Her first few bites of the salted crackers tasted amazing, much better than they should have. She sat down at one of the cafeteria style tables with them and took her phone from her bag, about to try her boss again.

"Hey."

She turned at the sound of a man's voice. Wheeler stood in the doorway. Something about his pressed white shirt made her angry. "Yes?" she asked.

"There's something wrong with my satellite phone. I have urgent matters that can't wait. Do you have one I can borrow?"

His words struck a chord, so similar to her own when they were at the base. Unless Wheeler had life or death concerns, she doubted his matters were as pressing as her own need to communicate with the CDC. But thinking that way might make her just as pompous and arrogant as him, so she pushed her dismissive thoughts aside and held her phone out for Wheeler.

Wheeler stayed in the doorway. "Just set it on the table there."

She set the phone down and backed up.

Wheeler pulled a disinfecting cloth from a packet he carried. He wiped Madeline's phone before picking it up.

If Wheeler had come a few minutes earlier, he would have seen the vials and the yellow biohazard tape. Good thing her portable incubator was still in her room.

"I'll be back with this in a few minutes," he said.

"I'll be here."

After Wheeler left, she found three packaged meals in the freezer, read the directions, and stuck them into the microwave. While waiting, and munching on more crackers, she thought about what she should do with the fluid specimens.

Wheeler returned quicker than she expected, clearing his throat as he placed her phone on a chair near the door. "I can't get a connection."

"I couldn't get one earlier." Madeline rested her elbows on the table and leaned forward. "It must be the storm."

▲▼▲

Hair still damp from her shower, Madeline contemplated making a carafe of the dorm's coffee. It tasted terrible, and it might keep her up all night. She wasn't one who could sleep a few hours and feel fine, and the time difference had already messed up her sleep cycle. With two strikes against the coffee, she stretched her arms overhead, deciding to push through her fatigue with sheer willpower. After a few more stretches, she removed the trays of fluid samples from the fridge and set them on the counter.

119

Quinn crossed the kitchen and embraced her. "Ben is already sound asleep."

"He looked adorable wearing your T-shirt. It went down to his knees." She rested her head against Quinn's chest. "What's going on with him? Where are his parents?"

"He only has a mother. She was in the hardest hit area when the tsunami came. So that's not good. But he was there, too, and he's okay. Maybe she survived. I don't know if he expects her to show up any minute, or...I'm not sure what he believes."

"If she survived, wouldn't she have found him by now?" Madeline lifted her head and met Quinn's eyes. "Maybe she's in the hospital?"

Quinn shrugged. "The woman watching the children in the tent didn't seem to think so. But could you ask about her tomorrow? Her name is Eve. Mermaid tattoo on her shoulder. Rainbow friendship bracelet on her wrist. Ben made it for her out of colored strings."

"I know what friendship bracelets are." Madeline smiled. "I'll check with Grace and Matthew and ask around."

"In the meantime, if we can make things a little easier for him while we're here...I hope you don't mind."

"Of course I don't mind. I mean...I don't know what Wheeler would do if we brought a bus full of children back here, and I can't get my work done if we take over child watching services, but if we can help one, or two, by all means."

"I can't imagine what's going to happen to him if his mother really is dead. And I probably didn't give him the best of experiences today." Quinn told Madeline about Mitch being gunned down. "Mitch was a totally different man today. The tusk thing, I think that was a psychotic episode."

Listening to Quinn, Madeline's fears intensified. The illness could be contagious and airborne. With Nate and now Mitch, Quinn had two prolonged, unprotected exposures.

"I know you weren't happy about people being locked up in that containment area," Quinn said. "But maybe it's best, you know, for their own safety."

She didn't answer.

"What are you working on now?" he asked.

"I have a hunch." She turned to face the samples she'd set out on the counter. "In just a few minutes, I'll know if I'm way off, in the land of make believe, or if I'm on to something."

"Let's not underestimate your hunches. Can I help?"

"You sure?"

"Whatever I can do, so you can get to bed soon." He chuckled. "I mean, so you can get some sleep."

She grinned as she handed him a small package. "These are the kits I found in the lab. Dozens of them. I'm betting they're expired, and a pharmaceutical company donated them to the island as a tax write off rather than discarding them. I hope they still work. I've already run a control on myself."

"What exactly are we testing for?" Quinn asked.

"Drugs."

Quinn scrunched his face, forming wrinkles along the bridge of his nose. He tore open the package and read the instruction sheet. "Okay, then. Looks straightforward enough."

Madeline opened another package and transferred Nate's fluids to a testing cup. She wrote his name across the top and pressed the cap down, then repeated the steps with Martina's sample, and again with the sample from Colonel Nelson. She twisted the key on each cartridge to initiate the tests, then started the timers. "Now we wait five minutes."

Outside the kitchen window, a bolt of lightning snaked across the sky. A thunderclap followed.

Madeline pressed her fingers into the back of her neck and massaged the tight muscles there. After two long exhausting days on the island, she was working on borrowed time. She needed sleep soon, or she wouldn't be of much good to anyone tomorrow. The workload had already worn out Grace and Matthew. They needed all the help they could get.

Quinn moved to stand behind her. He gently lifted her hands away from her neck and took up the massaging. Under the firm pressure of his fingers, Madeline felt her body relax. Her eyes closed. Her head grew heavier and dropped forward. She relished every second as she began drifting off.

The timer buzzed.

Madeline straightened. "That felt wonderful, but it was putting me to sleep. Back to work." She got up, selected Martina's test cartridge, and compared the adulteration strips from the test to the colors on the instruction chart. Quinn did the same with Nate's sample.

"Weird," Quinn said. "If I'm reading this test correctly, and if this thing works, Nate tested positive for three different substances. Methamphetamine, opiates, and cocaine."

Madeline double checked the test in her hand. "So did Martina."

Quinn picked up Colonel Nelson's cartridge and did another comparison. "Same."

Quinn and Madeline exchanged a look. "Let's check samples from a few more patients, and the specimens you took from the German Shepherd."

They prepared the tests and set the timer. Madeline paced the kitchen, waiting for the five minutes to pass.

The results were all positive for the same drugs. Even the dog tested positive, although at trace levels.

"Is this what you were expecting?" Quinn asked.

"I'm not sure what I was expecting, exactly, but not this. Not to this extent. But these results do explain their behaviors—the paranoia, hallucinations, and psychotic episodes." She turned back to the counter and grabbed her phone. "According to the directions, the results are only stable for sixty minutes. I'd better get photos for the patients' records." She opened her phone and snapped photos of the test results, then took a seat at the nearest table and ran her fingers through her hair. "How did they all end up with these drugs in their systems?"

Quinn slid Madeline's laptop across the table toward him. "I need to check something." He opened the laptop, pressed a few keys, and frowned. "No signal."

"Try again once the storm passes. Meanwhile, tell me what you were thinking."

"You sure you want to hear it?"

"Why wouldn't I?"

Quinn rubbed his hand over the stubble on his chin. "Honestly, as soon as I heard what was going on here, the moment you mentioned violent behavior on a secluded island, I suspected terrorism. Not surprising that my mind always goes there first, but in this case, I imagined a foreign government, or even our own government, chose this island so they could test something in an inconspicuous location."

"So…that would mean the tsunami has nothing to do with what's going on?"

Quinn shrugged. "I didn't say that, but what's running through my mind now has absolutely nothing to do with a natural disaster. I'm thinking about chemical weapons developed by Germany, France, the United Kingdom, Russia, and the U.S. See, countries didn't develop weapons *only* for use on their enemies. They created some for their own troops."

Madeline crossed her arms and leaned them on the table. "What are you talking about? I'm not following what that has to do with things here."

"Bear with me. It goes back to World War II. The Nazis were desperate for more soldiers because they had exhausted their existing military. So they came up with an alternate plan—create a wonder drug to give their soldiers superhuman performance. They thought they could produce robot-like soldiers who never tired. They called the drug Pervitin. Soldiers referred to it as tank chocolate. Those who took it stayed awake for days without resting. They didn't experience pain, hunger, or thirst. So, in a way…it worked. But Pervitin also caused extreme aggression and bouts of murderous behavior. I can't remember the drug's exact component. That's what I wanted to look up. But I think it was methamphetamine."

"Hmm. That's crystal meth," Madeline said. "It causes a dopamine surge. A euphoric high along with increased alertness. At least in the short-term. Then comes the crash."

"Exactly. A few days after taking the drug, the German soldiers were hallucinating, hungover zombies. Hardly the super soldiers the Nazis aimed to create. So, the Germans set out to improve on their drug with a pill code-named D-IX. I can't remember what it was exactly." He glanced toward the laptop again, obviously wishing they had a connection. "I think they added oxycodone, cocaine, and a morphine-based painkiller."

Madeline raised her brows as Quinn gestured toward the used test cartridges on the counter.

"The components of D-IX sound eerily similar to what we just found on the tox screens we ran, don't you think?" he asked.

"Yes." Saying it aloud spooked her. "It sounds like the same mixture."

"The Nazis experimented with the concoction on concentration camp victims."

"Oh, God. How horrible." Madeline shook her head. "But…you said Germany developed and used the drug, not the U.S."

"One thing you can count on, besides death and taxes, is that if Germany and Russia did something, we did it, too. To do otherwise would give our enemies an edge."

"If the U.S. created a similar super-power drug, what happened to it?"

A clap of thunder rattled the windows.

"Well, there's what's supposed to happen to our chemical weapons, and there's what might have happened. Besides conventional bombs, the United States produced chemical weapons, nerve and blister agents, as a deterrent against countries making similar weapons. We never used any in battle. They're obsolete and deteriorating and we don't want them back on our soil. Some of it got dumped in the ocean—I told you about the fishing trawlers. We buried some. And we have elaborate disposal systems, like Johnston Atoll."

"What's that?"

"A small island controlled by the U.S. Military. For years, it functioned as an airbase and a testing site for nuclear and biological weapons. Eventually it became a primary site for the storage and disposal of America's chemical weapons."

"If those drugs *were* stored here on Nalowale a long time ago, as some super serum chemical weapon, would anyone know?"

"Maybe not. As far as I know, it was over eighty years ago that we produced them. And that super drug would have been top secret. Maybe only a small group of people knew. And those people would be dead now."

"But if it was here, someone might have found it?

"Possibly. Or someone is testing something new."

Madeline lowered her head to think. It was a lot to take in. And she was exhausted.

"I better check on Ben," Quinn said after a few minutes. "Can you come to bed soon?"

"Yes. Definitely. I'm going to be out as soon as my head hits the pillow. I just need to put everything away first."

"Now that those drugs showed up in every sample you checked, at least you know what you're dealing with. That's good, right?"

Madeline looked over at the cartridges on the countertop, then swung her head back to meet Quinn's gaze. "Yes. I can narrow down treatment plans now. But I'm still confused. I have to think about what you told me and how it might relate to the outbreak. And the important question is, where is the source of exposure?"

Quinn leaned down for a kiss then left Madeline with parting words to ponder. "Maybe it's not a where, or a what, Madeline. Maybe you're looking for a *who*."

CHAPTER THIRTEEN

Under the warm sheets, Quinn turned on his side and touched Madeline's shoulder. Just enough contact so she would respond if she was also having trouble sleeping but wouldn't wake otherwise. His mind raced with thoughts. The toxicology test had its limits and could only test for known substances. Maybe other yet-to-be-identified chemicals were mixed with the drugs. The island could be the chosen location for an experiment with a new and powerful weapon. If so, that weapon was proving to be a colossal dud. Though it might have propelled some of the islanders toward heroic efforts after the tsunami, enabling them to work without stopping as Nate had done. But at what cost? Nate was essentially a prisoner now, losing his mind and uttering nonsense in the basement of the hospital.

Or was there a more specific or personal reason for sickening the island's people? He couldn't think of any purpose that would serve other than pure evil. An image of Wheeler appeared in his mind and stuck there, like a vision from a nightmare. Was Wheeler somehow involved?

Quinn grimaced.

Am I being paranoid? Yes. I'm being paranoid.

That thought didn't sit well with him. He vowed to let Madeline focus on her job, her very important job, without sharing his unfounded ideas. At least not until he had more evidence to back them up.

Madeline hadn't stirred, so Quinn quietly got out of bed. He grabbed shorts, a T-shirt, and his running shoes. The sun was rising, and he needed to get in a hard run to work off some of his restless energy. He dressed in the bathroom, and Madeline was still sleeping soundly when he came out. With so much pressure riding on her knowledge, he wanted her to have every minute of sleep she could get before the alarm went off. When he left their room, he shut the door behind him with a gentle click.

In the hallway, he cracked Ben's door open and peered in.

"Time to go?" Ben asked, his big brown eyes already wide open. He threw his covers off and sat up.

Quinn smiled at him. "Somebody's an early riser, huh? Good morning."

Ben stood and stretched his arms over head. "Where's Madeline?"

"Still sleeping."

"Are we gonna eat breakfast here?" Ben asked.

"Sure. Get dressed and we'll go find something." The workout could wait.

It took Ben less than a minute to get dressed and use the bathroom. In the kitchen, he perched on the edge of a chair and helped himself to dry cereal and fruit. Quinn picked up a banana, saw the brown spots, and put it back down. He wasn't hungry anyway.

Ben finished his juice and stood. "Can we go outside?"

"Good idea. How about a walk around the complex? We can check this place out. We've got about half an hour to explore before Madeline's alarm goes off."

Ben nodded with enthusiasm and skipped toward the exit.

The first rays of sun cast light through the trees. The storm had passed during the night, leaving behind a damp, earthy smell, plants glistening with moisture, and lots of mud. As they headed down the quiet path, the roar of machinery started up somewhere on the property. Exiting the trail, they saw the backhoe operating. Two men with green shirts stood near it.

"Let's find out what they plan to do with that giant hole over there," Quinn said, walking next to a muddy trench. "Yesterday, Madeline said it looked like an asteroid hit."

"Yeah, it does," Ben said. "And it looks like a different asteroid hit over there first and then the hole got filled up." Ben stared at an area in the center of the property. It was cleared of all the natural plants and trees and covered with what appeared to be fresh, overturned dirt. There were similar mounds of fresh dirt everywhere, though none as big as the one in the center.

The excavators watched Quinn and Ben approach. One pulled the rim of a blue cap lower on his head. The other stared out from behind long stringy hair that hung in his eyes.

"Good morning." The backhoe shut off mid-sentence and Quinn's greeting sounded like a shout in the ensuing quiet.

"Morning. What's up?" The man with the cap dropped a cigarette butt on the ground and mashed it with his boot. He was middle-aged and American, or at least sounded like it. Beside him, the younger man blew out a puff of smoke. Their green shirts had an insignia and the words Blythe Enterprises on the chest pocket.

"This rain really does a number on your work, doesn't it?" Quinn asked, eyeing the deep pools of mud in the channels snaking away from the large hole.

"What are you making?" Ben asked.

The older man smiled. "It's going to be a pool and a lazy river. A water ride with a slow current. People will float along it in rafts or tubes. This one is going to cover a half mile of territory."

"Cool," Ben said.

"It really will be, once it's finished." The man's eyes lit up as he pointed to one of the channels branching out from the center. "Each of the tributaries travels around a different part of the property. This one will take people underneath a waterfall and connect to a slide that drops into the lagoon."

Quinn motioned to the cleared area covered with fresh, wet dirt in the center. "Looks like you got started over there and then changed your mind on the location."

The younger man huffed. His colleague shot him a warning look before addressing Quinn. "Yeah. Investors said they wanted the pool to one side of the building. Wish they'd thought of that before we got it mostly dug up."

"Have to say, I think it would have been better located in the center where you started," Quinn said. "Shame all the plants and trees got razed for no reason."

Shouts of "Hey! Hey!" came from behind them. Quinn turned to see Wheeler jogging in their direction. He wore a mask over his face, but his narrowed eyes suggested he was frowning.

The younger man cursed.

"Shut up, Roger," the older man hissed.

"Can I help you?" Wheeler yelled. Mud had splattered his expensive leather boots, perhaps his idea of work boots. They weren't anything like the rigid, tough boots the other men wore.

Quinn wasn't sure if Wheeler was talking to him but answered anyway. "Morning. We're just out for a walk." He looked over to Ben and found him glaring at Wheeler, which made him wonder if the child would say anything about the reason his mother was fired. Now that would be interesting.

"We're all good here," the man in the cap said. "Just bragging about the lazy river we're building. Everything's fine."

"Mr. Traynor here is with the FBI," Wheeler said, standing a few yards away from the rest of them.

Quinn wondered when Wheeler had learned that information, considering their host didn't seem to know or care who Quinn was when they arrived. While Quinn hadn't kept his profession secret, neither had he mentioned it.

The younger man averted his eyes.

The man in the cap nodded. "We're all good here," he said again.

"I just don't want anyone getting hurt during the construction process. I'm sure you understand the liability issues." Wheeler's gaze moved back and forth between Quinn and the excavators.

Quinn recognized signs of lying. Wheeler was concerned about something, but Quinn doubted it was their safety. "Too bad you changed the location of the pool and river channels after you started," he said.

Wheeler's face hardened.

Quinn had touched on something significant, though he wasn't sure what.

Wheeler crossed his arms. "They had to redesign the initial plans after running into some natural obstacles."

"Oh. I heard investors wanted a different design." Quinn smiled at the excavators.

"That too." Wheeler fidgeted with his hands. "There's always something. Luckily, there's more than enough space on the property to allow for flexibility."

Quinn repressed the urge to grab Wheeler by the throat and shake him into spitting out his secrets. "So, I'm curious, how did Blythe Enterprise excavators end up staying behind while the rest of the contractors were sent away?"

"They weren't *sent* away." Wheeler's lips formed a constricted, tight-lipped smile. "I granted them time off. And perhaps saved their lives in the process. Some of them might have been shopping on Market Street when the tsunami hit, rather than safe at home with their families."

"You saved their lives, huh?" Quinn kept his voice light and forced his own smile. He was close to something and didn't want to back off. "It's almost like you knew the tsunami was coming."

"If I knew it was coming, I would have found a way to warn *everyone*. But the way it happened, when it occurred…a lot of contract workers got lucky with the timing of their departure."

"Why didn't you go, too?" Ben asked the excavators. His question came across as completely innocent, which it probably was, prompting Quinn to think, *good job, kid.*

Wheeler answered immediately. "They had the most work ahead of them. Especially considering the changes." He opened one arm, encompassing the landscape and focusing on a trench trailing off to his right. "Now, with the lazy river, don't think of it as an amusement park ride. It's nothing like that. It's going to be very upscale. Think of it as an extension of the island's natural beauty. Like a relaxing stroll through botanical gardens, except taken while floating in sparkling blue water."

"Sounds interesting," Quinn said, noting Wheeler had changed the subject.

"It will be once they can finish laying the foundations and landscaping. As soon as my crews can return." Wheeler gave Quinn a hard look. "Right now, it's a bit of an eyesore."

Ben looked up at Wheeler, his face completely serious. "I don't know what an eyesore is, but it used to be beautiful here and now it's kind of wrecked. Hope you can get all this put back together soon."

Quinn loved Ben's directness.

The look Wheeler gave the child was angry and a bit creepy. "There's nothing I'd like to do more. As soon as the quarantine is lifted."

132

"I should have introduced you," Quinn said. "Devon Wheeler, this is Ben. Ben Misowski." He studied Wheeler's face for some recognition of his last name. But there was none. Figured. "Speaking of quarantines…we better be on our way so Madeline can get to the hospital." Quinn turned to the excavation crew. "Nice talking to you. Have a good day."

"Same," the man in the cap said. "Watch yourself out there."

"We will. And by the way, the south shore would really benefit from your equipment right now. Even a few hours would make a difference."

Quinn and Ben left, and Wheeler went with them, keeping a good ten feet of distance and giving Quinn the feeling Wheeler didn't want him roaming the property without an escort.

The backhoe started up behind them.

Quinn's mind raced again.

Almost everyone working at Azure Cove was sent away quickly. Now, Wheeler is desperate to get them back. What changed? What is Wheeler hiding?

CHAPTER FOURTEEN

The annoying and repetitive ringing wouldn't stop.

Madeline's alarm.

It pulled her from the deep, dreamless expanse of nothingness where her brain was trying to recharge. She woke sprawled across the entire bed in the empty dormitory room. Her first thought—where was Quinn? Had he already adjusted to the major time difference? She certainly had not. If she was home, she'd smack that alarm off and go back to sleep. It took another few groggy seconds for her to remember the tox screen results. Without lingering another moment, she sprung out of bed and got dressed.

The drug test results from last night explained the outbreak symptoms. Despite the many questions still to be answered, that knowledge should have provided a small sense of satisfaction, …but it didn't. Something specific about the discovery bugged her. It bothered her last night, right up until she fell asleep, and now the troubling feeling had returned full force. Unfortunately, there were plenty of other things to figure out, like determining where the drugs came from.

She brushed her teeth and reviewed her list for the day. The first item was to compare concentration levels across patients to help narrow down the source of exposure.

She set her toothbrush aside absentmindedly. No. On second thought…concentration comparisons wouldn't work. Not in this situation. Most drugs had a half-life, the time required to reduce to half its initial value as it metabolized. Patients who had been in the containment area longest would show lower concentration of drugs, which would skew her results.

And…wait a minute…wasn't the half-life of meth less than 24 hours? She was almost positive it was. That's what bothered her about the tox results! If she hadn't been so tired, she would have picked up on the discrepancy immediately. Most of the patients had been in containment for more than a day. Why were the drugs still present in such high concentrations?

She sat on the end of the bed and powered up her laptop to check the normal metabolization rates for meth, cocaine, and morphine. Still no signal. She rebooted and tried again, checking her satellite phone while she waited for the computer to reboot. Same result. No way to communicate with the outside world or do research on the internet, which made her feel very alone. Outside the window, flimsy-looking clouds hung in a calm sky. The storm had long passed. So why couldn't she connect? "Could just one thing here work as intended?" she said aloud.

After taking a few deep breaths to curb her frustration, she opened the photo icon on her personal phone and scrolled between the test results for Martina, Colonel Nelson, and Nate.

What? This can't be correct.

She checked them again and again.

There must be a mistake.

Martina was the first patient to enter the containment area. The concentration of drugs in her system should be lowest. Instead, they were the highest. The Colonel had been in the containment area for two days. His levels were almost as high as Martina's. Nate had been there less than twenty-four hours and his levels were the lowest. How was that possible? The results should show the reverse.

135

Madeline stared up at the ceiling, searching for an explanation. There had to be one. She tapped her pen on the table and came up with a rationalization. Relative to the other two patients, Martina must have entered the containment area with a much higher amount of drugs in her system, and thus it was taking longer for them to metabolize. And that made sense. Martina was petite. The same dosage or exposure would affect her more.

Madeline reviewed the paper chart that came folded inside each of the test cartridges. The information she read killed her theory, leaving her utterly confused. According to the chart, Martina's nanogram per milliliter drug levels were dangerously high, approaching fatal toxicity levels. If those levels had been higher three days ago, Martina would have already died.

There was only one explanation for what she was seeing. The concentration of drugs appeared to be *increasing* the longer the patients stayed in the containment area.

That was wrong. Inconsistent.

No kidding, Sherlock. As if I didn't already know something about the outbreak was illogical.

So, what did it mean? Was Quinn on to something with the terrorist angle? Was the source of exposure somewhere in the basement? Or was someone inside the hospital intentionally drugging the patients?

▼▲▼

The morning drive from Azure Cove to the hospital now held familiar landmarks. Madeline recognized the mango and banana groves, a waterfall cascading down a steep, rocky cliff, and smaller falls close to the road, each of them photograph worthy.

"What do you two have planned for today?" she asked Quinn and Ben.

"My mom might need me...if she's there." Ben looked up at Quinn. "If not, am I still going to help you?"

"I'd like it if you could help me again," Quinn said.

Amidst they mystery of the outbreak and the patients' rising drug levels, Madeline wondered if they should help Ben cope with his mother's probable death rather than acting like it was only a matter of time before she magically appeared. Allowing him hope seemed both important and the kindest route. Eventually, if his mother didn't return, he would realize what that meant. But Madeline wasn't a psychologist. She didn't know how to best handle the situation. And now, she couldn't call a psychologist for advice or hop on the internet to research how to help a traumatized child through the death of a parent. The *possible* death of a parent. Once the island was functioning again, Ben and all the other children would need therapists to help them cope with their anguish and loss. Would that support be available to him on Nalowale? And would it be available before psychological trauma caused irreversible damage?

"Can you check if the bug spray is still in my backpack?" Quinn asked, interrupting her thoughts.

Madeline grabbed Quinn's bag from the floor. After a few seconds of rummaging through it, she answered, "Yes."

"Mosquitoes don't bite me," Ben said.

"You're lucky," Quinn replied. "The little buggers have always loved me. I read it has something to do with my blood. But you know, I didn't see any at Azure Cove. They must treat the area with an insecticide."

"Mosquitoes are attracted to carbon dioxide," Madeline said. "You're a big guy, Quinn. You might put off more carbon dioxide than others. Unfortunately, they're about to get a lot worse around here. Standing water is their ideal breeding ground. Use the spray, Ben, just to be extra safe."

"All right," Ben said. "If you say so."

When they reached the hospital, Quinn let Madeline out near the front door. On her way to the basement, she found

Matthew walking slowly down the first-floor corridor, reading a paper medical chart.

"Good morning," she said. "Glad I found you. I ran some tests last night. I know what's causing the symptoms."

"Really? Thank God," Matthew said. "We lost three of the outbreak patients overnight to respiratory and cardiac arrest. Two more are in comas."

Madeline's heart sank. The news wasn't shocking. Opiate toxicity could lead to coma and lethal respiratory depression. "Is Grace here?" she asked. "Could we steal a few minutes together so I can tell both of you what we're dealing with?"

"Yes. Come this way." Matthew headed down the hallway. "Grace went into the staff room a few hours ago to get some sleep. But I think she'd want us to wake her to hear what you learned." Matthew stopped outside a door labeled *Staff* and knocked. "I'm not really staff. I don't officially work here, you know that, right? I'm normally on the base."

"I know. I was wondering, has Grace heard from her fiancé yet?"

"No. She might never know for sure what happened. The sea pulled lots of people out with the receding water. I'm sure I've lost colleagues who were off the base when the wave hit, but without communications, we aren't even sure exactly who's missing yet. People with the sickness are scattered. Some of them hiding. And then there's the people in the containment area. Most are friends or at least acquaintances, so it's personal for me. I want them to walk out of this place as healthy and normal as they were last week."

Matthew opened the door into the staff room, which contained a cot, a couch, a table surrounded by six chairs, and a counter area with a small refrigerator and coffeemaker. Bottled waters were stacked next to the coffee maker. A row of lockers lined one wall.

Grace sat on the cot with a fleece blanket balled by her side. Whatever amount of sleep she got had left her looking less than refreshed. She stared at them with bleary eyes and adjusted her ponytail. "Did something happen?"

"I have news on the outbreak patients," Madeline said, leaning against the wall.

"What did you learn?" Grace asked.

"They're suffering from drug toxicity."

Grace frowned, causing creases to appear across her forehead. "What?"

Madeline removed her notes and one of the toxicology cartridges from her backpack. "The samples I analyzed were positive for high levels of amphetamines, cocaine, and opiates. We also found the dog from the base. He was dead. He tested positive for the same combination of drugs."

"That's just...I don't know what to think." Matthew opened his mouth again but said nothing.

Grace rubbed her hand over her forehead as she stood from the cot and walked to the coffee machine. "Where could the drugs be coming from? Are they ingesting them?"

"I think it's safe to say they didn't take them intentionally, or someone would have told us by now so we could help them." Madeline debated telling them about D-IX, the decades old, super-serum drug concoction Quinn had described. If it was nothing more than a random piece of trivia unrelated to the outbreak, it might limit their ability to see other possibilities. But considering the toxicology results and the specific drugs in question...the information seemed relevant. Relevant enough to share what she knew.

As the coffee brewed, emitting a weak hiss in the background, Madeline told them about the Nazi's super serum drug concoction. "It might be totally unrelated, but..."

"The bunkers on the base are storing old weapons," Matthew said, pressing his hands over his head. "It's possible there's something like that in there with the other stuff."

"Should we move everyone away from the base?" Grace asked, leaning her back against the counter.

"No," Matthew answered. "Because…the base can't be the problem. It can't. Some of our symptomatic patients, the civilians, have never been on the base. Which means they were exposed elsewhere. The drugs must be coming from somewhere else. Except…I asked my colleagues about Tank when I heard he was sick. We're sure he never left the base." Matthew shook his head. "This is…crazy. What are we missing?"

Grace stared above Madeline's head at a point on the blank wall. "I just…let me get this straight…back to what you said about their drug levels increasing. That means, somehow, they're continuously being exposed to those drugs. What if…what if the source is in the containment area? Should we be tearing apart the walls? Moving the patients out of there?"

Madeline had been thinking the same. "What else have they been exposed to in the containment area since they arrived?"

"Just what you've seen," Matthew answered. "Sedatives and antibiotics. Food and water, which they've mostly declined."

"What food and what water?" Madeline asked.

"The food is coming from the hospital's supplies and the Air Force's rations," Matthew said. "The water is bottled or comes from the supply volunteers are boiling in the kitchen here. And the sedative is the same stuff we've always used. We're opening sealed containers."

"We'll have to inspect everything they got." Madeline remembered Quinn's parting comment to her the previous evening. *Maybe it's not a where, or a what, but a who.* She had to choose her words carefully so as not to offend anyone. "Maybe more

140

important than *what* they're getting is this—who they're getting it from."

Matthew frowned as he rubbed his hands over his forehead and into his hair. "Aside from hospital staff, Captain Barstow has spent the most time helping in the containment area. But he's only been around since Colonel Nelson got here. The military obviously don't have family here, but the civilians do, so there have been family-member volunteers in and out. Look, I get where you're going with this. But if someone is slipping drugs to those patients, which isn't likely, or if there's something seeping through the containment area walls...that doesn't explain why they were drugged when they came in. That's why they're down there in the first place."

"You're right," Madeline said, although she was already putting together scenarios under which the assumptions could work. That's what her mind did in epidemiologist mode—played detective and devil's advocate with every potential means of exposure, piecing together supporting evidence and data, forging a path toward the truth. "There's something else at play. Something we still don't understand. But now that we know what we're dealing with, the drug part at least, let's prioritize our efforts. Grace, can you work on treatments, so we don't lose anyone else to toxicity?"

"Yes," Grace said. "I was thinking about that. We have Narcan to reverse the effect of opiates. But I don't know if anything exists to counteract the other drugs. That just takes time."

"You're right. We'll still only be treating the symptoms of those other drugs," Matthew said. "We can give benzodiazepines for their elevated blood pressures. If that doesn't work, we can try an IV nitrate."

Grace nodded at him. "Okay. If I work in the containment area, can you handle the patients on the upper floors with Lydia? At least for the morning?"

"Yes," he said, rolling his neck from side to side like it needed to be stretched. "I'll do my best."

Grace poured a mug of the fresh coffee and took long sips of the black liquid.

"I'd like to autopsy the three patients who died," Madeline said, wondering if the staff room coffee tasted any better than the brew she had in the dormitory. "Where are they now?"

"They're in the morgue," Grace answered. "They're together and labeled with tags that say outbreak. Or maybe they say containment area, I can't remember which. It's crowded down there. You'll have trouble finding them. I better go with you."

"No, don't worry. I'll figure it out. Are there forensic tools and a table I can use to conduct an autopsy?

"Yes," Grace said. "You'll have to move body bags around, but you should find everything you need. I'd help you, but..."

"We have to divide and conquer to get anything done." Madeline had her hand on the door, ready to head out, when she turned around. "Oh, one more thing. I almost forgot. Any chance either of you remember treating a woman with a mermaid tattoo? Her name is Eve? She probably would be in her thirties or early forties."

"No, not that I recall," Matthew said.

"Me neither." For a second, Grace's expression darkened. She stared down at her coffee mug like she didn't know what she was holding.

"If you don't mind, let me know if either of you see her or hear anything about her," Madeline said before leaving. "I'll catch up with you later."

She went to the basement, where desperate voices wailed from behind the containment area doors. She expected to hear them, and now she had a better idea of what the patients were experiencing, and yet they sounded no less disturbing.

Captain Barstow and Brian stood close together in the hallway. Barstow held a syringe in one bandaged hand and a large prescription bottle of sedative in the other.

"How's your bite?" Madeline asked Barstow. Now that she knew about the drugs, she was less concerned about the condition being contagious.

"It's fine." Barstow appeared calm and in control.

"And you're feeling okay?" she asked.

"I don't feel any different from yesterday. I'm sure of it. So far so good."

"How are the patients?"

"Worse," Brian replied without hesitation. "My brother didn't recognize me and isn't making any sense."

"I ran some tests," she told them. "Turns out they're all drugged. Cocaine. Meth. Morphine. And the levels are rising."

"What?" Barstow frowned. "That's...that's impossible."

"My brother doesn't take drugs," Brian said.

"I didn't say anyone took the drugs," Madeline clarified. "I said the drugs are in their systems."

"If they didn't take them, how is it they're drugged?" Brian asked.

"I don't know." Madeline locked eyes with Barstow and waited to see if he had anything more to say.

"I...I don't know." Barstow rolled the syringe between his fingers. "I was sure they had some sort of rabies or brain infection."

"I'll do more tests. And I'd like both of you to get tested as well." There was still so much Madeline didn't understand about

143

the situation, but the drugs' presence was indisputable. "I'm going to the morgue, but Dr. Wilcox will be here any minute. She'll start treating everyone for drug toxicity. And I'll be back."

She continued to the morgue at the other end of the hallway. Four small rectangular windows, each hazy with dirt, filtered light into the room. She flicked the switches by the door, but nothing happened.

She walked through the room on a narrow path, making her way around dozens of body bags. Someone had stacked the bodies with meticulous precision on the floor and against the concrete walls. Fully gowned and protected, Madeline's mask filtered some of the stench. She checked tags on several bags. Many had names. Several said *unidentified.*

An electronic hum came from the wall of refrigeration drawers. Far fewer bodies were kept cold than at room temperature, even though a look inside the drawers showed two and three bags filling spaces intended for one.

In one corner of the morgue, Madeline found the three body bags from the containment area and unzipped one.

Martina.

The autopsy table had body bags on top and underneath it. With a focused grunt, she lowered one from the table to the floor. Bending her knees and wishing someone could give her a hand, she got Martina onto the table. The others would be harder to maneuver.

Drug toxicity showed little in the way of outward symptoms, but Madeline examined Martina anyway. She took a nasal swab and was going for a throat culture when she saw something that made her look closer. In her pen light beam, small, translucent lesions dotted the inside of Martina's mouth and throat. Madeline was fairly certain the lesions hadn't been there during yesterday's exam. She used her phone to take photos of the anomaly. There were many causes of mouth lesions, but to the best of her knowledge, drug toxicity was not one of them. Not from any of the drugs that registered on the tox screening results.

Madeline recalled Martina showed hints of jaundice yesterday. Martina's abdomen appeared slightly swollen, which could be nothing at all, or an early sign of a compromised liver. Livers played a primary role in metabolizing and excreting drugs and toxins from the body. During the autopsy, Madeline found Martina's liver looked normal, with no signs of scarring.

"What I really need is information from blood tests," Madeline said, talking to herself as she stitched up Martina's abdominal cavity. Madeline was frustrated that she still didn't have that information and planned to head straight to the lab to get the tests done herself, as soon as she finished the other two autopsies.

After Martina's autopsy, Captain Barstow joined Madeline in the morgue and helped her move the other corpses onto the metal table, one at a time. He returned when she had finished conducting the internal examinations.

"Did you find anything?" he asked.

"Yes," Madeline said, scrubbing her hands with the water from the wall sink. "All three had lesions inside their mouths. All three also had subtle signs of a compromised liver."

"What does that mean?" Barstow asked.

"I don't know yet."

Drugs. Lesions. Liver issues.

Their presence together might not be a coincidence.

CHAPTER FIFTEEN

Madeline tapped on the staff room door, heard nothing, and entered.

Inside, a painfully thin, middle-aged woman sat on the couch with her head in her hands. A bright scarf covered her head. Slowly, she lifted sunken eyes to face Madeline. She wore a surgeon's mask, so Madeline couldn't see her complete face, but with one long look, her eyes said, *What next? Will this be the last thing I can handle?*

"Hello. We haven't met yet. I'm Dr. Madeline Hamilton. I'm here from the CDC."

"I heard you were here," the woman said, smoothing the scarf over her head then pressing her hand against her narrow hip. "I'm Lydia. An RN. I just needed a minute in here."

"I need a minute *and* some caffeine," Madeline said, crossing the room to the coffee machine. The carafe was almost empty. "I'd like to meet with all the hospital's caregivers tonight to talk about the outbreak. Would seven p.m. work for you? Here in the staff room?"

The woman flipped her wrist and looked at her watch. "Yes. If it's important, I'll make sure I'm here."

Madeline opened a cabinet door, searching for an unused mug or paper cup. "Lydia, while you were treating patients over the last few days, did you notice anyone presenting with mouth lesions?"

"Actually, yes. I have. Not as the primary concern, but several have had them. Once I noticed, I began checking for them."

"Really?" Despite posing the question, the answer surprised Madeline. "I'd like to have a look. Can you tell me where to find those patients?" She realized the difficulty of her request. Lydia had probably treated hundreds of patients recently and they were using a paper system for medical charts.

Lydia bit into her lower lip. "I don't know where they are. I'd have to go back and look through charts."

"Those with the mouth lesions, do you recall if they had any other symptoms of the outbreak? Aggression? Hallucinations? Hyper-alertness?"

"I'm well aware of the outbreak and its symptoms. I've been screening every patient for them. I don't believe any patients with mouth lesions had outbreak symptoms. Not the ones I saw. Oh, I just remembered. One was a cardiac arrest. One was a stroke. And there was also a couple. Their daughter went to school with mine, years ago. The father came in with a broken arm. Both the mother and father had lesions. They've left now. And several men and women from the air base had lesions. They came and went."

"Okay, well if you can think of anyone who is still here—"

"Wait…there's a man in one of the first rooms on the second floor. He has a leg injury. Last name is…" Lydia clasped her hands and tapped them against her forehead. "Fervin. His last name is Fervin. He's still here." She got up from the couch and went to the table where she picked up a plastic container of something that looked like pasta. It appeared untouched. "Have some, if you like. There's not much else to eat." She set it on the counter. "I better get back out there. I hope that information helps you. I'll see you later."

"Thank you. See you at seven."

Madeline washed a mug out and dried it carefully with a paper towel. She made more coffee using one of the bottled waters and sat down to drink some. It tasted far better than the coffee in the dorm kitchen at Azure Cove. When finished, she left to find the man whose last name was Fervin. She passed by a first-floor window. Woods surrounded the perimeter of the hospital's back lawn, and the grass wasn't completely trampled like it was in the front. She still hoped she and Quinn could enjoy a few hours on the beach in the sun before they left the island. Although there wouldn't be much enjoyment happening if she couldn't make progress with the outbreak.

Outside the window, two boys ran across the grass, shouting something. Madeline wondered if Quinn still had Ben with him. She hoped his mother had shown up. If not, what did it mean for Ben? Was it good for him to spend more time with Quinn? Or a negative because he was growing close to someone who would only be on the island for a short time? So many questions, too many questions, so much beyond her control...she should really sit down and try to meditate for ten minutes to clear her mind...but there just wasn't time.

She found Mr. Fervin in an upstairs room. He was awake.

"Hello. I'm Dr. Hamilton from the CDC. I'm here on the island because of an outbreak."

"The violent syndrome. I don't have it."

"Good. Lydia, the nurse who treated you, she mentioned you had mouth lesions. Would you mind if I took a look?"

"Go ahead. They're not bothering me none. Sort of feels like canker sores I get every so often. Not even so bad as that though."

Madeline used her pen light to confirm the presence of tiny, translucent mouth lesions. "We're trying to determine what's causing them. Can you tell me where you've been since the tsunami hit?"

"I was at the new resort up north, Azure Cove, delivering fruit when it hit. I drove straight back to Market Street. My son works at the Fresh Mart. The whole store is crushed." He choked up.

"You were in the floodwaters?"

"Yes. That's how I hurt my leg. I thought it wasn't so bad, but my daughter insisted I get treated. They gave me a tetanus shot and some antibiotics."

"Do you have any insect bites?"

He lifted an arm and studied it. "Maybe a few. I always have a few."

"Animal bites? A dog by any chance?"

"No. I didn't see any dogs around the flooding. I think the animals perished, just like so many people." Tears welled in his eyes. He looked away to face the wall. A silent sob racked his body. "I'm sorry."

"It's all right." She wanted to be compassionate and give him time to compose himself, but time wasn't on their side, not for the patients in the containment area. "Do you know anyone else who also has mouth lesions?"

"I don't know. Why do I have them?"

"They might result from a virus that's going around. Its symptoms appear to be very mild, not significant enough for people to register amidst the larger problems they're facing on the island."

"Right. Then why do you care about them?"

Good question. "I'm seeing a correlation between the presence of this virus and a problem involving other chemicals. The violent syndrome, as you called it."

"So, because I have the lesions, I might get the violent syndrome?"

Madeline hesitated before answering. "I don't know."

CHAPTER SIXTEEN

Sitting on the passenger seat of the truck with his head down, Ben swiped his finger under his eyes and sniffed. "Sorry."

"What are you sorry for?" Quinn asked.

"Crying."

Ben had been holding in tears since they checked in at the tent, and the woman with the nose piercings said his mother hadn't been there.

"There's no reason to apologize."

Ben sniffed again and twisted the rope in his lap. "Have you ever cried? You know, like not a long time ago?"

"Of course."

"When?"

"When my wife died."

"Huh? Isn't Madeline going to be your wife?"

"She is. But I was married to someone else a few years ago. Her name was Holly."

"How did she die?"

Quinn's left leg bounced as he drove. "She was sick. It was very sudden and...I couldn't help her. And pretty recently, I cried because someone kidnapped Madeline."

"For real? She was kidnapped?"

"Yes. For real." Remembering the situation gave him chills. "I thought I might lose her. It scared me. Made me angry and frustrated. Then I cried when I found her because I was so grateful."

"You want to talk about it?" Ben let his hands be still. "When Madeline got kidnapped."

"It's a long story."

"We've got time before we get to the base. Don't we?"

"I suppose we do." He kept his smile to himself, so he didn't appear dismissive. He really liked the kid's confidence and curiosity. "Here's how it happened. Madeline was in Washington. D.C., which is the capital of America, where the President lives. The children of some powerful people were sick with a mysterious illness no one had ever seen before."

"Hey…just like people here are sick with a mysterious illness."

"Exactly. It's a different sickness, different symptoms, but that's why she's here. She's an expert on infectious diseases, plus she's smart and very persistent. She graduated from college when she was only nineteen."

"That's early?"

"Yes. In Washington, D.C., turns out a criminal had made the children sick on purpose so he could bribe the government. Madeline and her team figured everything out and ruined his plans."

"And did the children get better?"

"Yes." Quinn didn't need to be brutally honest. Most of the children had recovered, thanks to the team of neurological and pharmaceutical experts Madeline had put together. That's all Ben needed to know.

"You think she'll figure out the sickness here, so everyone gets better?" Ben asked.

"I hope so. I can tell you for sure that Madeline is very good at what she does. She's like a disease detective. And she knows how to bring out the best in others, the people she works with."

No one was perfect, not even Madeline, although she sure seemed like it most of the time. Quinn didn't want anyone to have unreasonable expectations. Not every situation can have a happy ending. Life was tough and rarely was it fair. Yet he had a strong feeling, almost like a premonition, that Madeline and the other health care workers would prevail against the current outbreak.

"Here we are again," Ben said as they neared the entrance to the base. The Airmen manning the gate differed from the previous day. Wearing masks, they spoke to Quinn from the doorway of the guardhouse. "Sir, what can we help you with today?"

Quinn showed his identification and explained the purpose of his visit. "I have specimens that need to be flown off the island for immediate testing. How do I make that happen?"

The Airman shook his head. "We have orders…"

"I know. Nothing on or off the island."

"Yes, sir. Not my call. We're on lockdown."

Quinn understood there was a chain of command to be followed. He understood that well. But it didn't keep his curiosity and determination in check. "We need to look at the bunkers," he said. Now that he suspected what they were dealing with, he was eager to confirm or disprove his ideas.

"Yes, sir. Just wait until I get someone to go with you."

"Ask whoever it is to bring an inventory list." Quinn said.

They waited much longer than the last visit. It was Airman Williams who came with them again.

"We want to check out a few more of those Hobbit Holes," Quinn said with a grin. "Starting with the one closest to the ocean."

Williams studied the stack of papers he brought with him, flipping pages until he handed one to Quinn. "That would be this one."

"Take us to it," Quinn said, accepting the paper and scanning the inventory. The list was simple but long. Bombs were categorized by type. Each individually numbered with a manufacturing date and other information. They were all old. None of them stored for rapid access. Empty chemical shells were listed along with the bombs.

Quinn started the truck's engine. "How often do you go in to verify the inventory?"

"Every week we enter each bunker, verify the type of munition and then perform a count to ensure everything is still there," Williams said. "We inspect each crate or box to ensure nothing has been damaged or tampered with. Which we don't expect to happen since we're doing our jobs to guard the base."

After a short drive with Quinn following William's directions, they parked the truck and walked across the nearly deserted base in the ocean's direction. Quinn carried the crowbar again, in case they ran into a sick animal or a violent person. He also had his gun. When Ben picked up his pace, Quinn and Williams jogged along with him. They slowed when they came to flattened grass and plants crusted with salt and sand—the edge of the tsunami's reach.

Ben pointed. "There's another bunker."

Tucked into the side of a hill, only the front of the bunker was visible. A carpet of moss dotted with purple wildflowers covered its top. A pool of muddy water flanked a patch of level ground by the entrance.

Ben skipped down the incline.

"Ben, wait!" Quinn shouted. "Come back."

Ben returned to Quinn's side. "Aren't we going to look inside it?"

"Not today. Listen, let's get back to the truck. I'm going to put on protective gear and come back to take some samples."

"Do you have protective gear for me, too?"

Quinn shook his head. "Sorry, buddy. Even if I did, I just really want you to be safe."

"I want you to be safe, too. If it's not safe, neither of us should go."

"Well…" Quinn laughed. The kid's logic was sound. "It only takes one person to get the samples, and since I'm the adult, I'm going. I've had training that helps me be extra careful." Ben looked eager for more information, but Quinn knew better than to expand on the topic and begin educating a ten-year-old about bioterrorism. No reason to give him nightmares for the rest of his life.

Back at the truck, Quinn sifted through the box of tools in the back and selected a trowel. He removed surgical gloves and two lidded containers from his backpack.

"Wait here," he said before jogging back to the bunker, where he scooped up soil and water and deposited it into the containers. Williams watched him.

Quinn took off his protective gear and bundled it into a bag before he reached the truck.

"What are you going to do with the samples?" Ben asked.

"Give them to Madeline. She'll test them for contaminants."

Ben nodded and repeated the word contaminants, whispering it as they got back into the truck. He scooted back on the seat, his feet dangling a few inches from the floor mat. "Can

155

we go by my house again and see if we can get through now? I want some of my stuff."

"Sure. We'll go there right now."

Quinn prayed they would find some sign Ben's mother was alive.

After dropping Williams back at the checkpoint and leaving the base, Ben directed Quinn northwest, avoiding the flooded areas. Eventually they turned in a southern direction and the streets quickly became undrivable. On the road leading to Ben's neighborhood, someone had moved the power lines, and the floodwaters had mostly receded or evaporated, but debris still covered the roads. The truck's old tire treads were almost bare. It wouldn't take much to pop them. Quinn parked, and they walked the rest of the way.

Water had flooded the modest bungalow homes and left a mess behind. A man shoveled mud and shards of broken pottery from his porch. Couches and chairs cluttered the lawn, drying in the sun like an unorganized yard sale with broken merchandise. A minivan blocked the entrance to someone's house.

"That's my house," Ben said, hurrying ahead. "The white one with blue shutters."

Across the street, an older couple dragged a mattress out of their front door. The woman's eyes lit up when she spotted Ben. "You're all right!" She held out her arms.

Ben went over and allowed the woman to hug him for a few seconds before he stepped away. "Have you seen my mother?"

"I haven't," she said. "When did you last see her?"

"Before the wave. She was in a store on Market Street. I don't know which one."

"Oh, dear," the woman said. "What about her friend, Joyce? You should stay with her until...until we know where your mother is."

"Joyce was with her when the wave came," Ben said.

Quinn moved closer and introduced himself to the couple.

"From the military base?" the man asked. He grabbed his wife's arm and pulled her farther from Quinn. "Because people there are getting sick."

"No. I'm visiting the island."

"We're getting some of my stuff," Ben said before running off to his house.

"Anyone else Ben should contact until his mother is located?" Quinn asked the woman. He wondered if she would offer to have Ben stay with her.

"It's just the two of them. Ben and Eve. That house used to belong to Eve's parents. Her father passed last year. Her mother a year earlier." The woman shook her head. "Eve and Joyce were the best friends you've ever seen. Joyce was like another mother to little Ben. Anyway, now I'm remembering that Joyce lives closer to the ocean than we do. She might not have a house to live in right now. Not for a long time, if she's lucky. But if Eve and Joyce were together on Market Street, then…" She let her words trail off.

A woman with wiry gray hair exited the nearest home carrying a pile of blankets, the quilted kind Quinn's grandmother used to make, and tossed them onto a mound of objects on her lawn. So far, everyone Quinn had seen in the neighborhood was elderly.

"I'm going to leave my phone number at Ben's house, somewhere his mother can find it when she gets back," Quinn told the couple.

"All right," the man said. "Though it won't do much good if the phones don't work. The cell towers got flooded and the transformers blew. Even when the electricity gets restored, we don't got a crew here to fix those."

157

"We're just desperate for our phones to work again." The old woman rested her hand on her ample hip and leaned to one side. "I'll keep an eye out for Eve, but…" Her solemn expression conveyed she didn't expect to see Ben's mother again.

Quinn crossed the road to the little white house with bright blue accents. Ben was standing on his tiptoes and reaching into a dried-up hanging plant on the porch. He spun around and held up a key, then unlocked the door and waited for Quinn before going inside. "Ew!" he shouted. "Why does it smell so bad?"

A few steps into the living room and a powerful musty odor hit Quinn. He scanned the living area, taking in a couch, a television on a stand, and a desk along one wall. The rugs and furniture were sodden. Water had ruined the wood floors. Otherwise, the house was lovely. As he walked around, the small space didn't feel cramped because of white walls and light pouring in through the back windows. The kitchen, with its sea foam-colored cabinets, was old and more dated than the kitchen Madeline and Quinn were remodeling in Atlanta, but somehow charming. It gave off the vibe it was exactly as it should be.

A canvas portrait hung above the kitchen table. A beautiful, raven-haired woman had one arm around Ben, pulling him close. She had a contagious smile, both serene and smart-alecky at the same time. And something about that smile was familiar.

Ben caught Quinn staring at the painting. "My mom painted us from a photo Joyce took."

"It's great," Quinn said, rubbing his fingers against his cheek. "Your mom is beautiful and talented, huh?"

"Yeah. I already told you she was. Want to see something?"

"Sure."

Ben went to the kitchen counter and took the lid off a porcelain canister. He dipped his hand in and drew out a rusting copper coin. "My mom found this at Azure Cove. The very first people who lived on the island probably used it. Thousands of years ago. She was going to bring it to the historical museum. She says it's an important find."

"She found it recently?"

"Yup. Before she got fired. When she was finishing the mermaid mural."

And that's when Quinn knew where he had seen Eve's beautiful smile before. The mural.

Ben pocketed the coin. "I'll keep it safe for her." He bolted from the kitchen and bounded up the stairs. "I'm going to my room to get some stuff."

While Ben was upstairs, Quinn moved the living room couch outside, under an awning where it would get fresh air without getting further doused by rain. Next, he dragged out a carpet, a throw rug, and two mats from the kitchen floor. Although, in his opinion, the mildewing couch and carpets weren't salvageable. But what would happen to the house if Ben's mother didn't show up? Who would help Ben clean it up, take care of it, or sell it? And more importantly, who would take care of Ben?

Quinn went back inside and climbed the narrow staircase to check on him. A hallway separated two bedrooms and a bathroom. Ben was in the smaller room. Soccer posters covered the wall behind his twin bed. A bookshelf held dozens of books stacked every which way.

"This is my room," Ben said, yanking off his shirt. "I've worn this T-shirt for so many days that I don't ever want to wear it again." He tossed the shirt into an almost full clothes hamper and pulled a fresh shirt from a dresser.

The simple act of Ben tidying up after himself made Quinn sad. How long would those clothes sit in the hamper if Ben's mother didn't return? Not that Quinn cared deeply about unwashed clothes. He cared that life as Ben knew it might never be the same.

"I should pack some stuff, right?" Ben asked.

"Yes. Take your hamper, too, so we can wash your dirty clothes. Pack the things you use the most."

"That's my phone and my soccer ball. They're both gone."

With Quinn following, Ben left his room, went to his mother's, and opened her closet door. He stood on a stepstool, but it wasn't enough for him to reach the suitcase on the top shelf.

"Here, let me get that for you." Quinn got the bag down.

Ben dragged the suitcase back to his room and carefully placed things inside. "I'll take two pairs of shorts and two T-shirts. And three socks. Plus the clothes from my hamper. And a book." He grabbed the one on top of the bookshelf. "I'm reading this one." He selected another from a lower shelf. "And this one because it's my favorite." He slid his fingers over the spines and pulled out a third. "This one is good. Maybe someone else will want to read it."

"You like to read, huh?" Quinn rubbed his cheek again, aware of an odd sensation in his mouth.

"Yeah. I like to read while my mom paints. Especially on Sundays, after we get a bagel and two chocolate donuts." Ben finished packing and crossed his arms. "Should I pack stuff for my mom, too? In case she needs them?"

"Um, if she needs them, I'll drive you back here."

Ben nodded and headed downstairs with his suitcase. He left it by the front door and went into the kitchen. He opened a cabinet and took out a box of crackers. After eating a handful, he offered the box to Quinn. "Want some?"

"No, thanks. I'm fine." It was already late afternoon, but Quinn wasn't hungry.

Ben opened the fridge. "Oh, no!" He covered his nose with his hand. "It smells so bad!"

Quinn scrunched his nose. "We need to throw this stuff out." They emptied the fridge, throwing its contents into trash bags

160

and dropping those into the bins outside. Quinn hoped someone would collect them soon, but he doubted that. He left a note with a few words and his phone number on the kitchen counter. Ben left his own note, telling his mother he was okay and with Quinn from the FBI.

"Come on, we've got to get these soil samples to Madeline at the hospital," Quinn said.

On their way out, Ben relocked the front door and returned the key to its hiding spot. Quinn carried the suitcase as they made their way back to the truck.

"I hope no one here gets sick."

"It's going to be okay, buddy." Quinn wasn't sure what sparked his confidence. He had that same feeling he often got before a big game, when he knew his team had every advantage. Focused and feeling invincible. Some might even call it cocky.

He would protect Ben. He would help Madeline.

Everything would be okay.

Quinn winced as he accidentally bit the inside of his lip for the second time that day.

CHAPTER SEVENTEEN

With dim light streaming through the lab's upper windows, Madeline felt she'd entered a time warp into the past, back to the days where she'd visited a foreign location and helped in any way she could. After familiarizing herself with the hospital's very basic lab equipment, she'd essentially resumed the tasks of a young CDC epidemiologist and researcher—smearing and streaking specimens onto slides and preparing cultures. Even with the bare minimum of equipment, she much preferred this work—the actual *doing* of things—to the administrative decision making perpetually influenced by politics that occupied her time recently. Yet there was nothing enjoyable about working in the lab alone now, not with recent deaths and comas proving the patients couldn't get much worse before succumbing to fatal toxicity.

Mr. Fervin's tox screen results were negative for drugs but Madeline wasn't ready to drop the possibility of a correlation between the aggressive behavior and the lesions yet. Not if the other outbreak patients had the same lesions. If they did, there had to be a connection.

Lydia poked her head in the door. Her bone structure was clearly defined, though between her scarf and mask, Madeline still had little idea of what the woman looked like.

"Oh," Lydia said. "Are you...I was looking for...I need some lab work." A small tray between her hands held vials of dark fluid.

"I'm the only one here." Madeline hoped she wouldn't get asked to take on additional lab work in the absence of laboratory staff. She would hate to say no, but she had to stay focused. "I'm doing the lab work on the outbreak patients."

Lydia set the tray down. "Lab work? What are you finding?"

"I'm ruling out all the things that it's not...that's about all I can definitively say."

"But I thought someone drugged them."

"We don't know if someone drugged them, only that they're drugged...but there's something else going on. Something is compromising their livers and causing lesions, at least in a few of the patients. Something is preventing them from metabolizing the drugs."

"Well, I heard none of the antibiotics they were given had any effect on their condition."

"That's right. Whatever is affecting them, in addition to the drugs, the culprit doesn't seem to be bacterial or fungal. Although it will take two to three days to confirm that with these cultures. I ran every test available to us. They're negative for all of them. I also checked for abnormal pathogenic proteins in the brain sections from the autopsy patients but found none."

"Can't believe this is happening," Lydia said. "I better get upstairs. I'll see you later tonight?"

"Yes. Seven p.m. In the staff room."

"I'll be there."

Madeline checked her watch. Her hand shook. Not a lot, but enough that she noticed. She wasn't feeling herself. Could be stress or low blood sugar from not eating, or the urgency of the situation gnawing away at her composure.

Before checking on the outbreak patients, she had time to prepare one more test. A test on herself to see if she'd also been exposed to the drugs. The timer started counting down the necessary five minutes. In the silence, her pulse thumped methodically behind her temples. Suddenly she couldn't focus. She lowered herself onto a stool and rested her head in her hands.

The timer buzzed.

She swallowed hard, her mouth dry, then lifted the cartridge and scanned the results. Negative for all the drugs. So, what did that mean? The source of the exposure wasn't in the hospital? Madeline wasn't susceptible? Or she'd just gotten lucky so far?

She stuck three cartridges in her bag for later.

▼▲▼

On her way to the basement, Madeline tried to reach Patrick on her satellite phone. She got a signal right away but only heard annoying static. There was no time to be frustrated. She put on protective gear and entered the containment area, ready to focus on her patients.

"Red licorice. Red licorice. Red licorice!" A woman grinned eerily at them from behind the bars. Legs spread wide, she jumped from one foot to the other in what looked like a football practice drill.

"Dr. Hamilton!" Nate shouted, pulling on the bars. "Something's burning! This entire place is going to burst into flames! We have to find the fire and put it out."

Madeline concentrated on differentiating the foul smells filling the space to determine if something really was burning, or if Nate was suffering from phantosmia, an olfactory hallucination. "I don't smell anything burning."

"I don't care if *you* don't smell it!" Nate shouted. "I do! I smell it! Something is burning! Let me out and I'll find it. You can't keep us in here. You can't get away with this!"

Madeline moved along the row of cells.

164

Captain Barstow stood on the other side of Colonel Nelson's bars, speaking in a hushed tone as Nelson paced the tiny space with his head down and his hands together.

Grace was in the next cell with a woman who wept in the corner, producing no tears. The woman opened her mouth and Grace swept her penlight around.

"Any progress with treatments?" Madeline asked the doctor.

"No," Grace said. "No one is eating. Or drinking. Or sleeping. Going on three days with no sleep for some of them. We're still only treating the symptoms. Sedatives and beta-blockers, that's about it.

"What about the Narcan?"

Grace exited the woman's cell. "It had a transient effect on opioid levels, but it didn't last. Nothing we're doing is really helping them. And none of them know anything about the drugs, or how they came to be drugged, as far as we can tell." She lowered her voice. "Though some of them also don't know where they are right now or how they got here." She let out a tired sigh. "Lydia told me about the lesions."

"Oh, good. We need to check for them."

"I have been. So far, most of these patients have them."

"They do?" Madeline still didn't know what it meant, but it confirmed her suspicion. "Then there has to be a correlation between the lesions and the outbreak symptoms. There has to be...even if some people are experiencing one without the other. The lesions don't seem to be much of a problem on their own, but combined with the exposure, we have a problem. If only we knew where the exposure was coming from." Madeline sighed as she checked the time. "It's almost seven. I know how busy everyone is and don't want to keep anyone waiting."

Madeline and Grace left the containment area, leaving behind Nate's screams of, "We're going to be burned alive!"

165

They removed their protective gear, and Grace slid her bag over her arm. "When I moved here, never in a million years did I imagine myself in this situation."

"Where are you from originally?" Madeline asked.

"Maine. I'm not much of a tropical beach person. You probably can't tell that from my deep tan." Grace's solemn expression disappeared for a second, replaced by a slight smile as she lifted her hand, showing fair, lightly freckled skin. "I prefer the mountains and shade. I'm in the hospital most of the time, anyway. When I'm outside, the sun is either rising or already set, and that works for me."

"What brought you to the island?" Madeline asked as they started up the stairs.

Grace flinched, a flash of discomfort before squaring her shoulders. "My fiancé is an anthropologist and received a grant to work here. Nalowale needed another physician, so here I am. I followed my soulmate. I've been here almost five months. We've got another seven to go."

"Oh. I'm engaged as well. No wedding date set, though. We're working on it. Things keep happening…in fact, we just decided to forgo the whole traditional wedding and have a small private ceremony. I'm not sure why we didn't decide on that sooner. It's kind of a relief now that we have."

Two men came through the door at the top of the stairwell, letting in a burst of daylight. They carried a body covered by a worn blanket. The door shut behind them, shrouding the stairwell back into darkness. Madeline turned sideways, giving them room to pass. The men were a few stairs below the women when Grace turned and said, "Hold on, please."

Grace flicked her flashlight on. She descended a few stairs to the men and lifted a corner of the blanket. Seconds passed with her beam of light hovering above the corpse, illuminating coal-black hair and just the top of a forehead. With the slowest

166

movement, Grace peeled the blanket back further. The bloated face barely looked human.

Grace dropped the blanket. Her flashlight fell from her trembling hand and hit the stairs with a loud clang. It rolled and clattered down two more steps.

"Grace?" Madeline touched the doctor's arm.

"You know her?" one of the men asked.

Grace didn't answer.

"I'm really sorry," he said before continuing their descent to the morgue.

Without a word, Grace ran up the stairs.

"Grace!" Madeline said.

Grace stumbled near the top. She got up and kept going.

Saddened, Madeline made her way to the staff room alone. Matthew, Lydia, and Juliette, the other nurse, were already there, hovering around the coffee machine.

"How are you feeling?" Matthew asked Lydia as she poured water into the carafe.

Lydia offered a weak smile.

Matthew turned to acknowledge Madeline. "Grace was in the containment area. I can run downstairs and get her."

"No. I was just with her. She recognized a woman being carried to the morgue. She was very upset. I don't know where she went."

Matthew grimaced. "Was the woman petite? Long black hair?"

"Yes."

"Sounds like it could have been Heidi, Grace's fiancé."

Madeline couldn't imagine the pain of losing Quinn now. Just thinking about it made her ill. And the tsunami had been so sudden and unexpected, leaving no time for goodbyes.

Gripping coffee mugs, Lydia and Juliette dropped into seats around the table, looking exhausted. As hard as Madeline had been working, they'd been working harder and longer.

"Grace might have found her fiancé," Matthew told them.

The staff room door opened. Grace entered. Her skin was ash gray, her cheeks streaked with tears. But she held her head up and her eyes blazed with determination as she took a seat.

"They found Heidi?" Lydia whispered.

Grace squeezed her eyes shut. The top of her cheeks quivered.

"I'm so sorry." Lydia wrapped her thin arms around Grace as others offered similar condolences.

Madeline kept silent for several minutes while they grieved. She debated saving the update for later, considering Grace's personal tragedy, even though the outbreak patients didn't have the luxury of waiting.

"We've got work to do," Grace said. "Go ahead, Dr. Hamilton."

"You're sure?" Lydia asked.

"I'm sure." Grace placed her hands on the table. "Go ahead. Please."

"I'll be as brief as possible," Madeline said. "I want to share the findings we have so we're all on the same page and can expand on that knowledge together. I have nothing typed up for you, but once we have internet or printing capabilities back, I'll compile my data and send it out. Right now, any time not spent on direct patient care or researching their disease seems like wasted time."

"I agree," Lydia said. "Let's share what we have now."

Madeline continued. "I autopsied the three patients who passed. Their cause of death was drug toxicity. All of them, as well as all the patients in the containment area, have dangerously high levels of opiates, cocaine, and meth. But I don't think they're dealing with the drugs alone. There's something else. A significant number also have unexplained mouth lesions. Some of you have seen this." She looked at Lydia and Grace, who both nodded. "Based on my lab results, the patients have high T and B cell counts. Also, elevated bilirubin and liver enzymes."

"Okay, so your lab results suggest they're mounting an immune defense against a foreign organism," Matthew said. "Sounds like a virus. What virus causes mouth lesions and affects liver functions?"

"None I'm aware of," Madeline answered. "As you've all suspected, they're suffering from something new. Something for which diagnostic tests don't exist."

"And how does that explain the drugs, or even relate to their presence?" Matthew asked.

No one had the solution.

"We saw Covid-19 cause bizarre side effects like anosmia and parosmia in mild cases, but there are physiological explanations for how the virus affected taste and smell," Grace said. "How does a virus manufacture cocaine, meth, morphine?"

"As far as we know, it can't," Madeline said. "And yet it appears to be happening."

"How are they catching this…whatever is happening to them?" Lydia set her coffee mug down. A deep frown etched her face. "You know, I think it has something to do with Azure Cove. I think that's why the person in charge there told most of the contactors to leave the island."

Madeline sighed. They all had the same questions. None of them could see the answers. Meanwhile, she couldn't quit thinking about the super serum drug concoction Quinn mentioned. Taking a deep breath, she changed their focus to some relatively good news. "One thing is that the disease doesn't seem to be transmissible. A patient bit Captain Barstow. He didn't get sick. Not yet, anyway. I think they're all suffering from a common source of exposure. As soon as communications open up, I can consult with the NIH and my colleagues at the CDC. Until then, it appears we're on our own. We need to put our heads together to come up with more effective treatment plans."

"To come up with a way to keep them alive," Lydia said.

CHAPTER EIGHTEEN

Outside the hospital, Madeline threw her arms around Quinn and held him tight. After witnessing Grace's raw grief and imagining herself in Grace's position, she didn't want to let him go.

"Rough day?" Quinn asked, holding her and smoothing her hair over the back of her head. As usual, Quinn's gentle strength reminded her not everything was strange and unpredictable. There were still solid and dependable things in her life.

"Three of the outbreak patients died," she whispered.

"It's not your fault," he murmured. "You just got here. It will be okay."

She moved away from his embrace. It would not be okay for everyone, that much was obvious. Eventually, they would figure out what was going on. But that could take months. It would require resources and equipment the island didn't have at the moment. Mostly they needed time. It took years to understand AIDS and decades to develop effective HIV treatments. Once eliminating the Covid-19 virus became a global priority due to sickness, death, and the impact on the global economy, the world developed vaccines in less than a year. But Nalowale was different. On a small, secluded island, as long as it remained cut off from the rest of the world, the outbreak would eventually die out on its own. Eventually there would be no one left to get sick or to spread the sickness. The outbreak would die off with its hosts. Thoughts of it made goosebumps rise over Madeline's arms.

"Let's go back to Azure Cove," Quinn said. "There're some things I have to check on."

Ben patted Madeline's arm in a consoling gesture.

"So…what did the two of you do today?" she asked once they were in the truck, doing her best to sound upbeat.

"We went to my house," Ben said. "Are we going to make something to eat when we get back? Because Quinn didn't eat all day."

"He didn't?" Madeline turned her satellite phone on. "I guess I didn't either." She sighed. "Still no signal on this thing, and I really need to speak with the CDC. This is not a great time for technology issues. Can you look at it when we get back? Maybe I'm doing something wrong."

Quinn frowned the way he did when something was bothering him.

"What?" she asked.

"It's not an issue with your phone or laptop. Or with anyone else's. Multiple devices turning on but failing to connect indicates jammed signals."

"What's jamming them?" she asked, noting Ben was following the conversation with wide eyes.

"The question is…who is jamming them?" Quinn said.

"Seriously?" Madeline let the information sink in. "Why?"

"To keep information from getting out. To avoid panic and another recession. My guess—there's a few CIA operatives on a clunky fishing boat, or maybe a rusty cargo ship, about a dozen miles from the island. It may look like a normal ship but it's full of black budget electronic warfare equipment and it's jamming communication frequencies so the world doesn't find out about this outbreak. Notice it happened shortly after your last call to Wallen. You told him you didn't understand what was going on, but knew it was serious."

Quinn sounded a little paranoid. She could understand the quarantine, not letting anyone off the island until they understood how to control the outbreak. The world was still reeling from Covid-19. No country wanted to bring a new and deadly disease onto their shores. But shutting down all communications? Cutting the island off from the rest of the world to avoid panic? That seemed drastic. Although, it would allow the outbreak to run its course without the rest of the world finding out.

Madeline suddenly became aware of Ben's attentive stare. It occurred to her that perhaps this wasn't an appropriate discussion for adults to have in front of children and she should change the topic. "Today I discovered most of the outbreak patients have lesions. As do some of the other hospital patients. I think it's a virus. Possibly related to the floodwaters." As she finished her sentence, it hit her that even though she dealt with issues such as this regularly, it might also be a frightening topic for Ben, perhaps even more worrisome than jammed satellite signals.

"What are lesions?" Ben asked.

"Tiny sores that might hurt a little." Madeline tapped her cheek. "The ones I saw are in people's mouths."

Ben stuck his finger into his mouth and probed it around.

"Something is annoying me a little," Quinn said. "Nothing hurts. It's like my mouth is swollen. I keep biting my lip." He pinched the corner of his mouth and pulled it away as he leaned toward the truck's mirror. The truck veered off to one side of the road, but Quinn righted it in time.

"We'll check as soon as we stop," Madeline said. And then she worried the rest of the way to Azure Cove. She didn't understand what was causing the lesions or how it related to the drugs. She thought of Nate. The floodwaters. The base. Mitch. Mosquitos. Sick animals. So many potential sources of exposure.

173

As soon as Quinn put the truck in park, Madeline opened her door. The cabin's overhead light came on. Ben scooted forward as Madeline leaned toward Quinn.

"Shouldn't we wait until we get inside?" Quinn asked.

"I don't want to wait." She turned on her penlight and moved the beam over his inner cheek, revealing small, translucent spots. She never would have seen them if she wasn't looking, but there they were. "You have them." A heavy weight constricted her chest, making it hard to breathe. Despair-inducing what-if scenarios came at her from all directions. If only they were still back home in Atlanta, where their biggest worry had been managing without a kitchen for a few weeks or months.

"What about me, do I have them?" Ben stretched his mouth open.

Madeline moved the penlight's beam around the lining of his cheeks. "I don't see any."

"So, what do they mean?" Quinn asked.

"Maybe nothing," Madeline said, willing her words to be true. "A slight infection. A mild immune response."

"But you said it might be a virus and the outbreak patients have it," Quinn said.

Frustration mixed with mounting fear as she crossed her arms in front of her chest and carefully chose her words. "Several people have lesions and no other symptoms. Maybe the majority. I don't know. I don't have numbers. The lesions might be separate from the outbreak symptoms."

"Okay." Quinn tapped out a rhythm against the steering wheel. One slow count, three fast. "If you aren't worried, I won't be."

Ben seemed to study her, waiting to see what she said next. "Are you worried?" he asked.

"I'd like to test both of you when we get to the dorm," Madeline said. "But no, I'm not really worried."

She had just lied to a child and the man she loved.

▲▼▲

"That tasted better than it should have." Madeline glanced at the empty container from her microwave meal. "I was famished."

Quinn pushed his chair away. "There's something I want to check on outside. I'll be back. The sample you asked for...the cup is in our bathroom on the back of the toilet. I wrote my name on it, but it's pretty obvious what it is."

Madeline watched him rise from the kitchen table, searching his eyes for some clue about what he was going to do outside. As he walked past, she wrapped her hand around his arm and gave it a quick squeeze.

"Need help?" Ben asked him.

"Not now, but thank you for offering, Ben."

"You can help me with my tests." Madeline smiled and tried to focus on Ben and not worry so much about Quinn. "Right after we scrounge up some dessert from the cabinets. I think I saw cookies somewhere when I was looking for plates."

▼▲▼

Feeling as if he'd been cooped up for the past few hours, Quinn left the dormitory and strode down the trail to the resort's main building. No sign of workers. The machines were quiet. Waves lapped softly on the sand below the cliffs. The smell of the ocean mixed with tropical flowers. All of it—the scents, the sounds, the cool breeze on his skin—seemed enhanced as he marched to the offices and guest check-in on the side of the main building. Light shone from one of the front rooms.

He should have questioned Wheeler on the spot in the morning, but he'd been in a rare, edgy mood and just wanted to get

175

away from him. Wheeler made him angry, and he sure didn't want to have it out with the man in front of Ben.

The door to the guest check in area was unlocked. Quinn entered an elaborate foyer. The Azure Cove logo stared at him from the back wall. *Azure Cove. Exclusive luxury meets unparalleled beauty.*

Surrounded by chest-height glass walls, a detailed model of the resort community filled the center of the foyer, offering visitors a bird's-eye view. Each luxury home in the elaborate replica had a small rooftop pool overlooking the ocean. Wrap-around balconies provided ocean panoramas for the condos, which were built above retail boutiques and restaurants. The main pool sat in the exact center of the complex. There were no lazy rivers.

Quinn read the placard next to the model.

Wheeler Properties is proud to strengthen its global portfolio with this unprecedented debut resort. Azure Cove welcomes exclusive travelers into a world of exceptional luxury, unparalleled beauty, legendary service, and unforgettable experiences.

President and Brand Leader–Devon Wheeler

A shoe scuffed the floor, coming from a room off the foyer.

Quinn spun around.

Wheeler glared at him with cold eyes.

Quinn's neck and jaw tightened. Heat flashed through his body. What was it about Wheeler that made Quinn want to humble the man? To physically hurt him? Over the years, in the FBI's anti-terror division, he'd dealt with some of the worst criminals— sociopaths and brainwashed zealots. Even when they infuriated and disgusted him, rarely did he have trouble controlling his emotional response.

"Can I help you?" Wheeler asked, still hovering near the doorway.

"I'm just exploring." Quinn gestured to the large model as he paced around it. "The place is impressive when you see it laid out like this. Though I'm not one to know what *exclusive travelers* expect these days. In any case, if this here is the end goal, looks like you've got a lot of work to do before your opening."

"Yes, I'm aware." Wheeler entered the room and moved clockwise around the model, staying equidistant with Quinn.

"So why did you send your contractors away?" Quinn's gaze locked with Wheeler's.

"Why is that bothering you?"

"I'm curious."

"You're going to keep asking me the same questions, hoping to get the answer you want. Is that how it works with you?"

"That's about right." Quinn stopped moving. So did Wheeler. They stared at each other, unblinking.

"Okay." Wheeler rested his fingers on the edge of the glass case and made a big show of sighing. "You're probably not going to believe me, but this is the truth. I had a premonition about the tsunami."

"You're right, I don't believe you." Quinn scoffed. "If you thought anyone was in harm's way, you would have been the first one hightailing it out of here, wouldn't you? And why would you send away people working here, on high ground, and not warn those on the south side of the island?"

Wheeler shrugged and stepped away from the model. "Suit yourself. I gave you an answer. I can't control your satisfaction level with the information. But did you ask yourself why they're closing the base and returning the land to the island? And why so many of the infected are military? That's what you should find out." Wheeler motioned toward the front doors. "I'm locking up and you need to leave."

177

"Good luck with this." Quinn took a last look at the model before walking toward the door. "You're going to need it."

CHAPTER NINETEEN

Madeline handed Ben a glass of water and a bag with seven pills. "These are antibiotics for your stitched areas. You'll take one of these every day until they're gone. Okay?"

"Okay." Ben popped one into his mouth, took a gulp of water, and swallowed.

"Do you like science, Ben?" she asked.

"You mean like experiments?"

"Yes. That's exactly what I was thinking."

"My mother got me a chemistry set for my birthday. We haven't used it yet. We opened it…there were a ton of parts. But…yeah, I like it. I can get the set tomorrow, if Quinn takes me to my house, and bring it here, if you want."

"That could be something. But meanwhile, I've got some real-life experiments here. I'm testing the soil you and Quinn brought from the base. Would you like to help?"

"Quinn didn't want me to go near the bunker where he got it from. He said it wasn't safe."

"Oh." What had she been thinking? Here she was, suggesting Ben help her with a potentially toxic substance. Was she going to be the worst mother ever? "You know, Quinn was right. I'll wear gloves and a face shield when I handle it. And maybe I'll have you test something else."

"What?"

"A test for chemicals inside you, like I'm doing for people at the hospital."

"I feel fine," Ben said.

"And that's good. That's important. But sometimes we can have a disease without symptoms. I just want to be sure." And what if he tested positive…then what would she tell him? The whole idea about entertaining him with her "work experiments" was turning into a terrible mistake of judgement on her part.

"What if I am sick? What if I have the disease?" he asked, as if reading her mind.

"Then we can treat it." Except that they had no treatment. She felt terrible, but she couldn't be brutally honest with a kid about something like that. Why had she even brought any of this up? None of what she was working on was appropriate for a child to be involved with. She tried not to be too hard on herself. Everyone makes mistakes. When she and Quinn had children of their own, they'd have years to figure things out before getting to this point. Starting with the right crib, the right sleeping position, covers over the electrical sockets, gates across the top of the staircase. That much she knew. She'd have time to read up on the rest.

"What's Quinn doing outside?" Ben finished his question with a yawn.

"I'm not sure. You know, it's probably past your usual bedtime, isn't it?"

"Yeah. Way past. And I didn't get to sleep much when I was in the tent. Too much noise and stuff."

"Why don't you get washed up and ready for bed? I'll be in soon to tuck you in. I mean…is that a thing? Do you want to be tucked in?"

"You don't have to worry so much about me. My mom had to work a lot. I'm pretty independent."

"I know. I can tell." She smiled, thinking his mother must be so proud of him. "But if you don't mind, I'd like to tuck you in. So, I'll be in later. Okay?"

"Okay," he said.

"One more thing. This is for the test. Quinn also did one." She handed him a cup with a lid. "I need you to pee in this. Then put the cover on. Got it?"

He laughed. "Got it. Like at the doctor's office. Oh, right! Because you're a doctor."

"Yes, I am." She smiled again. "I'll come back for it later. Meanwhile, I'll be right here if you need me."

"Okay. Be careful," he said before turning to go.

He was so sweet and considerate. His mother had raised him well.

When he was gone, Madeline set up her equipment on the countertop and began with a test of the dorm's water as a control. It was negative for all toxins. Next, she mixed the soil with the tap water and prepared a separate sample with the floodwater from the base. The results from both tests were positive for the same array of drugs as the other samples, though the concentrations were less pronounced.

Was the entire base contaminated? Or was the contamination localized to that one bunker?

Still thinking about all the research she needed to do, the additional areas she needed to test, and all the questions that required answers before she could draw any conclusions, she went to Ben's room. A soccer poster now hung above his bed. His suitcase was in one corner of the room. T-shirts hung on hangers in his closet. A red triangle of material stuck out of a dresser drawer. Ben was making himself at home and for that, she felt a little

181

guilty. How long would he stay with them? And what would happen when it was time for them to leave?

"I left the pee cup in the bathroom." Ben chuckled. "It's on the back of the toilet. Cap is on."

"Good job," she said, appreciating the sound of his laughter. She sat on the edge of his bed and pulled the sheet up to his chin.

"Is Quinn back yet?" he asked.

"Not yet."

"I hope he's okay."

She'd been wondering why Quinn left and what he was doing outside in the dark. "I'm sure he is. Quinn can take care of himself."

"I know. He's FBI and fought in the longest war ever. I didn't mean it like that. I meant when you test his pee."

She smiled, touched by Ben's concern, then told him what she wanted him to hear. "He'll be okay." More than anyone, she hoped Quinn was fine, but it was nice that she wasn't alone in hoping his results were normal.

After saying goodnight to Ben and retrieving the fluid sample Quinn left behind, she returned to the kitchen. Alert for sounds of Quinn's return, she prepared the tox screens.

While waiting, she took a seat at a table and stared down at her notes. Twice she looked over at the toxicology test on the counter, anxious for the timer to go off. The five-minute duration seemed to take longer and longer. When the timer finally buzzed, she scanned Ben's results first and let out a little sigh of relief. His sample was negative for all the screened substances.

It was time to check Quinn's test.

She picked up the results, blinked, and checked again. "No," she whispered.

Detectable levels of every drug were present.

Her knees went weak. She swayed as the floor and all solid ground seemed to drop out from under her. She had to steady herself against the counter.

Anger, helplessness, and guilt battled inside Madeline. Quinn was sick because of her. That's what he got for being the most supportive and caring partner she could imagine and accompanying her to Nalowale Island.

Regardless of precautions, risks, albeit small—an infected needle piercing a glove, blood spatter finding a vulnerability in your mask—always existed when treating patients. There was always the remote chance of contracting the disease and becoming its next victim. Accompanying Madeline into territory with a known outbreak had extended that risk to Quinn. So why was she so shocked he got infected? Why was she trying to rationalize that his results, and his alone, might be erroneous? No matter how strong he appeared, no matter how invincible...he was human. And humans were vulnerable.

Years ago, when Madeline went to Africa to work on the Ebola outbreak, her parents were terrified for her. Now she understood what they'd gone through. It was easier to take a risk and accept the consequences with oneself than with someone you loved. The fate of Quinn's health now eclipsed everything else. It gave her work even more purpose. She wanted to monitor him continuously. But under no circumstances would she take him to the containment area and see him locked inside a cell. That was for certain. She wished she hadn't even tested his sample. To go back only a few hours in time would be bliss, but she couldn't undo her knowledge. She needed to alter the outcome—for Quinn and everyone else afflicted.

Was Quinn feeling the effects of the drugs yet? Maybe not. The levels in his sample were detectable but still low. Lower than any of the other patients in the containment area. But if his condition followed the path of the others', his drug toxicity levels would quickly rise over the next few days.

She checked her phone again, which had become a habit. She was desperate to consult with her colleagues. Everything else could wait, especially the contractor. Suddenly the entire kitchen remodel seemed stupid and superficial. Who cares if she had a kitchen at all, never mind an updated one, if there was no Quinn to use it with her? She'd sell the house. She didn't want to live there without him, wouldn't be able to bear it. At least the new kitchen would help sell the house quicker. She couldn't imagine ever being happy again if anything happened to Quinn. They'd never have children now…

Stop!

She was getting way ahead of things. Negative, self-indulgent thoughts about kitchens and offspring did nothing to help the situation, yet there they were, popping into her head right and left, distracting her. Quinn was still alive, and she would die trying to keep him that way.

She squared her shoulders and went outside to find him. He appeared from the hidden path. She waved and watched him walk toward her. He was so handsome and kind and brave it made her heart ache. He did not deserve this.

"Hey," he said. "Everything okay?"

Something rustled the bushes. Quinn jerked around and scanned the area.

"You hear that?" he whispered.

"Probably an animal." But just in case, she wouldn't have this conversation outside. "Let's go in and sit down for a minute." That's all it would take for him to know something was wrong.

Inside, suddenly lightheaded and needing to sit, she lowered herself into one of the foyer chairs.

"What is it?" He sat across from her, scooted his chair closer, and grasped her hands.

"I ran the tox tests on the three of us today. You, Ben, and myself."

"Are you all right?"

She struggled to contain the tears welling in her eyes. She didn't want to scare him. She had to tell him. "Yes, I'm fine. My test was negative. So was Ben's. But…you were positive for the same drugs we saw in the other samples. I'm so sorry, Quinn." She moved closer to embrace him. "We'll get through this."

He dropped her hands and jumped up from his chair. "If a virus has something to do with this…you don't know how it's transmitted yet. You need to stay away from me."

"I can't catch drugs from you. And if I could, if whatever is happening was somehow contagious, I would have it by now. Or I soon will."

"We don't know that. We don't know what's going on with this outbreak We don't know how I got it, or where I got it, or if I got it from someone else." He paced the foyer. "At least I can tell you I didn't take drugs or allow anyone to experiment with me. We know that for sure."

"Can you tell you're affected? Have you been feeling any different?"

"Maybe. I'm feeling extra restless. No appetite." He snorted and laughed. "I thought about running a marathon. Or two. Not because I wanted to, more like I need to."

"I'd say that's a yes. For the record, your levels are still low. Much lower than the others we tested." *If he felt like running a marathon now, what would he feel like later?*

"I can tell you exactly where I've been, who I've been with, and what I've done since we arrived on the island. This might give you the break you need."

185

Those were his first thoughts? Could he be more selfless? She'd rather remain clueless than have Quinn suffer…but he was right. While he was still rational and level-headed, his case might prove extremely helpful to everyone else. At the moment, she cared much more about eliminating his drug toxicity than understanding how it came to be, but the more they understood, the better chance they had of defeating the outbreak. Maybe, hopefully, before Quinn got really sick.

She pushed herself up from the chair. "Let's go back to the kitchen and talk."

"I'll be your canary in a coal mine," he said, walking several feet away from her and attempting to keep his tone normal. "But Madeline, after we hash through this, if I start to act aggressively, you need to lock me in one of these rooms with some sedatives until you know how to handle this. Mitch was out of his mind when the Airmen shot him. I don't want to hurt anyone. Especially not you. Or Ben."

Madeline shuddered as they walked into the kitchen. "We aren't at that point yet. And if I can help it, we won't get there."

"But everything you've seen so far with the other patients tells you otherwise, doesn't it?"

She met his gaze. "So far, yes."

Quinn resumed pacing back and forth. "There has to be something going on at the base with the south side of the island in the rubble or floodwaters. Because those are the only places where I've been, and you and Ben haven't. You're sure Ben is okay?"

Madeline grabbed a notepad and took a seat. "I'm sure. And you're right about the base. The soil samples you gave me from outside the bunker tested positive for the same drugs."

Quinn strode across the room, making large arm gestures. Whether or not he recognized it, he wasn't his usual, calm self. It amazed her he wasn't feeling sorry for himself or acting angry at his misfortune. She had expected no less, but his response filled her heart with love and pride.

"We need to have a look inside that bunker. I'll get someone to search it." He stopped moving and shook his finger. "It could also be the mosquitoes." He tapped several bites along his bare arm. "Or it could be something here on the site. Something Wheeler is hiding."

"What are you talking about?"

"They say it has nothing to do with the outbreak, but we need to be sure."

"I don't know what you're...back up. They who? Tell me what you heard."

"Something to do with the excavators. Those ditches and trenches and areas with overturned dirt. They either dug up something that they shouldn't have, or they buried something. Without a doubt, my gut tells me Wheeler is hiding something."

"No one here is sick. Not the excavators. Not the guards. Not Wheeler. Not as far as we know." She studied Quinn. "How are you feeling right now?"

He let out a curt laugh. "Like I'm about to play in a bowl game and I know I'm going to win. Sharp, focused...a little cocky. I'm feeling great, to be honest. I guess that's the lure of illegal drugs and why so many people do them."

"I've never tried drugs, never cared to, but that's what I hear."

"Neither have I," Quinn said. "Between football and the military, too many drug tests to risk it. Not that I wanted to, either." He shrugged and grinned. "Guess I'm about to get a huge taste of what it's all about."

"Glad you can joke about it." Madeline felt so bad for him. She'd never seen him drink more than two or three beers in an

187

entire night. He hated being out of control, and now…it was coming.

"Where's Ben?" he asked.

"Sleeping."

"Did you tell him I'm…uh, whatever this is?"

"No. I didn't tell him anything. I did the tests after he went to bed. We should tell him tomorrow."

"Okay. Then, unless I can help you, I'm going to go for a run around the complex. That's what I need."

"Don't leave the property, okay?"

"I don't plan to."

"I love you, Quinn. And we'll figure this out."

CHAPTER TWENTY

Morning light shone through the kitchen windows as Madeline finished her coffee.

Ben pattered in, stretching his arms overhead. "Good morning."

"Good morning. Did you sleep well?" she asked him.

"Yes. Where's Quinn?"

"Sit down, honey." She passed the basket of cereal boxes toward him.

Ben pulled a chair away from the table. "What's going on? Where is he?"

"You know how I did some tests on the chemicals in our bodies yesterday?"

"Yeah."

"You and I both tested normal. There was nothing unusual inside us. But Quinn has some drugs inside his body that shouldn't be there."

Ben sat up straighter. "Like Mitch had?"

"Yes. But not as much as Mitch had." *Not yet, anyway.*

"What's going to happen to him?" Ben sat on the front of this seat and gripped the edge of the table.

"He's going to stay here and rest while I work at the hospital." That's what came out of her mouth when she answered Ben. In truth, in the state Quinn was in, and the condition he was heading toward, rest and sleep would be near impossible.

Ben nodded. "He'll be safe here. If he leaves, people might shoot him."

"No one else is getting shot," Quinn said from the doorway.

Madeline caught her breath, studying Quinn for any signs that he wasn't okay. "Were you able to sleep?"

"A little."

"That's a good sign." Her gaze fell to the gun in his holster. He was rubbing the handle as if polishing it with his fingers. "I think I should take your weapon when I go," she said.

"I'll leave it in your room," he said, his fingers still moving methodically.

More than anything, she wanted to go to him, hold him, and tell him everything would be okay. But Quinn wouldn't allow her to get close enough to hug him. "Ben and I are going to the hospital. There are a few more toxicology screening kits in the kitchen. Use one now and another this evening so we can monitor what's going on with you. I wrote down a value for the opiate levels. If your results get close to it, use the Narcan. It will give you a temporary reprieve."

"You have it here?" Quinn asked.

"Yes. I didn't know any of us would need it, but I brought it with me, just in case. There's also sedative in our room. In the blue bag. I left instructions for when to use it and how much to take. But I don't think you'll need it today." If Quinn got bad enough to need it, he might not have the wherewithal to take it, so there was probably no point in telling him. She stared into his eyes from across the room, wishing more than anything that she could make him better before he got worse. "We're going to beat this. I'll figure it out."

Quinn knocked on the wooden doorframe. "I know. I have faith in you, Madeline."

Ben jumped from his chair and ran toward Quinn.

Quinn's hands flew up as he took hurried steps backward. "Ben, stop. I don't want you to get too close until I'm better."

Ben slid to the floor on his knees. He flung his arms around Quinn's leg. "I don't want you to die."

"I'm not planning to die, buddy." Quinn tried to step away, but Ben hung on.

"I've already been with you for a long time," Ben said through tears. "And I'm not sick."

"I know, but there are some things we still don't understand yet." Quinn extricated his feet and sprung away.

Ben stood up, wiping his tears away with the back of his hand.

"Ben," Madeline said, keeping her voice calm. "Come over here with me." The poor kid had been through so much. Maybe they shouldn't have told him Quinn was sick. But how would they have explained the need to keep their distance?

"Don't say anything about me to Wheeler or his security guards," Quinn said.

"I won't." Ben sniffled as he walked backwards toward Madeline.

"You know what to do with the tests and where to find the sedative, right?" Madeline asked. If only their cell phones were working, she could just check on him every hour.

"I'll figure it out. I'm sure you left me excellent instructions."

Madeline blew him a kiss. "I love you, Quinn."

191

"And I love you. I'm glad you're the one working on this."

Quinn left the doorway, and Madeline stared into the space. She was so emotional she could barely think straight. Every patient had someone who loved them the way she loved Quinn. Mothers. Fathers. Significant others. Children. The disease was now personal. Not just knowing, but truly understanding exactly what was at stake for all of them, escalated the urgency of the situation. She berated herself for sleeping at all since she arrived. She should have stayed in the lab. She should have driven to the airstrip herself, found a pilot, and insisted they send the samples out for testing. She should have demanded to know what was going on with the satellites. But who would she give her demands to? She couldn't communicate with anyone off the island...everyone on the island appeared to be in the same situation...victims of circumstances.

Stop, she told herself. *Focus.*

Ben was staring at her.

She took a deep breath and centered herself. "Let's get going."

She drove to the archway, where two burly guards marched over to them.

"Where's Quinn Traynor?" a guard asked.

"He stayed behind to get some work done here."

"What kind of work?"

"The classified kind. If you wouldn't mind moving those roadblocks, we have work to do."

▼▲▼

Determined, but with a heavy heart, Madeline parked the old truck in the crowded hospital parking lot and climbed out.

Ben shut the passenger side door. "I have to see if my mom came. And if she didn't, am I going to...can I help you with stuff in there? Help you figure out how to keep Quinn from getting sicker?"

She'd been so concerned with Quinn and the other outbreak patients and the tests she needed to run that she hadn't considered what to do with Ben. Having him around was starting to feel natural. He'd proven to be independent and self-sufficient, but he was still a child. She couldn't watch over him with all she had to do. And she couldn't put him at risk of becoming sick inside the hospital.

"Madeline!"

Matthew was walking toward her. Good. She had so much to tell him, and now he'd saved her the trouble of trying to find him. He was still unshaven, and the circles under his eyes had darkened. But there was also something different about the medic, something she hadn't seen before. The tight, worried look that previously represented his mood no longer dominated his expression. He wasn't quite smiling, but almost.

"Morning," she said. "I want you to know...I found the drugs in a sample of soil from the southern tip of the Air Force base. The tsunami floodwaters reached a bunker. I don't know how widespread the contamination is or how transmission occurred from the soil to people and to at least one dog. But we've got to check out the bunkers."

"I'm going back there now. I can collect more samples." Matthew lowered his bag to the dusty pavement. "And I have news for you. Good news and bad news. Which do you want first?"

"The bad news."

"Two more deaths. And one more patient in a coma."

The news was devastating, particularly considering Quinn's situation, yet she couldn't say it was unexpected. Not when all their treatments had failed, and the patients' toxicity levels were steadily rising. "And the good news?"

"One patient is recovering. His drug levels dropped. He's lucid and no longer in the containment area. He's going to hang around for more tests."

Madeline allowed herself a glimmer of apprehensive hope.

"That means maybe Quinn will get better, too," Ben said.

"Yes," she said. "I hope that's exactly what it means."

"Who is Quinn?" Matthew asked.

"My fiancé," she answered. "Last night, he tested positive for the same concoction of drugs as the patients in containment."

"Oh. I'm sorry." Matthew met her eyes. All traces of his slight smile disappeared.

It's not a death sentence, she told herself. Not yet. They still had time. But her panicky heartbeat and the acid-laced knots churning in her stomach were firm representations of the urgency. "Which patient improved?"

"Colonel Nelson."

"Did he receive any treatments the others didn't?"

"I gave him cephalexin for his leg infection. And a tetanus antitoxin. It's in his chart."

"I'll find his chart. We need to give others the same meds and see if any improve."

"Grace is working on that. She was going to give the coma patients the antitoxin asap." Matthew hoisted his bag up and looked back toward the building. "Aside from the outbreak situation, things are calming down a bit at the hospital. I'm going back to the base for a few hours."

"Yes. You should get some sleep."

"If you want to examine Colonel Nelson or speak with him, he's outside, behind the building. We asked him to stay for observation, but I doubt he'll hang around for long. He wants to get back to the base."

"I'll go find him now," Madeline said. "This really is fantastic news."

Matthew said goodbye and walked away.

Slightly giddy with the news Colonel Nelson had recovered, Madeline faced Ben, still deciding if she should keep him with her and try to find things for him to do or send him back to the tent with the other children. She glanced at the collection of tents. The smell of cooking meat rose from the grills, even though it was early. Why did she already feel responsible for this child she barely knew? Quinn was even more attached. That was obvious. But if Quinn became aggressive or delusional later, he would be enough to handle without worrying about keeping Ben safe from harm. Perhaps Ben should return to the tent. She probably should have told him to pack his belongings from the dormitory and take them with him.

"Madeline!" Matthew jogged back toward her. "I almost forgot. You asked about a woman with a mermaid tattoo. A diver brought her in last night and someone identified her. She's in the morgue." With a single wave of his hand, Matthew turned away again.

Ben's mouth hung open. His jaw trembled.

Oh, no, no, no! Madeline wrapped her arms around him, pulling him close. "Ben," she said softly.

"It's not my mother. It's not!" Ben wiggled out of her arms and bolted off, running across the lawn.

"Ben, wait!"

Weaving between tents, suitcases, and people, Madeline yanked her backpack off and clutched it against her chest so the contents wouldn't bounce around as she chased after him. A man emerged from a tent, stepping right into her path. She jumped to her left, crashed into a grill, and knocked it over. She looked in the direction Ben ran. The kid was fast. He'd almost made it across the lawn and was heading toward the woods. She turned to the man next to her. "I'm so sorry. I was following a child. I'll come back and help pick this up."

The man grunted as he bent over and started scooping up charcoal. "Just go. Find your kid."

She backed away, straight into someone else. "Excuse me," she said, without even turning. Her eyes scanned the edge of the woods, where she'd last spotted Ben. She couldn't see him. She ran to the edge of the trees. "Ben! Ben!" she shouted between gulping breaths. She still couldn't see him. She trampled into the brush, pushing aside tall shoots of bamboo, and calling his name.

"Ben!"

Almost out of breath, she quit running and looked around. Quietness pervaded under the canopy of trees while the soft buzz of conversation and car engines still came to her from the hospital, muted and seeming farther away than it was. Hardly any sun shone between the bamboo shoots and spiraling, parasitic vines. There were no cleared paths. Which way had he gone? "Ben! Please come back! Please let me help you!"

No response.

She did not know which direction to take, didn't even know for sure if Ben was in the woods. While she stood listening for twigs snapping or branches rustling—any sound he was nearby—something brushed against her ankle. She jumped, scanning the ground for a snake or rat, but it was only the sharp leaves of a bush. Lowering her head into her hands, she fought the urge to let out a primal scream. She felt so sorry for Ben.

Her sense of helplessness and frustration rose. Nothing was happening as it should. Everything was going wrong. The Colonel was better—a positive—but they did not know why or what they could do to help the others, including Quinn. Especially Quinn. Was that terrible to think? She couldn't help it. She loved him and couldn't bear for him to be ill. She dropped her bag and dug her fingernails into her fists. As long as she stayed there waiting for

Ben, she wasn't making progress. She needed to remember why she was here and take control over the things she could control.

"Ben! I have to get back to the hospital. Please find me there. I want to help you. It's going to be okay." She couldn't fix things for Ben. His mother had died. But what else was she supposed to say?

Madeline picked her bag up and slung it over one shoulder. Could Ben hear her? Feeling like a complete failure, with sweat pooling between her breasts, she tried to compose herself.

Time to make a difference and stop making things worse.

Still looking around for any sign of Ben, she trudged out of the woods. When she passed a teenager, she stopped him, told him what happened, and described Ben.

"Please, could you keep an eye out for him? If you find him, take him to the tent and ask him to wait for me there."

She headed straight to the basement, planning to go to the containment area. At the bottom of the stairs, she made a split-second decision and went to the morgue, donning a mask and gloves as she walked. She had to see for herself, just to be sure.

The morgue was cool compared to the upper floors of the hospital, but the smell of decomposing bodies permeated the air. Breathing slowly through her mask, she read the handwritten labels on the drawers, pulled one open, and unzipped the white body bag. The corpse had long, dark hair and skin a few shades darker than Ben's. Despite the battered, bloated, and filthy condition of the body, Madeline could tell the woman had been young when she died. Perhaps younger than Madeline was now.

She raised one shoulder away from the bag. Mud and wounds covered the corpse's skin. She lifted the other. There it was. The mermaid. A tiny version of the one on the wall at the Azure Cove complex. To be sure, she unzipped the bag farther, revealing the hands. A filthy friendship bracelet, well-worn and fraying, surrounded one petite wrist.

197

Madeline closed her eyes and said a prayer for the young woman she didn't know. Taken too soon, leaving her sweet child behind. After zipping up the body bag, Madeline pushed the drawer back into place. She felt this woman's loss and Ben's loss deep inside her soul. It wasn't right. It wasn't fair. Ben's mother wasn't coming back. There was nothing anyone could do to change that. But Madeline *could* change other things. Someone had sent her to Nalowale Island for a reason.

▲ ▼ ▲

Madeline hurried upstairs and out to the hospital's back lawn. She gulped in the fresh air, looking every which way for Ben but stopping short of shouting his name.

The Colonel was still outside, and for that she was grateful. He stood against one of the awning's support beams, away from the other hospital patients and their family members. He put a cigarette to his lips and inhaled. He had showered and changed into a T-shirt and shorts. A clean bandage surrounded his leg. As she drew closer and they made eye contact, Nelson pinched the cigarette butt with his fingers and put it out. His eyes had a calm thoughtfulness to them that Madeline hadn't seen before. He straightened, though still favoring his injured leg. His eyes moved to the butt between his fingers. "Sorry. Not a good habit. I haven't smoked in years. My wife would not be happy. But right now, it's exactly what I need."

"Please don't apologize. You've been through a lot. I'm Dr. Hamilton from the CDC."

He smiled. "I remember you, doctor."

"I wasn't sure if you would."

"I do. Unfortunately, I also remember my recent behavior. It was inexcusable. It wasn't me. Forgive me." He had a humble sincerity to his manner. Nothing like the man who cornered Grace in the hallway and screamed about iguanas. He reminded her of Quinn. A man used to being in control of his emotions no matter how dire the situation.

"I saw your tox screen. It's completely understandable why you behaved as you did. I'm glad you're feeling better. And now we've got to learn why." As she spoke, she scanned the edge of the woods for Ben. "I don't know if we got something right, or if your body's own immune system prevailed, but we need the same thing to happen for everyone else."

"I wish I could tell you how I got sick and why I got better. All I know is that once it started, it felt like I was trapped and losing my mind. It got worse and worse until yesterday. In the afternoon, I just started feeling a little less crazy and a little more like myself."

"How is your leg? You had a pretty serious wound."

"As I started feeling sane again, my leg throbbed. Until then, I felt nothing."

"That pain is a sure sign the drugs, particularly the morphine, have metabolized. Right now, would you mind if I checked inside your mouth?"

"No. Whatever you need to do, go ahead. Please. I want to help. With so many of my men and women sick…that's what's killing me now."

Madeline put on a mask and gloves, removed a penlight from her bag, and moved closer.

The Colonel lowered his head and opened his mouth.

She flicked the light on and scanned the inside of his cheeks and his gums. "No more lesions," she announced, turning the light off and stepping back. "I believe a virus caused those lesions. It appears the virus left, and with it…the drug toxicity."

"So, how can I help? You need more blood from me?"

"Yes. That's a start." She looked toward the woods again. "There's something I have to do and then I can meet you inside the lab in about fifteen minutes."

They started walking together, but with the Colonel limping, Madeline quickly outpaced him. She went on by herself, walking the perimeter of the hospital's property and then around the large tent, searching for Ben. His name was still on the board, with Quinn's name and phone number next to it. But Ben wasn't there.

Madeline walked straight into the middle of the crowded lawn, between the tents, and yelled, "Ben! Where are you? Ben!" Shouting in public would normally garner the attention and concern of everyone nearby. Barely anyone took notice now. Those who did merely cast a sad, sympathetic look her way. Madeline was simply one of many people desperate to find their loved ones. She waited another minute then went to meet Colonel Nelson in the lab.

▲ ▼ ▲

The Colonel leaned against the counter with the microscopes, waiting for her. "I'm ready to be your guinea pig."

Tests confirmed his temperature, blood pressure, and heart rate were slightly elevated but almost normal. Only trace amounts of drugs were detectable in his urine. In contrast, testing the new specimens showed no one else's drug levels were coming down. They were rising to dangerous levels of toxicity incompatible with life. The coma patients wouldn't last much longer. Even if they didn't die, the physiological damage might soon be irreparable.

The colonel left, and Madeline was again alone. She took out the viral and bacterial cultures she'd previously prepared. She added the meds the colonel received, each to its own sample, to test them individually for effect. It would take some time. All the while, she wondered where Ben was. The poor kid. What a terrible way to find out his mother died. And she worried about Quinn. How was he doing? If only she could call him to find out. She'd also have to tell him about Ben.

It was past noon when she created a medical chart for Quinn and pocketed another vial of sedative and the same array of meds the Colonel got. She wanted to take several toxicology cartridges. There were only a few left. She took one.

Before leaving, she checked the tent again for Ben. Then she told the woman in charge what had happened. She expected a rebuke but received none.

"We'll keep an eye out for him," the woman said. "Just like we're doing for everyone else."

Driving back to Azure Cove alone, she sweated as the fan vents spewed warm air, but making her even more uncomfortable was the empty seat next to her.

CHAPTER TWENTY-ONE

There had always been something strange about the Azure Cove resort. The property remained deserted aside from the security guards, the omnipresent Wheeler, and the excavation crew working unusual hours. They were working now. Quinn put on a mask and marched toward them, straight to the man in the blue cap who appeared in charge of the crew. "We need to talk. And as Wheeler pointed out, I'm with the FBI. What's your name?"

"Barry." The middle-aged man stuffed his hands in his pockets. "What's this about?"

"That's what you're going to tell me, Barry." Quinn pointed to the man with the long stringy hair. "And you're next. Don't go anywhere."

Behind them, the Bobcat shut off.

Quinn's mouth was dry, his heartbeat racing. "There's an illness on the island. It's killing people."

"We know," the younger guy said. "Everyone on the island knows about the disease."

"I need to find out if it has anything to do with what you accidentally dug up while excavating the first giant ditch here." Quinn cracked his knuckles. "So, tell me what you found."

Barry shook his head and looked back at the main building.

"Expecting Wheeler to race over here and advise you to shut up?" Sweat trickled down Quinn's face and between his shoulder blades. He felt ready for anything.

"Look, I told you—"

Quinn got right in the man's face. "No, you look. If you or your company accepted money under the table, if you aren't paying taxes on your work, if there's an unexplained transfer of funds into any of your accounts or any of your close family's accounts, I'm going to find out. I can make your life a living hell and see that this is the last hole Blythe Enterprises ever digs. Or you can cooperate." Quinn's voice rang out across the empty resort, louder than usual. He didn't sound like himself. This wasn't how he did things, going right to the threats. He worked using a calm and rational approach, making a suspect feel the need to cooperate. If that didn't work, he had other ways. But straight to big-guy posturing and making threats—that had never been his style. And yet it felt right.

Barry scratched at his arm and then the back of his neck. "It has nothing to do with the illness."

"Yeah," the younger man said. "There's no sickness up here. None of us are sick."

"Let me be the judge of that. What doesn't have to do with it? What did you find under the dirt?" Quinn flexed his arms. He was fast losing the small measure of patience he still possessed. Adrenaline joined the other drugs swelling within him, fueling his agitation.

"My wife has stage three breast cancer, and our son is going to college next year," Barry said. "I need this job and the ones that will come from it at Wheeler's other resorts, and so does every member of my crew. We can't afford to be replaced. If you have questions, why don't you ask Wheeler? This is *his* project. I'm just doing what I'm told."

"I'm asking *you*, not Wheeler. You'll be much better off with me on your side. Tell me what's hiding under all this dirt." A

203

twitchy feeling coursed through Quinn, like a microscopic pinball zipping through his veins.

Barry wiped his forehead with the back of his hand. "Look, the people building this complex, the investors, they're powerful people."

Quinn grabbed Barry's shirt. His hat tumbled off, leaving his balding head exposed.

"Tell me what happened here!" Quinn shouted. His muscles quivered, straining under his skin, the same way they used to do before the whistle blew and the game was on...except he was even more hyped. Blood pounded in his ears, fueling the need to dominate and destroy. It felt good. He felt incredibly alive. With one hand still holding Barry's shirt, he grabbed the man's neck.

Barry whimpered.

A flash of rational thought and judgement crept into Quinn's resolve. *What the hell am I doing?* Cops and Feds got rough with suspects when they needed to, but this was different. Quinn had experienced countless instances when he couldn't control the situation, but he could always control his own response. Using physical force with Barry wasn't something Quinn had *decided* to do. It wasn't part of a plan or a strategy. It had just happened without thought or reason.

He hadn't hurt Barry in an irreversible way yet. But he was close. So close. Barry's face was red and turning purple.

"Let him go!" shouted the younger man. He was thin and wiry. Quinn could toss him away with one hand.

"I can take the two of you." Quinn said, his mouth turning up with a smile that didn't reach his eyes.

Barry clawed at Quinn's hands and kneed him in the groin. It should have hurt, but Quinn felt nothing.

"It was dead people! Human remains," the young man shouted. "They're everywhere. Now you know, so leave him alone!"

Quinn loosened his grip, then forced himself to let go and back away.

CHAPTER TWENTY-TWO

On Azure Cove's entrance road, Madeline spotted Quinn walking across the property, taking long, sure strides and pumping his arms. He wore athletic shorts, a T-shirt soaked with sweat, and his gun in a shoulder holster. Her stomach knotted. Did he seem okay?

She parked in front of the main building and waited for him. "Hey," she said. "Have you been exercising this whole time?"

"Yes. It helps." Quinn's eyes darted between her, the building, and the woods.

"Strenuous exercise might facilitate metabolism of the drugs. Just make sure you're also hydrating. The more bottled water you drink, the better." She waited for him to answer, all the while studying him for signs his condition had worsened in her absence.

"Will do."

She leaned out the window. "I have good news. Colonel Nelson is feeling better and out of containment. We don't know why, but I've got all the meds he took. One of them might have worked. If you haven't done a retest yet, let's do one now."

Quinn narrowed his eyes, peering into the truck's cab. He came closer. "Where's Ben?"

"I don't know." Madeline told him what happened. "I'll look again as soon as I go back."

Quinn grabbed the door handle. His eyes appeared brighter, more intense. "Get out. I'm going to his house."

His tone startled her. He'd never raised his voice at her before. There was no longer any question in her mind that the drugs were having a major effect on him. "Give me directions and I'll go," she said. "As soon as we get you retested."

Muscles corded in Quinn's neck. "I'm not waiting. I have to find him."

She hardly recognized the manic look in his eyes. "We barely know Ben. This island is his home. I'm sure he has other people he can go to."

"He doesn't," Quinn snapped. "Get out of the car, Madeline."

"Quinn, I don't—"

"Madeline, move! I need to find him."

She couldn't stop Quinn from having his way, if it came to that. "Okay. But I'll drive. Remember when Nate was hallucinating and he thought—" She quit talking because Quinn wasn't listening. Taking powerful strides, he stormed around the front of the truck. Madeline was never more aware of his strength and athleticism. A Herculean concoction of drugs was churning inside him, but he acted as if he was fueled by pure testosterone. He slid into the passenger side and slammed the door. "Go."

"Hold on. I brought a tetanus antitoxin. No one else in containment had one except the Colonel. It might be what made the difference." She got the meds from her bag and depressed a needle into the vial.

Quinn was looking past Madeline, out the window. "Look who's here," he snarled, his voice guttural.

Madeline quickly administered the shot to Quinn's arm, then lifted her gaze. A few yards from the truck, Wheeler had his hands on his hips, watching them. Aviator glasses hid his eyes, but she guessed his stare was hard and cold. She didn't know how long he'd been standing there or how much he'd seen or heard.

Quinn threw his door open and leaped from the car. A drop of dark blood dripped from the site of the needle stick.

"Quinn, wait!" she cried. He was in no state of mind to have a conversation. The way he was approaching Wheeler would set off alarms for anyone. His palm moved to the grip of the weapon. He didn't draw the gun, but his hand was so close it made Madeline paralyzed with fear.

Wheeler slid something out of his pocket as he backed away. A weapon? No. He lifted a two-way radio transceiver to his face.

"I know why you sent everyone away," Quinn said, still moving forward as if he was desperate to get in a fight. "All so your *boldly conceived* complex could open on time."

What was he talking about? Madeline didn't know and didn't like what she saw. She placed her hand over her coat pocket, feeling the outline of the sedative bottle.

Wheeler kept backing up, moving faster now. "You're sick!" His tone held no compassion. He pressed a button on the hand-held radio. "I need help here. I've got a problem with Traynor. He's got the violent syndrome."

Madeline got out of the car. "Quinn! Get in! If you want to find Ben, we have to go now!"

Quinn hesitated, looking between Madeline and Wheeler and rubbing his fingers over the top of his gun. He settled his steely, unforgiving gaze on Wheeler. "We're not done."

To Madeline's relief, Quinn stormed back to the truck, yanking the door open so hard she thought it might rip off the rusting hinges.

208

"Don't come back here!" Wheeler shouted. "Find somewhere else—" His last words got lost in the distance growing between them.

Quinn hadn't stopped rubbing his gun. His lips pulled back. His jaw clenched. "I'd like to kill that SOB."

The violent comment shocked Madeline. "What happened?"

He finally moved his hand away from his gun, scooped a tire pressure gauge off the dashboard, and tapped it almost spasmodically against his leg. "There are bodies buried all over the property. Hundreds. That's why Wheeler sent everyone away. The excavators told me."

Quinn was ranting. Spewing random nonsense. And yet she asked, "Dead bodies? Whose?"

"I don't know yet."

"Why would the excavators tell you that, Quinn?"

"Because they're weak." He accented his point with a loud and uncharacteristic snort.

Madeline's thoughts swirled. Quinn's comments were random and delusional. But what if his words were true and there really were bodies on the property? She allowed herself to consider the possibility. "The dead bodies—could they have anything to do with the outbreak?" she asked, mostly thinking aloud.

"You're the one who said the dead don't usually harbor disease and that viruses need a live host."

"I did say that. *Usually* is the key word. Nothing on this island is happening as usual."

Madeline slowed the car to a stop at the archway, wishing the roadblocks weren't there and she could speed through. If the guards gave them any trouble, she could only imagine how Quinn might react. He was fired up for an altercation.

The bearded guard stared at them. A crackle of static came from his radio device. Wheeler's angry voice followed. "Once Hamilton and Traynor leave, do not allow them to come back under any circumstances. Do not let them back onto the property. Is that clear?"

The guard met Madeline's gaze as he responded with, "Understood."

Quinn clutched the edge of the bench seat and glared at the guards as they moved the barriers. Afraid Quinn might leap out of the car, Madeline rested her hand on the vial of sedative again. Was it time to use it? She knew Quinn hated feeling out of control and violent but being helpless and ineffective would be even worse for him.

As soon as the road was clear, Madeline pushed her foot on the gas pedal.

Quinn pressed his hands against his temples. "I'm not handling this situation like I thought I could. The drugs. I'm not handling it well. I'm sorry."

His comment surprised her. She was grateful the man she knew and loved hadn't completely turned into a drug-fueled maniac. "It's okay, but I'll feel much better if you give me your weapon."

He handed her his gun, and she slid it into her bag.

"We should stay closer to the hospital anyway," she said. "I need to spend as much time as possible there." And yet here she was, driving around the island to find Ben and to keep Quinn from harming himself or others. "Quinn, I'm a little afraid of what could happen. I have a sedative with me and I—"

"No. First, we find Ben. And I already gave you my gun, but no sedative. I need to be ready for Wheeler if he comes after us. I won't let anything happen to you."

If he comes after us?

210

Quinn's voice was relatively calm, but now she could add paranoid and delusional to the rest of his symptoms. The notion of Wheeler coming after them didn't concern her. What worried her was Quinn's health and what *he* might do to Wheeler.

CHAPTER TWENTY-THREE

Quinn was silent along the narrow road, giving Madeline time to think about his condition, the work she needed to do back at the hospital, and the clothes and personal items they'd left behind in the dormitory. At the first intersection, he moved to the front edge of his seat, strangely close to the windshield, and said, "Turn right."

The right turn took them in the opposite direction of the hospital. From that point, they covered a few more miles, traveling south. "Left after that sign," he said. "We're almost there."

"How would Ben get all the way here?" Madeline asked.

"He's resourceful. Stop at that embankment area. We walk the rest of the way."

Madeline parked the truck in a grassy turnoff beside the road. "If he's not here, we go back to the hospital, okay?"

Quinn didn't answer her. He marched down the quiet street, his skin flushed. Sweat beaded his forehead, trickled down the sides of his face, and darkened the fabric around his armpits. Madeline offered him a bottled water as she hurried to keep up. "Please drink some. It will help."

He waved the bottle away.

She took in the small homes, with their bright shutters, all with their windows open. Most had furniture outside. One had a van blocking the front door.

With a single stride, Quinn jumped from the bottom stair onto the porch of a small white bungalow with blue shutters. "Ben! Are you in there?" he shouted.

No one answered.

Across the street, an elderly couple sat outside, smoking on a covered porch. They watched Quinn pound on the door.

Quinn took a key from a brittle hanging plant in desperate need of water, unlocked the front door, and went inside. "Ben!" He stormed from room to room, went outside, back in, and barreled up the stairs, shouting Ben's name as Madeline followed. Just as quickly, he marched out. After gesturing for Madeline to hurry, he locked the door and ran down the street.

"Where are you going?" Madeline called after him.

The elderly couple stared at them. Madeline offered them a half-hearted wave as she hurried after Quinn, not wanting him out of her sight. When she reached the end of the street, he had climbed a hill and was standing near a large rock, shouting up into a tree. "Ben! If you're up there, please come down."

"Quinn, he's not up there." Madeline felt weak with fear. First, the story about dead bodies at Azure Cove. Now this, imagining Ben was up in a tree. Another psychotic episode?

A flicker of color and movement in the branches above caught her attention. It was Ben. Relief flooded her, not only because they'd found him, but because there had been some logic involved with Quinn's decision to yell up into the tree.

"I'm staying up here," Ben shouted. "Let me be alone. My mom isn't around anymore. I can climb as high as I want and stay up here forever. There's no one to be afraid for me."

213

"That's not true," Quinn said. "I care, and if you're staying, I'm going to go up there with you. So come down or I'm coming up."

"Quinn, you're scaring him," Madeline said.

Using brute upper-body strength, Quinn snatched a thick gnarled vine and hauled himself up one branch at a time, muttering, "When I told you I'm not a fan of heights, I meant it." His breath came in loud huffs as he ascended higher.

"Quinn, don't...you're a lot heavier than him." When Quinn kept climbing, Madeline appealed to Ben. "Ben, please come down so we can talk."

A sudden cracking sound made her gasp. At least twelve feet above ground, the branch supporting Quinn's weight hung by peeling strands of wood.

"Quinn!" she shouted.

"Oh, no!" Ben cried. "Hang on!"

With a tearing sound, the branch ripped away from the tree. Quinn slammed to the ground, his shoulder hitting first. He was back on his feet in seconds, already brushing dirt from his arms as Madeline rushed toward him.

"Are you okay?" she asked.

"I'm fine," he said, looking up into the branches.

Madeline ran her hand over his shoulder. "You may feel fine, but it's dislocated." She wished he registered some discomfort, rather than being oblivious to pain.

"I'm so sorry," Ben cried, still scrambling down the tree.

Quinn laughed—a quick cackle followed by hysterical laughter that ceased as quickly as it began. "Hey, at least it got you down here."

Ben hurried to his side. "But you got hurt."

214

"I'm not hurting. It's happened before. In a game against USC my first year of college and against Navy when I was a junior." Extending his arm, he turned to Madeline. "Just fix it."

Madeline looked around. "I'm trying to think where to go so we can—"

"Just do it here," Quinn snapped as he sat on the ground.

Madeline applied firm pressure, moving the lower part of the shoulder blade toward the middle of his back. Quinn didn't flinch. When she finished, he bounded back onto his feet as if nothing had happened and said; "Good as new."

Ben flung himself at Quinn. "I'm so sorry. My mom…And now you almost got really hurt."

Quinn wrapped his arms around the child. "I know about your mom, Ben. It's not fair. I'm sorry she's gone."

Madeline let them stand that way for a long time. The sight of the two of them holding each other was bittersweet. Quinn clutched Ben tighter than necessary, although Ben wasn't complaining. She was heartbroken for Ben. But his situation would improve with time, Quinn's would only get worse. If she had any hope of helping him, she had to return to the hospital.

Ben lifted his head and stared up at Quinn. "Weren't you supposed to stay at Azure Cove? Does this mean you're better?"

"I'm not better yet," Quinn said. "I sort of got us kicked out of Azure Cove. Wheeler doesn't like me much." He laughed. Again, there was an edge to the sound that didn't sit well with Madeline.

"My mom didn't like Wheeler." Ben sniffed. "And neither do I." He turned to Madeline. "I'm sorry I ran away."

"It's okay, honey. You don't have to apologize." She embraced him and stroked his hair. "I understand. I'm so glad we found you. We're both so glad we found you."

215

Ben clutched her tightly until she had to go. "Quinn, stay here…with Ben…at his house. I'll give you a sedative and I'll come back as soon as I can."

"Yes. He can stay with me," Ben said. "I'll take care of him."

Quinn lifted his head to the sky and raked his fingers down his cheek. "Not sure that's such a good idea."

"Quinn, let me help you. I have to figure out what I can do about the outbreak, and I can't do it if I'm worried about you. I need to know you're somewhere…" She was going to say safe. But was Ben's house safe? Was anywhere safe?

He nodded. "Okay."

Madeline trailed back to Ben's house behind them. With every stride, Quinn's power and energy were apparent. As they approached the house across from Ben's, the elderly couple got up from their seats and went inside. Before the front door clicked shut, the man peered out at them with a wary expression. Quinn's condition wasn't fooling anyone. They knew he was sick.

Quinn suddenly spread his legs apart and raised his arms, almost like he was surfing a giant wave.

"What is it?" Madeline asked.

"Another quake," he said. "The ground, it's still shaking."

Ben looked alarmed. "I didn't feel it."

"I didn't feel it either," Madeline said.

Fear passed over his eyes, but he kept moving, walking unsteadily now, as if he was crossing an unstable suspension bridge rather than solid ground.

Inside Ben's house, Madeline looked around the empty living room.

"Out here." Quinn lurched and swayed through the house and onto a back porch, where he sank onto a dank-smelling couch.

A continuous tremor of motion moved through his body, causing him to twitch and fidget uncontrollably.

Madeline took his vitals. Her stomach clenched with worry. His heart rate was sky high. The simple act of sitting still had to be almost unbearable for him. She checked his mouth next. The lesions had multiplied and were clearly visible, even without her light. "I'd like to check another fluid sample," she said, doing her best to keep her expression neutral. She removed the collection cup from her bag and gave it to him.

"I'll be back." Still unsteady on his feet, Quinn smiled at Ben as he got up. But there was something about that smile— forced, uneasy, his teeth bared. It was anything but comfortable.

Once Quinn left, Madeline crouched down to face Ben. "I'm going to give Quinn some medicine to help him calm down. He'll still be sick, but he won't hurt you or anyone else. He'll sort of be in a trance. I need you to make sure he stays here and doesn't wander off."

Ben nodded. "I won't let him leave. He'll be safe here."

"And he should drink fluids. Do you have any bottled waters?"

"No. Wait...yes! We have a whole case."

"Great. Maybe one bottle every hour. He won't want it but keep offering it to him."

"I'll do it," Ben said, his face scrunched in seriousness. "I promise."

It was a lot to ask of a child. Especially a child who had just lost his mother. What he'd been through...Madeline admired him so much. "Thank you, Ben. I'm really proud of you. I'll be back as soon as I can. Before the sedative wears off."

Quinn returned to the couch. "I left the cup in the bathroom." He rolled up his sleeve, baring his shoulder. "Go ahead."

217

She prepared the syringe and administered the sedative. Nothing less and nothing more than the recommended amount for his body weight. Sedation would slow his bodily functions, including his metabolism, possibly allowing the drug concentrations to accumulate even faster. But it was a risk she had to take to prevent him from hurting himself or others. She administered a dose of Narcan next, then left to test his drug levels.

"Do you feel better? Is it helping?" she heard Ben ask Quinn as she ducked into the small half bathroom on the main floor. The wood was damp and puckering under her feet. The musty stench filled her nostrils. She unlocked a window above the toilet and pushed it up, letting in fresh air. Quinn's sample cup sat on the side of the sink. There wasn't much in it. He was already dehydrated. She chastised herself for not bringing an IV drip.

Madeline unwrapped the test cartridge—possibly the last one—and prepared the test. She dreaded the results, and yet she had to know.

Waiting, she stared into the mirror at her reflection to gather her nerves. She felt like crying, but there wasn't time to let go now. She turned on the faucet. Brown liquid spurted and sputtered out. When it cleared, she splashed her face with the cool water. Maybe Quinn's drug levels weren't that high. Maybe the tetanus antitoxin was already helping. He wasn't acting like himself. He had imagined the ground moving when it wasn't. But he could still follow directions, cooperate, and uphold a conversation. In that respect, he acted more clear-headed than most of the patients in the containment area.

How am I going to walk out of here and leave him with Ben?

She closed her eyes and prayed hard. *Please let us figure this out. Please don't let anyone else die. Please protect Quinn.*

The timer buzzed.

She didn't want to see the results. She didn't want his condition to have worsened, and the tox screen would be

218

irrefutable proof. She forced herself to grab the cartridge and scan the results. Her stomach sank, a startling queasy sensation like the first drop on a roller coaster. Panic swelled, tightening her chest around her hammering heart, and choking her. She closed her eyes, waited as long as she dared, making sure she composed herself before leaving the bathroom.

Quinn's levels were high. Extremely high. It was a sheer testament to his willpower and self-control that he was behaving even somewhat normally.

They were running out of time.

CHAPTER TWENTY-FOUR

At Ben's front door, Madeline went over instructions with him one final time. "You know what to do?"

"Yes. Don't let Quinn leave. Get him to drink water. Go to the neighbor's if he gets violent and starts imagining things."

"That shouldn't happen. The sedation should last until I get back. But just in case…the last thing he would want is to harm you."

"I know," Ben said, scuffing his foot across the floor.

"Questions?"

He looked out across his porch to the home across the street. "No…I mean…How come Quinn got sick when he's strong and healthy, but none of these old people got sick? They're so old. And they smoke. That's supposed to be terrible for you."

"It probably has more to do with where they've been rather than how old or how healthy they are."

An idea suddenly exploded into her thoughts. She grabbed Ben's arms with more force than she intended. "Ben!"

He whimpered and leaned away from her. "What did I do?"

She smiled and hugged him. "You just pointed out something the rest of us failed to consider."

"What?"

She was already looking across the street. "Your neighbors. The smoking. I've seen a lot of people smoking on the island."

"So?"

"We've been analyzing Colonel Nelson's treatment to figure out what made him better. Maybe it wasn't the antibiotics, or the tetanus shot. Maybe it was because Captain Barstow shared his tobacco in the containment area! There might be a component in the tobacco that affected the virus."

"Nelson and Barstow? Who are those people? I don't know them."

"They're—it doesn't matter. What matters is that I need to find something with tobacco. Did your mother smoke, Ben?"

"No. But most of the neighbors do."

Madeline ran out of the house and straight across the street. She banged on the door. "Please! I need some of your cigarettes. It's important."

There was no response. She'd probably frightened them.

"Please," she said, lowering her voice and speaking quietly when she really wanted to kick the door down and run in there. "I'm a doctor and I need a few of your cigarettes for medicinal purposes." She realized how crazy that sounded.

"Please go away. We know you've got the violent syndrome. We don't want to catch it."

"My fiancé is sick. I'm not. There's a chance the cigarettes might help him. If you could just put some out here…"

She backed off the porch and stared at the front door, willing it to open. The wait was unbearable. She glanced at the other houses. Was anyone else in them? If so, they'd probably heard her pounding and already had their own doors bolted. She was about to knock again when she heard, "Doctor. Over here."

She hurried over to the next house, tripping over broken pottery. The door cracked open. A wrinkled hand set a small tin on the weathered porch.

"You treated my granddaughter at the hospital. Dominique. She had carbon monoxide poisoning. I hope this helps you."

"Thank you so much!" Madeline grabbed the tin and raced back to the house, feeling giddy with anticipation but trying to temper her expectations.

Ben was waiting for her. "Did you get some?"

Madeline opened the tin. Neatly rolled cigarettes filled it like tightly packed sardines. "Do you have matches here?"

"Yes. For the firepit." Ben ran to the kitchen and rustled through drawers while Madeline went out to check on Quinn. He was trudging in slow circles around the firepit. His eyes were glassy. He muttered words she couldn't understand.

"Found them!" Ben burst outside carrying a long tube of fireplace matches.

Madeline lit a cigarette and held it out for Quinn. "I need you to smoke this. Please." She held the burning cigarette to his lips. He smacked it away.

"Please, Quinn." Madeline's pulse pounded behind her ears. This new theory might be nothing more than a waste of precious time. But she was desperate. "This might help you."

Quinn shook his head and turned away.

Ben pulled on his arm. "You have to trust her and do what she says."

Quinn stared at Ben as precious time ticked away.

"Please, I need you to try this," Madeline said.

Quinn snorted, took the cigarette, and inhaled. A coughing fit erupted. The cigarette fell to the patio floor.

Madeline scooped it up. She rubbed Quinn's shoulder as he coughed. He shrugged her hand away and stared at her as if he'd never seen her before. She tried not to be upset. Who knew what was going on in his mind? When the coughing subsided, she placed the cigarette between his lips again. He inhaled.

"You think this will help him?" Ben asked as Quinn blew out a puff of smoke.

"I don't know." Madeline felt a little crazy forcing a cigarette on someone. "Sometimes we don't know for sure what will make a difference. We have to try things until we find what works."

Quinn muttered something unintelligible.

"Quinn?" She bit down on her lip. "I want you to smoke a few more over the next hour. Do you understand?"

She wished she hadn't given him so much sedative. She wanted to stay and monitor him for changes, although without additional tests, she could only track his behavior and vitals.

"I'll help him. I know how to light a match and get the cigarettes going." Ben gripped the tin of cigarettes. He looked so serious, as if his life depended on taking care of Quinn. Maybe this is exactly what he needed right now—a purpose. A surge of gratefulness mixed with her other emotions and brought tears to her eyes. Was this insane? Leaving a ten-year-old alone and in charge of matches and cigarettes with a powerful man high on cocaine, meth, and morphine?

Madeline hugged Quinn hard. "I love you so much, Quinn Traynor." *You hang on*, she pleaded silently.

"I love you, too." He moved his lips again, slurring his words, and said something that sounded like, "The cigarettes. Destin and our how you."

Madeline leaned closer. "What did you say?"

He bit down on his lip and squeezed his eyes shut. This time, his words were decipherable. "Desperate. You're desperate, aren't you?"

Tears threatened to fall. Yes. She was desperate for a miracle. And if this worked, it would be nothing short of one.

CHAPTER TWENTY-FIVE

Madeline eyed the faint yellow circle inside the gas gauge. Almost empty. Unless the gauge worked as well as the air conditioning and the needle had hovered next to the E the whole time. With so much on her mind, she hadn't been paying attention. Had they passed a gas station on the way there? She couldn't recall seeing one anywhere since they arrived on the island. She reached for her phone, as she'd done so many times already, about to press the home button and say, "where is the nearest gas station," before remembering that wasn't an option. Nor was calling AAA, or anyone else.

She entered the roundabout and blanked on which exit to take. Had they had taken the first or second one? She got off on the first, having a fifty percent chance she'd guessed correctly.

For her entire driving life, she had access to navigation systems or Ubers. Even when she was traveling in the jungles of Africa, someone knew how to get where they were going. Now, when she could least afford to get lost, she was without guidance. Nothing looked familiar. The inside of the truck was mercilessly hot. Then she saw a billboard ahead. Wheeler's smug profile and *Azure Cove-the Luxury Vacation Complex. Now hiring.* There was no way anyone could miss that prominent sign, so out of place amidst the natural landscape. Which meant she hadn't been on that road previously. At the first opportunity, she pulled over, turned around, doing an unimpressive eight or nine point turn on the narrow road, and went back to the roundabout to take the second exit. The gas gauge may have been empty, but she was still driving. Another few miles and she came to the intersection leading to the hospital. She felt a bit of tension drop from her shoulders. She was close. Only another mile or so. Surely the gas would hold out.

The truck sputtered and slowed.

She smacked the steering wheel. "No!"

After coasting to the side of the road and putting it in park, she began jogging the rest of the way to the hospital. At least she was wearing running shoes, but that was the only positive she could find in the situation.

"How did it come to this?" she muttered to herself aloud. Her life so suddenly disrupted, as if something had shaken all the solid pieces around until they broke apart. One minute her biggest worry was how she would get through not having a kitchen for a few weeks, and now…she couldn't bear to think it…but she had to. Quinn's days were numbered.

Sweat tricked down between her breasts and shoulder blades as she went from a slow jog to a power walk, furious about wasting more time.

A compact sedan pulled up alongside her. A stranger, a woman about her same age, rolled down the window. "Need a ride?"

"Yes, please. To the hospital." Madeline jumped into the car and sank into the passenger's seat. Cold air whooshed from the car's vents, chilling her sweaty skin.

At the hospital, Madeline charged through the stairwell door and into the basement. Captain Barstow and another man were outside the containment area. She headed straight toward them. "Any improvement with any of the other patients?"

Barstow shook his head. "I heard there aren't any more of those tests you were using to screen them, but it's pretty obvious they're still drugged."

"To your knowledge, are any of them smokers? Or snuffers? Any of them?"

Barstow stared at Madeline for a few seconds before shuffling over to the names written on the board. "I don't know." He turned to the Airman with him. "Does Williams smoke?"

"Nope." The Airman moved closer, looking at the board over Barstow's shoulder. "Neither does DeShaun. Or James. Or Gunthrup. None of the guys or women in there are smokers."

"Do you know anyone who uses tobacco and *has* gotten sick?" Madeline asked.

The Airman shrugged. "I smoke. I'm not sick."

"Neither am I," Barstow said.

"How many times did you give tobacco to Colonel Nelson?" Madeline asked, the pitch of her voice rising. So far, her theory was gaining traction.

Barstow widened his eyes. "You think—?"

"I don't know. It's a hypothesis, but an easy one to test. Was it just that once when we were doing exams, the day a patient bit you? Or were there other times?"

"Wow…" Barstow stared past her, thinking. "The first time was when I helped you and Martina bit me. After that, the Colonel asked again, said it was helping him calm down, and I gave him my entire stash."

"How much do you have with you?" Madeline asked.

Barstow removed a container from his pocket and looked inside. "Not much. But I can get more."

"Round up as much of that exact type as you can," Madeline said. "I'm going to take a sample and run some tests

227

with it. Meanwhile, start giving it to the patients now. Replicate the amount you gave your Colonel. Record everything. Names, time, amounts given."

"Yeah. Okay," Barstow said.

"How will we know if it's working?" the other man asked.

Madeline pressed her lips together. "We're at the point where if no one else dies today...it's working."

She prayed her theory would prove true.

▼▲▼

Daylight waned, challenging visibility, as Madeline leaned against the lab's countertop and added ground tobacco to vials to test out her theory. Behind her, the laboratory door swung open. Grace's presence surprised Madeline. She'd assumed the doctor had finally taken a day off to mourn. Grace had washed her face clean, free of makeup. Her scrubs also looked fresh, probably thanks to Maria's ongoing efforts to keep up with the hospital's laundering.

"Clever idea about the tobacco products," Grace said. "Barstow rounded up a huge stash. All red-coded patients got some. If it doesn't work, we may go down as deranged health care providers." She chuckled, but there was no warmth in the noise, only sadness. "Maybe I should shred my medical license now. But if it does work..."

"Any changes?" Madeline asked.

"Not yet." Grace pursed her lips together. "I also switched to ketamine for the sedative. I did some research on it during my residency. It might keep them alive and out of comas longer. The problem is that if it works...we don't have much of it." Grace dropped into one of the metal chairs and slid her back down it. She sighed and it came out like a soft whistle through her nose. Her eyes were barely open. "How on earth is this happening?"

The doctor wasn't expecting an answer, but Madeline grabbed the opportunity to test her thoughts out loud. "I'm convinced there's a virus. An unusual one."

"I agree," Grace said. "And obviously it's unusual."

"The virus is damaging their livers, impeding metabolization. That condition would keep some level of drugs present. But it doesn't explain why they're increasing. This virus…I think…" She hesitated because saying it aloud seemed almost absurd.

"You think what?" Grace asked.

All along, Madeline had the sense they were missing something. Not only because they lacked the proper equipment and the time it would take to sequence and study the virus. It went beyond that. They needed to stretch their current beliefs and take a leap of faith. Maybe it was necessary to let go of everything she knew and embrace the impossible to discover the truth. She crossed her arms, perhaps a subconscious need to protect herself from Grace's reaction, since she was about to suggest something outrageous. Something that would sound more implausible than Nate's delirium-fueled idea about radio signals controlling their brains. "What if both the virus *and* the drugs must be present? And then…" Madeline struggled to finish.

Grace lifted her palms, a signal for Madeline to get to her point.

Madeline blew out a breath, summoning courage. "What I'm suggesting is…the virus encapsulates the drugs and replicates them along with its own genetic material."

Grace sat up in the chair and tilted her head, her eyes fully open now.

"I know it sounds far-fetched," Madeline said.

"It's exactly what appears to be happening." Grace smoothed her hand over her ponytail. "If the virus is replicating the drugs, while compromising the liver, it's created a perfect storm."

Grace's face fell. "A storm that patients have no chance of surviving."

"I know." Fear gripped Madeline's heart once again. "We still have to find out where the drug exposure is coming from. But right now, if I'm right, all of that has to take a back seat to figuring out how to eliminate the virus and rid the patients of the drugs."

"We defeat the virus first, understand it later," Grace said.

"We need something to explode the infected cells. Something to break through their protective barriers."

"And you're hoping that's the tobacco," Grace said.

"Yes. Until we have another solution. The patients I autopsied show no liver scarring, which means liver functions are reparable. If we can get rid of the drugs, the patients might be fine." Madeline's every thought now related to Quinn and what it meant for his condition. Without warning, a lump formed in her throat, and she had to fight back tears.

"Are you okay? Grace asked. "What's going on?"

Madeline covered her face with her hands, nodded, and swallowed hard. When she uncovered her eyes, Grace was studying her. "Remember I told you my fiancé is here with me, staying at Azure Cove?" Madeline asked.

"Yes."

"He was helping with rescue efforts on Market Street. Now he's infected."

"I'm so sorry." The empathy in Grace's eyes shone through. She truly understood what Quinn's condition meant for Madeline. First the suffering he would endure, and then the pain of losing him.

"I didn't bring him here. To the hospital."

"I don't blame you. He's at Azure Cove?"

"No. He's…with a friend. Sedated. And I gave him the tetanus antitoxin and had him smoke cigarettes before I left. I need to leave and check on him."

"Yes…go."

"I can't. I need a ride."

"Come on." Grace pushed herself up from the chair. "I have to get out of here, if only for a few hours. We've done all we can for the moment. Now we wait. Tonight is the next test of time. Either more patients get better like Colonel Nelson, or the rest will die."

▼▲▼

Loud knocking on the front door startled Ben as he walked through the house.

Is Madeline back?

The sound came again, right away. *Bam. Bam. Bam.* Madeline wouldn't pound that way.

"We know you're in there. Open up!"

The person at the door sounded furious and reminded Ben of the wolf from the three little pigs threatening to huff and puff and blow the door down. Ben squeezed his eyes shut. His mother wouldn't know if the door blew down or not. Still, this was her house. He had to protect it. And Quinn. He ran out to the back yard.

Quinn was smoking cigarettes and trudging around the backyard, swaying as if he didn't quite have his balance.

"Stay out here," Ben told him "Okay?"

Quinn muttered something. He didn't seem dangerous, or like he might hurt anyone. He was acting a little spacey. That was probably because of the shot Madeline gave him.

Ben slid the patio door shut and pulled the curtains closed. He hurried through his house to the front. He twisted the lock, cracked open the door, and peered out.

A gigantic man with yellowish blond hair stood on Ben's porch, holding a gun. Ben recognized him. A guard from Azure Cove. Behind the man, the survivor truck waited in the street. Ben didn't know what to do, but he wasn't getting in the truck.

"Hey, kid." The man didn't smile. "We're here for Traynor. He in there?"

Ben couldn't let them take Quinn, either. "He's not here."

"I'm sure you won't have a problem with us coming inside and looking around," the man said.

Ben slammed the door, but before it closed, the blond man pushed it open and shoved Ben so hard he staggered across the living room and fell on his back.

The man stormed through the family room and into the kitchen, pointing his gun ahead of him.

Ben jumped up. "He's not here! Get out! You can't come in here!"

The man laughed, a mean and frightening sound. He charged back to the family room, pulled the curtains aside, and spotted Quinn in the yard. "There he is."

Ben rushed at the intruder and grabbed his arm. "Get out of my house!"

The man swung his arm, catching Ben across the chest. Grunting in pain, Ben sailed across his empty family room and smacked into the wall.

"Hey, hey! Enough!" someone shouted from the front of the house. Another guard from Azure Cove stood in Ben's doorway. The one with the beard. "Don't touch that kid again, Ronnie," he hissed.

The blond man snorted. "Just get in here and help me with Traynor."

"Leave Quinn alone!" Ben screamed at the top of his lungs. "You can't come in here! Get out of my house!" He scanned for something he could use to hit the men. Remembering his mother kept an old golf club in the coat closet for protection, just in case of something exactly like this, Ben ran and grabbed it. He raced toward the bearded man, ready to swing the club.

The bearded man easily grabbed the club in his giant hand. Ben couldn't move it at all. "Calm down," the man said. "We aren't going to hurt him."

"Like hell we aren't," the blond man said.

Still holding the club, the bearded man glared at the other guy, then turned back to Ben. "We have to take Traynor. If you all cooperate, no one gets hurt. Got it?" The bearded man was even bigger than the blond, but not as mean. Something about his voice almost made Ben believe him.

"That's not what the other guy said!" Ben shouted as hot tears fell from his eyes. "Madeline is a doctor. She knows what to do, and she's coming back! She already gave him medicine so he could stay calm and wouldn't hurt anyone." Ben tried to jerk the golf club out of the bearded man's grip, but he was so much stronger. Feeling helpless, Ben surrendered his weapon and ran outside.

The blond man pointed his gun at Quinn.

"Quinn!" Ben shouted.

"Ben, go upstairs, now," Quinn said.

"He's already sedated," the bearded man told the awful blond man. "Take it easy."

"Sedated? Then I'm going to make this really easy for you, big guy," the blond said to Quinn. "Come with us without making trouble, and no one gets hurt." He swung his gun around, pointing it at Ben. "Otherwise, the kid gets a bullet in the head. Or maybe the stomach. Maybe both. Capiche?"

"That's not going to happen," the bearded man said. "No one is going to get hurt." He spoke each word slowly, as if he wanted to make sure everyone understood. But he also had his gun pointed at Quinn.

"Like I said, no one gets hurt if everyone cooperates," the blond man said. His creepy grin scared Ben. He was sure the blond man didn't want their cooperation. He *wanted* to hurt them.

CHAPTER TWENTY-SIX

Grace tied a scarf around her head and slid on large sunglasses before starting the Mustang. With wisps of hair escaping from the sides, she reminded Madeline of a movie star. Or a blonde Jackie Kennedy.

"You said you don't really like the sun, but you drive a convertible?" Madeline asked.

"This was Heidi's car."

Madeline couldn't see Grace's eyes behind the sunglasses. She could only imagine the pain they harbored.

They drove slowly out of the hospital lot, stopping and waiting for the myriad of people milling about. The wind whipped Madeline's hair back as they reached the main road and picked up speed. "That's where I ran out of gas," she said, pointing to the abandoned vehicle.

"Someone in my neighborhood will have a gas can I can borrow. I'll bring it to the hospital, and we'll get you back out there tomorrow." Grace spoke in a flat monotone. "Unless...is there any gas on the island? There might not be. I don't know. I barely left the hospital all week. We were slammed but that wasn't the only reason. If Heidi was okay, I knew she would find me there."

A large truck, green with an open back and rattling sides, approached from the opposite direction. Muscular men carrying rifles stood in the back. They stared down at Grace and Madeline as they passed.

"Great...that was more outbreak patients." Grace sighed. "Poor Matthew and Lydia. At least Barstow is still there. But I should probably turn around and go back."

Madeline couldn't get back to Quinn fast enough. If the truck hadn't run out of gas, she would have left to check on him much earlier. She couldn't allow Grace to turn around, couldn't bear it if she did. "As a physician, I'm ordering you to take a break before you go back," Madeline said, rubbing her cuticles in small, fidgety movements. "You need to get some sleep. And I'm sure there are personal things you need to take care of."

"I need to call Heidi's parents...but I can't until communications are restored. Anyway, I'm actually more worried that truck might not be taking outbreak patients to the hospital. We said we were full. I don't know where else they would go. I don't know who is in charge of that truck."

"Tell me about Heidi," Madeline said, grateful Grace hadn't turned the car around. "What sort of work was she doing here?"

"Heidi's passion was anthropology. Particularly historical mysteries. She was close to finishing her graduate dissertation. Her great, great grandparents lived on Nalowale, so she'd always been interested in the stories about the first settlers. The mystery of what happened fascinated her. She had her own theory, that some group massacred the original inhabitants and buried them at sea or somewhere on the island."

Madeline debated telling Grace about the bodies Quinn mentioned. She had no proof what he said was true. He might have been delusional.

"There was a small cultural museum on Market Street," Grace said. "That's where Heidi did most of her work. The museum housed the artifacts from the island's first inhabitants, the ones who came before the first Polynesian ancestors in the late

1600s. The people responsible for the monoliths. You must have seen those along the entrance to Azure Cove."

"Yes. I did."

"The tsunami destroyed the museum. Crushed it." Grace bit down on her lower lip and blinked repeatedly. "As a physician, I know life is precious, and we never know how much time each of us has…and still—" her voice broke "—I'm shocked Heidi is gone. Absolutely shocked. I just can't wrap my head around it. I don't want it to be real."

"I'm so sorry," Madeline said.

A few seconds passed before Grace spoke again. "Once everything calms down, I'm going to sort through Heidi's work and submit her thesis so she can receive her doctorate posthumously. It was important to her."

Madeline decided to tell Grace then. "Did you hear that Devon Wheeler, the man in charge of the resort, sent almost everyone working at Azure Cove off the island the day before the tsunami?"

"Yes."

"Quinn said it's because the excavators found bodies on the property. Hundreds of them."

"How did he hear this?" Grace's mouth hung open.

"He said the excavators told him. He might have been delusional. But now, after hearing about Heidi's research, I thought you'd want to know."

Grace took her eyes off the road to look at Madeline. When she turned back, there was a choking sound in her throat, and then the tears came, sliding out from under her dark glasses and streaming down her cheeks. "It's exactly what Heidi was hoping to find to prove her theory. It has to be the indigenous people who lived here first." Grace's voice suddenly grew angry. "This island has a well-defined process in place for finds of that nature, and there's no way Wheeler didn't know about it. Development at Azure Cove was subject to a National Historic Preservation Policy. If he found human remains, or any artifacts, the investigative process would have sidelined development of the Azure Cove resort for months. Or shut it down permanently." She slapped the steering wheel, then gripped it hard. "So, I understand exactly why Wheeler would want it covered up. I get why he sent all his workers away except the excavators so he could finish digging without worrying about what he uncovered. But he's not going to get away with it."

"Turn left here," Madeline said, feeling guilty about interrupting Grace's intense anger and sorrow to give directions. "Considering the timing, if it's true, the discovery might have something to do with the outbreak."

Grace clenched her jaw. Anger radiated from her body. "We're going to find out."

They'd reached Ben's neighborhood. "This is it," Madeline said. "You can let me off here."

Grace slowed the car to a stop and put it in park.

"Thank you," Madeline said. "Go home and rest. I'll see you tomorrow."

Madeline jogged down the street to Ben's house, completely focused on getting to Quinn. She'd prepared herself for all possibilities. He may be worse...but he may be better. She didn't have a cartridge to test his levels, but small signs of improvement would be apparent. And if his condition had worsened...that too would be obvious.

She had her hand on the door handle when Ben burst out.

"You're back!" His eyes were red and puffy, his face streaked with tears.

"Is everything all right?" She braced herself for Ben's response as she headed toward the back porch, where she'd last seen her fiancé.

"He's not here! They took him."

"He's not here?" She could barely think straight, couldn't process what he'd told her. "Who took him?"

"The same men who took me. In the survivor truck."

"One of your neighbors must have ratted us out," Madeline said, anger and frustration building inside her.

"Quinn couldn't do anything about it. He couldn't fight because of the medicine you gave him. I told them you were a doctor. I said you were coming right back. But they took him anyway. And they had guns."

"Then it's probably better that Quinn didn't resist," Madeline said, trying to get her wits about her.

"Come on, we have to get him back before something bad happens to him." Ben hurried through the house and exited a side door. "Follow me! Hurry!"

Ben exited the yard through a side gate and ran across a flattened patch of bamboo. Madeline followed him without knowing why. They came out on a narrow path between two homes and walked around to the front of one. The floodwater had deposited a blue Volkswagen Beetle on the muddy yard.

Ben handed Madeline a key.

"What's this?" she asked.

"The key to my mom's bug. I forgot Joyce picked us up and took us to town the day the tsunami came. My mom's car was here all along, just not where she left it."

Madeline snatched the key from Ben's outstretched palm. "Let's go."

She prayed water hadn't flooded the engine.

CHAPTER TWENTY-SEVEN

Come on. Come on.

The bug's engine sputtered when Madeline turned the key. "That doesn't sound good."

"It always does that," Ben said, shifting to the front of the passenger seat. "You have to start it a few times before it wakes up and goes."

On the third try, the engine rumbled to life and Madeline shifted into gear. "Thank God my parents owned stick shifts when I was in high school."

"Hurry," Ben said.

"I passed that truck when I was on my way here. It has an enormous head start. If only I'd known."

They sped across a lawn and onto the street, driving as fast as the old car would allow. The bug wasn't an original. It was a newer model, but at least thirty years old and with over two hundred thousand miles on the odometer.

"Do you know where the truck takes people?" Madeline asked. "Besides the hospital? Because Dr. Wilcox wasn't sure if it was going to the hospital. Do you know where else it goes?"

"They took me to the hospital. But I don't know about everyone else. How would I know?" Ben looked alarmed and Madeline realized she needed to calm down, stop shooting questions at him as if he was on trial. "Sorry, Ben. I'm just nervous about getting to Quinn. I didn't mean to snap at you."

"It's okay. I'm nervous, too. The men with the survivor truck, they were also the guards from Azure Cove. You know, the big ones guarding the entrance."

Wheeler's men. She should have known. Wheeler must have sent them to find Quinn. But why? She felt a chill as it occurred to her that the truck wasn't taking Quinn back to the resort or to the hospital. Maybe Quinn wasn't being paranoid about Wheeler coming after them. And maybe there really were bodies buried on the Azure Cover property and not all of them were ancient. So many were missing because of the tsunami. What if the sea wasn't solely responsible for all the disappearances?

Please let Quinn be at the hospital.

When she arrived there, they ran inside and down to the basement, rushing past Maria, who was delivering a load of clean blankets and towels.

"Wait right here. Don't go anywhere else," Madeline told Ben, positioning him outside the containment area doors. Not stopping to put on protective equipment, she pulled her shirt up over her mouth and nose and burst through the doors.

"Hey," Matthew said. "Glad you're here. I could use a hand."

Madeline barely registered Matthew's words, nor the haze of cigarette smoke in the containment area, as she hurried down the center corridor, scanning the cells for Quinn.

"Madeline?" Matthew called after her. "You okay?"

"I'm looking for my fiancé. Armed men came and took him. Is he here?"

"No new patients today. Our numbers are dwindling. Almost everyone has their own room now." Matthew had consistently called them rooms. Hardly. All Madeline could think of was prison cells.

Her stomach in knots and feeling like she might throw up, she reached the end of the corridor without spotting Quinn. She rushed back the way she'd come, peering into each cell again in case Matthew was mistaken and in case she'd missed Quinn. She hadn't.

Where was he?

▼▲▼

Ben was talking to Captain Barstow and another Airman on the other side of the containment area doors when Madeline charged back out.

"I heard what happened," Barstow told her.

"Please, help me find him." Madeline wrung her hands, unsure of where to go next. "I think Wheeler has something to do with this. I don't think he'd want Quinn back at Azure Cove, since he's sick. I don't know the island. Where could they have taken him?"

Matthew joined them in the hallway, where he removed his mask, gown, and gloves. "Calm down. We'll find him." He turned to Barstow. "Someone must have seen the truck."

Barstow nodded. "We'll ask around. We'll find it."

Matthew glanced at the containment area behind him before saying, "Lydia will be here soon. I'm going with you."

The other Airman agreed to stay and monitor the patients.

Already moving, Madeline gestured for Ben to follow. She heard someone say "wait" but she didn't stop.

"Wait! I can help you!"

This time, they all stopped and turned to face Maria. She lowered her head, as if embarrassed about shouting. Her skin was fast turning a deep shade of red.

"You know where they took him?" Madeline asked.

"I don't know for sure," Maria said. "I might be able to find out. Come with me?" It was more a question than a command. Maria scooped up a large bag of dirty linens and carried it with her up the stairs, with Barstow, Madeline, and Ben in tow.

Madeline didn't want to waste any more time. "Thank you, Maria," she said, ascending the stairs. "What do you know? How are you going to find the truck?"

Maria marched to the next landing without answering. On the first floor, she entered the staff room and opened a locker. She removed a handheld radio and turned it on. She pressed the talk button. "Lucas? It's Maria."

A crackle of static and then, "You ready for a ride home?" The man's voice was familiar, though Madeline couldn't place it. Despite his directness, he sounded concerned for Maria.

"I might not need one today. Are you at the resort?"

"No. I'm not there. What's going on?"

"I need the car for something. A friend offered to drop me off. Tell me where you are. I'll come get the car. Then you won't have to get me later."

"That would be good because I don't know when I can leave here. I'm at the old orchard. I'm parked near the barn. Wheeler won't want anyone from the hospital to come around. Have your friend drop you off at the end of the road and walk to my car. Go right to it and then leave. I'll put the keys inside. Understood?"

Maria pressed the talk button one last time and said, "I understand." She lowered the radio, avoiding eye contact with the rest of them. "That was my brother. He works for Wheeler."

"I know where the old orchard barn is," Ben said, bouncing on his toes. "Come on. We have to go."

"You coming?" Barstow asked Maria.

She shook her head and looked away.

"Thank you, Maria," Madeline said. "Thank you for helping me."

▼▲▼

Barstow steered off the road and straight into the underbrush, leaving his vehicle partly concealed. Barstow and Matthew got out. Both carried weapons.

"Stay here," Madeline said to Ben.

Barstow looked at Madeline. "You should stay, too. We don't know what we're going to find. And no one wants you getting hurt."

Madeline felt the weight of Quinn's gun in her bag. Thanks to him, she knew how to use a weapon. She didn't want to. She saved people, healed them. She wasn't a killer. But she would use it if it meant saving Quinn. "You don't know what Quinn looks like and he doesn't know you. I'm coming."

Barstow opened his mouth to speak and looked like he was about to protest. Instead, he said, "Get between us."

"We look suspicious," she whispered, her nerves making her a little lightheaded. "Maybe we should pretend we got a flat tire and need help."

Barstow snorted and whispered back. "If they see us, especially if they see you, they'll know exactly why we're here."

He led the way, pushing giant plant leaves and branches aside as they marched along the edge of the road. Matthew pulled up the rear. Both men acted capable and confident. Madeline was grateful for that. Hope spread through her, though tempered because the only thing they knew for sure was that one of the truck's drivers, Lucas, was there. They didn't know if Quinn was with him.

They came to the barn, a faded, weathered structure. The top was open and tobacco leaves were drying in the rafters.

Someone had parked a compact car with a dented fender on one side of the barn. Near it was the green truck with the tall sides. The survivor truck. There was no one inside and the truck bed was empty.

Barstow left the shelter of the trees and ran to the barn, angling his back against its walls. He edged to one end, looked around the corner, then waved the others over. When they reached him, he held a finger to his lips. "Two of Wheeler's men."

Madeline couldn't see the men, but all Wheeler's guards were massive, and always armed. She heard voices.

"You gave him a cigarette?" someone said.

"He keeps asking."

Madeline held her breath, straining to hear every word. The second voice sounded like Maria's brother.

"Fine. Last wishes and all," the first voice said. "But don't talk to him. The feds know stuff to mess with your head."

The man who sounded like Lucas grunted. "He can't cause much trouble as sedated as he is."

Madeline whispered to Barstow. "Can you see them?"

Barstow nodded. "Just the two."

"Anyone else? Do you see Quinn?"

Barstow shook his head.

▼▲▼

Lucas was uncomfortable. Sick to his stomach with sweat trickling down his skin. He stroked his beard and stared off into the tobacco fields. With nothing to do but wait for instructions, which was the nature of his job, he couldn't stop thinking about what was about to happen. "Why didn't we take him to the hospital?" he asked.

"He knows too much." Ronnie smoked his third or fourth cigarette since they arrived. "Wheeler thinks the excavators told him."

"The excavators told him what?"

Ronnie laughed. "It's best for you to know as little as possible, Luke."

No one called him Luke. Only Ronnie and Wheeler, who thought they could change people's names to suit their whims.

"You ever killed a man?" Ronnie asked.

"Not intentionally." Lucas gulped. He couldn't let Ronnie know what he was thinking, but for once, he couldn't stay silent. "That FBI agent has the violent syndrome. My sister said the doctors can't do anything about it. Only one patient has gotten better. The rest are dying. If we hold him here long enough, he's going to die on his own. Nothing anyone can do about it."

"Not my call, Luke. And it's not yours either. They're gonna ask you to do it. To prove yourself." Ronnie had a sinister gleam in his eyes, reminding Lucas of why he hated working with the man. He'd hated watching him pummel the sedated and restrained agent. He wished he'd pulled Ronnie away sooner.

"What about the woman he's with? The doctor?" Lucas asked. "She might know everything he knows. We going to kidnap her next? And then the excavators?"

Ronnie shrugged. "We do what we're told, Luke. Get that and you'll have a long career with Wheeler."

"People will look for him," Lucas said. "Americans. The FBI. They'll want to know what happened to him."

"Nah. Too many people missing. And like you said, he's got the syndrome. Besides, no one else in the world knows what's happening on Nalowale right now. Wheeler can do whatever he wants. So can we." Ronnie grinned and it made Lucas's stomach turn.

Even if the violent syndrome had already doomed Quinn Traynor to death, Lucas would not murder him. Neither was he about to let Ronnie do it.

A noise came from the other side of the barn. Ronnie didn't seem to hear it. Was Maria there already? Lucas had made a terrible mistake telling her she could come and pick up their car. He didn't want her anywhere near Ronnie. He waited a minute but heard nothing besides the shuffling noises his coworker made pacing back and forth. "I'll be back."

"Where are you going?" Ronnie asked.

Despite the question, Lucas could tell Ronnie wasn't interested in a response. "Taking a dump," he muttered.

Ronnie laughed. "You're always pissing and dumping, man."

Only as an excuse to get away from you.

Lucas walked toward the end of the road. He tried to reach Maria on his radio. No response. Maria was kind and hardworking. He shouldn't have told her to come here. He didn't want her to see something she couldn't unsee.

▼▲▼

"One of them left. He's walking down the road," Barstow whispered. "Stay here, Madeline. We need you to watch our backs." He faced Matthew. "Ready?"

Matthew nodded. "Let's go."

Barstow and Matthew ran from the side of the barn. Madeline got the gun from her bag and moved to the edge of the building so she could see what was happening. The Airmen had their pistols aimed at the guard with the blond hair before he could take his gun out.

"Don't move," Barstow screamed.

The guard made a move for his weapon.

247

Madeline cringed, closing her eyes as Barstow fired. Two shots. When she looked again, the guard was lying on the ground. Matthew approached him and kicked his weapon away.

Madeline ran over.

Matthew and Barstow stood looking around, their weapons readied. The other guard would have heard shots fired and would be back any second.

The guard was still alive, moaning on the ground.

"I don't think it's a fatal wound." Madeline pulled off her shirt and pressed it against the hole in his chest. She looked up, alert for the other guard's return. That's when she got her first glimpse inside the barn door. Someone was there, in the back. Tied to a chair. "Quinn?" She squinted and the figure became clearer. "Quinn!"

She couldn't let pressure off the wound if she wanted to save the guard, but she wanted to go to Quinn.

"I'll get him," Matthew said, jogging into the barn.

After Matthew untied him, Quinn stood and walked out, looking a little unsteady. A sheen of sweat coated his forehead. Blood and bruises covered his face.

"Oh, my God. Are you okay?" Madeline asked.

"Yeah. I still feel wired and disconnected, but guess what? I think the cigarettes work because my face hurts like hell."

"That's so great!" Madeline said.

She had a second to feel relief before Barstow shouted, "Stop right there!"

Lucas marched toward them on the path, with Ben by his side.

Oh, no! Please don't hurt Ben.

"Don't worry, don't worry." Ben broke into a run, coming toward Madeline and Quinn. "Lucas is on our side. He's not a bad guy."

Lucas dropped his gun and put his hands out. "No one else needs to get hurt," he said. "I never wanted anyone to get hurt."

CHAPTER TWENTY-EIGHT

Quinn paced around the firepit in Ben's backyard, inhaling on a cigarette.

"Stop moving for a minute so I can give you another dose of Narcan," Madeline said. "How are you feeling now?"

"Terrible. Hungover and high at the same time." When he lifted his arm, it was shaking. "My face and shoulder hurt."

"Yay!" Ben said, jumping around. "That means you're getting better."

Madeline checked his vitals. "Your pulse and blood pressure are down. All good signs. I know you want to storm Azure Cove with Barstow and his people, but I need you here, where I can monitor you. I do wonder what they'll find there."

"Ancient remains," Quinn said. "Must be the first settlers."

"That's what I figured. What I hoped. Except you didn't say *ancient bodies* or *skeletons* when you first told me. You just said bodies."

"Do I have a lot to apologize for? Because I'm really not sure what I told you, or what the excavators told me. Can't trust a hallucinating druggie, now can you?"

Madeline smiled, grateful Quinn could joke, and turned to Ben. "Come on. Let's go inside and try to find some food."

Ben climbed onto the kitchen countertop and got a box of mac and cheese from the cabinets. "How about this?"

"That looks good." Anything would have to do. As long as Quinn was getting better, she didn't care what she ate or where she ate it.

"So, we're all staying here tonight, right?" Ben asked.

"If you'll have us," she answered.

"Yes! And this time, no one will take Quinn and he won't die because he's getting better, right?

"Yes, Ben. I think he really is. And no one will take anyone else. Captain Barstow and the Air Force will make sure of it."

▼▲▼

Wearing protective gear in a misty drizzle, Quinn and Colonel Nelson walked the concrete walkway toward the bunker. Still coming down from the flood of invasive chemicals, a hungover feeling dwindled inside Quinn, though it dissipated with each passing hour. The Colonel understood exactly how Quinn was feeling. In the brief span of a day, the two men had developed a bond discussing and dissecting the insanity of their drugged-out ordeal. The experience even trumped their shared military backgrounds.

A strong breeze made the purple flowers tremble above the bunker.

"When did someone last go in here?" Quinn asked.

"Not since the tsunami hit. Despite the chaos on the island, my men and women kept up their patrol shifts. The inventory is safe." Nelson reached under the steel plate with his key and unlocked the padlock. He pulled on the door, dredging the bottom through filmy mud. It opened with a metallic groan and light spilled into the bunker.

A thin layer of foaming water coated the bunker's concrete floor.

"Not so impervious after all," Nelson murmured. "It wasn't like that before the tsunami. The last check of this bunker noted moisture and mildew, but that was all. Must be cracks in the concrete somewhere under the pallets."

On the other side of the bunker, building materials, worn sacks, and smaller crates littered the ground in no semblance of order.

Colonel Nelson opened the top of the first massive crate. They looked in on exactly what they expected to see—a 250-pound Mark 81 general-purpose bomb surrounded by a wooden framework. Nicknamed Firecracker. The smallest of the Mark 80 series.

After consulting the inventory list, Quinn turned to a stack of much smaller crates. "These contain the inert chemical shells. Let's move a crate outside so we can look at it."

Working together, their breath loud and wheezy behind their masks, they each lifted one end of a crate. Its rotten bottom fell away, and a metal canister tumbled out. Quinn braced himself for an explosion, but nothing happened except the dented and rusted canister clattering against the floor. A skull and crossbones symbol marked the canister's peeling placard. Under that, a date: November, 1938.

Quinn would bet anything that he knew what was inside the damaged canisters, and they weren't empty like it said on the inventory list. "I think these containers are the source of what's making everyone crazy. It appears we beat Germany to developing what was supposed to be a super-power serum."

Colonel Nelson stared at liquid droplets on the rusted metal. "If some of my men and Tank were exposed to this serum before the tsunami, that explains why they were acting wired, but then they recovered. But how did it spread all the way into town and get caught up with the virus?"

Madeline sat on a bench next to Nate. She held her handwritten notes and a pen. The largest tree on the hospital lawn enveloped them with shade.

"I feel like crap," Nate said. "Like the worst headache and the worst hangover ever." He was emotionally and physically exhausted, dehydrated, and yet he smiled. "But that's nothing compared to what I felt like two days ago. That was a nightmare, and I can hardly believe I survived it. Who would have thought cigarettes or nicotine, whatever it is, could fix us? Can't thank all of you enough. You and Matthew and Dr. Wilcox. All the nurses. And Maria."

Madeline smiled. "Now that you're thinking more clearly, you can thank us by answering my questions despite your headache. Ready?"

"Go for it."

"Did you experience any symptoms before the tsunami hit?"

He closed his eyes in concentration. "No. I don't think so."

"Tell me where you were before having symptoms."

"I didn't leave the base during the week. I was on patrol."

"Can you elaborate for me?"

"We have defined routes around the perimeter of the base. The routes take us past the bunkers. Twelve of us make the rounds on every shift. We're spread apart in groups of two. Half drive. Half on foot."

"When did you leave the base?"

"Soon as we got word about the tsunami damage on the south shore. I headed straight there with a bunch of Airmen. I was part of rescue efforts right until I picked you up at the airport and brought you to Azure Cove."

"Were you mostly in one specific location? Or all around the south shore?"

Nate trailed his finger over the nicotine patch on his arm. "I was mostly on Market Street. What was left of The Mercantile, The Fresh Mart, The Pharmacy. After rescuing people, we tried to salvage products in case we ended up short on food and supplies."

"Was anyone handing out food or water there, that you recall?"

"No. Actually, we went a long time without eating or drinking anything."

Madeline continued through her list of questions, including, "Did you spend any time at Azure Cove? On the property?"

"I've dropped people off there from the base, like I did with you. Never walked around the resort or anything like that."

Madeline jotted down the last bit of information and looked up. "Thank you, Nate. That's really helpful. And I'm glad you're feeling better."

"Yeah, so am I. I never want to go through *that* again. Thank you again for helping us."

As Nate walked away, Madeline scanned her notes. Now that the patients were coherent, not drugged out of their minds and spouting paranoid theories, she had confidence in the information they provided. It was time to find out what that data had to say about the outbreak. Based on the day's interviews so far, Nate was the eighth patient who had functioned as a first responder at the south shore. Colonel Nelson made nine. And Martina had been working in the pharmacy there. The Market Street location, particularly the west side, was fast emerging as statistically significant.

In the back of his office, Colonel Nelson unlocked an old armoire-style cabinet and removed a stack of crumbling charts. Holding the edges with the tips of his fingers, he unfolded one and gently spread it over his desk. Flecks of dust floated into the air as he leaned his hands on either side of the yellowing paper and stared down at the map. "Someone created these drawings long before we built the base. This one encompasses most of the property." He scanned the latitude and longitude lines, then hovered his finger over a southeast point. "The bunker with the leaking canisters should be right around here."

"What's this?" Quinn asked, looking at the dotted line connecting the bunker's location to the south shore. "A trail? I don't remember a trail there."

"There isn't one. Maybe there used to be, but not anymore." Nelson blinked at the map's legend. "I can't read the key. It's faded."

When Nelson straightened, Quinn leaned into the unoccupied space and tried to decipher the legend. "I can't make it out either. What lies at the other end of that dotted line now?"

"That's where Market Street begins." Nelson walked to the cabinet, returned with a magnifying glass, and held it over the old paper. He squinted, closed his eyes, then squinted again. "It says aqueduct. The dotted line represents an aqueduct. An old underground tunnel. Maybe a pipeline for drinking water?"

"We need to follow the coordinates and find out exactly what's there," Quinn said.

They left the base and drove in a misty rain. Sun peaked out from behind clouds and a rainbow appeared over the road. Near the south shore, they got out and walked to the same location where the dotted line stopped on the map. The floodwaters had receded, leaving behind the tsunami's carnage.

"Here it is," Quinn said, standing with Colonel Nelson at one end of Market Street amidst debris. "That old aqueduct ends underground right here."

Nelson looked around. "It makes sense to me now. When the tsunami hit, the floodwater mixed with the drug serum leaking from the canisters in the bunker. The mixture traveled down the old tunnel and into Market Street."

"And somewhere in the floodwater, the virus was waiting," Quinn added.

An electronic chirping sound came from Quinn's backpack, startling him. Something he hadn't heard since they arrived on the island. It was his phone, notifying him of a message. The noise repeated, one electronic chime after another as his messages poured in.

Communications were back.

CHAPTER TWENTY-NINE

Sitting at Ben's kitchen table, Madeline finished checking her emails and moved on to check her phone messages. Beside her, Quinn tapped his own keyboard. Ben was outside on the couch, reading a book about the universe.

Madeline's satellite phone battery was almost dead from talking for hours with her colleagues at the CDC. She was using her personal phone now—roaming charges be damned—she'd worry about those when they got back to Atlanta. Loss of communications had worried Patrick Wallen. Though the situation wasn't his fault, he'd apologized profusely. Once he and others at the CDC learned the specifics of Nalowale's outbreak, Madeline had dozens of messages with questions and advice.

She had to go back several days to find the calls and texts from Fred, the kitchen contractor. She played the final one now.

"Neither you nor Quinn have returned my calls or responded to my texts," Fred said, his irritation coming across loud and clear. "I can't proceed without hearing from you. I have other clients waiting. You've left me no choice but to move on to my next project."

From what Madeline could glean from Fred's previous messages, nothing had happened with the kitchen in their absence. Nothing. And she didn't care. Quinn was okay. That's all that mattered. As she counted her blessings, he caught her staring at him. He sat back in his chair and smiled.

"How are you feeling?" Madeline asked, well aware she sounded like a broken record or a song with an irritating repeated chorus. Even though Quinn was acting like himself, only three days had passed since he was dangerously close to death.

"I feel great." His eyes twinkled, which meant he was excited about something.

"Great? You sure about that?"

"Well, not great. You know. More normal. Listen, I think I found what I was looking for."

"What were you looking for?"

"Remember when we were talking about bringing something home with us? Something to remember the island by?"

"Yes."

"What I've found is going to make leaving a whole lot easier."

▼▲▼

Under a clear sky on Colonel Nelson's porch, with the sun descending on the horizon, Quinn stared out over a grassy area of the base. It was no longer a ghost town. Now that the outbreak was under control, he could see Airmen coming in and out of their barracks.

Madeline sat nearby in one of Nelson's patio chairs, between Matthew and Grace. Captain Barstow handed her a beer and grabbed another for Quinn.

"Not tonight," he said. It might be a long time before he wanted drugs of any sort in his body, other than the patch dispersing a small but steady stream of nicotine into his system. Madeline wanted him to wear the patch for a few more days to eliminate any last traces of the virus and the drugs.

A melancholy mood descended as they remembered deceased loved ones, friends, and coworkers. Some taken by the tsunami. Some from the outbreak.

Quinn left the group and walked over to Ben, who was playing with a German Shorthaired Pointer. The boy heaved a ball across the green and the dog raced after it.

"You've been at that for a long time," Quinn said. "You're going to have a sore arm tomorrow."

Ben rubbed his shoulder and laughed. "Nah, I'm not giving up until he does. He loves it."

"Mind if I have a turn?"

"Sure. I bet you can throw really far."

"I used to."

When the dog returned, Quinn picked up the ball and drew his arm back for the throw. The discomfort was immediate, making him acutely aware he'd recently dislocated his shoulder. He welcomed that normality. Bringing his arm back down to his side, he said, "Changed my mind. Instead of going for far, I'm going for accuracy. Think I can hit that flagpole?"

"Yes! Try it."

Quinn lined up his throw, then let the ball fly. It nailed the pole with a solid thwack as the dog raced after it.

"You did it!" Ben yelled.

Quinn watched Ben give it a few tries, always coming short of the pole. "Don't give up, kid. If not today, there's always tomorrow. And if not tomorrow, don't worry. No reason you need to hit a pole to live a good life." Quinn tousled Ben's hair before returning to the group.

Quinn sat down next to Grace. "I contacted a society Heidi worked with in Maine," Grace said. "Archaeologists are coming from several groups to study the remains at Azure Cove. They'll finish the work she started."

"That reminds me—," Quinn said, still watching Ben, "— based on something Ben told me, I figured his mother got fired because she ditched Wheeler's sexual advances. Now I think otherwise. She was on the island's historic committee. I bet Wheeler thought he got rid of her in time…but he didn't. She'd found something while she was there. An ancient coin. She planned to bring it to Mitch. If it weren't for the tsunami, I think they would have exposed Wheeler."

"We had him in custody for a few days until his attorney arrived," Nelson said. "He didn't speak to anyone. Then he was whisked off to somewhere on the mainland. The future of Azure Cove is uncertain."

"I'm sure the complex will still open. Eventually. The shareholders will see to that." Matthew took a drink from his beer. "Just not with Wheeler in charge. Attempting to conceal a historic discovery wasn't the best PR strategy, now that it's all out in the open."

"Neither was having his guards kidnap and beat up my fiancé," Madeline added.

"That too," Matthew agreed.

"Not to mention that Wheeler's failure to follow the National Historical Preservation Policy when he discovered those remains means imprisonment and millions in fines," Grace added.

It was getting dark when Quinn finally exchanged glances with Madeline and stood to go. "Well, everyone, it's been a wild ride."

Colonel Nelson got up. "Air Force versus Army next year. You still game? We can go together but sit on opposite sides."

"You bet." Quinn shook the Colonel's hand.

"We'll be in touch," Grace said to Madeline.

"Absolutely." Madeline responded.

"Safe flight tomorrow," Matthew said as Quinn and Madeline made their last goodbyes.

CHAPTER THIRTY

The smell of warm chocolate chip cookies filled Madeline's kitchen as she opened one of the dark cabinet doors and grabbed a large plate. No, she didn't have the gleaming white cabinets with the simple silver pulls she'd selected, or the white quartz countertops with the wispy gray lines that made them look like marble. And that was okay. The dated kitchen no longer bothered her. Especially not when someone told her it was the biggest and most beautiful kitchen he'd ever seen.

The contractor had installed all the new appliances. The rest of the kitchen could wait.

She scooped the cookies off the baking sheet and slid them onto the plate. The garage door went up so smoothly that she might not have heard it if Maddie hadn't jumped up barking and galloped to the door. Footsteps clopped against the mudroom floor. Madeline's mother entered the kitchen first, followed by Ben.

"Welcome home." Madeline always had a big smile for the child.

Mrs. Hamilton put her hand on Ben's shoulder. "Someone had a good day at school."

Ben nodded as he unzipped his backpack. "Yep. We talked about immune systems in science class. I knew *a lot* of stuff."

Madeline gave him a hug. "I'll bet you did."

Ben set his lunchbox on the counter and grabbed a handful of cookies. "I'm going up to my room to start my homework."

"Sounds like a good plan. I'll let you know when Quinn comes home and dinner is ready. It won't be long."

Ben jogged out of the room and up the stairs.

Mrs. Hamilton watched him go, then turned to her daughter. "He's a great kid."

"He is," Madeline replied. "I'm grateful we were able to get him a good therapist for ongoing counseling. It must be helping."

"What happened when you spoke to his father's family?"

"They want to meet him. They sounded genuinely excited. They want to be involved, but also made it clear they aren't in a position to care for him, which is great news for Quinn and I."

"Any more news on the adoption front?"

Madeline shook her head as she picked up a cookie and bit into it. "No, but thank goodness Quinn found out about the emergency foster license. Don't forget, Ben's only been with us a few months. The longer we foster him, the better the chance of the adoption going through."

"Good. Because I couldn't stand for all of us to lose him."

"I know." Madeline gazed into the living room at the beautiful portrait of Ben and his mother. They'd brought it back with them and hung it up in a prominent position. "He's lost enough already. Surely the adoption agency will see it that way. Plus, he really wants to be with us. He's going to be the ring bearer when we get married. I bought him a suit yesterday."

"You and Quinn are lucky."

Madeline smiled. "You have no idea how lucky, mom."

"Everything going okay with work?"

"Yes." Madeline picked up the plate of cookies and offered it to her mother. "With this new research, I won't be traveling for a long while. I've got a big presentation tomorrow."

"What about?"

"The virus."

▲ ▼ ▲

Madeline set her hands down on either side of the podium and stared out at the gathering of her CDC colleagues. Her computer projected the title of her presentation onto the wall behind her. *Epidemiology, Evolution, and Pathogenesis of the N-1 Herculean Virus in One Epidemic Wave.* The slides represented the results of her research since returning to Atlanta.

"Thank you for coming. Four months ago, I began researching an outbreak caused by a previously unidentified virus. We've named it the N-1 Herculean Virus. It's the first in a new genus of Herculean viruses. Essentially, super viruses, capable of replicating in ways previously unimagined."

Madeline glanced at her notes.

"An earthquake may have unleashed the virus from beneath the ocean's floor, or it was there all along. As you know, there are more viruses in the ocean than stars in our galaxy. Even one milliliter of ocean water can contain up to ten million different viruses. Mutations occur every day at warp speed, and it only takes one random mutation to enable infection of a human host. I believe the pathogen spread inland via a rogue wave. Alone, the virus was relatively harmless. Those infected with only the virus in its simplest form suffered mild to zero symptoms—mouth lesions and a mild impairment of liver function. Alone, we might not have registered the existence of this virus. But it wasn't alone. The virus combined with a toxic chemical mixture that had leaked into floodwater. And here's where the virus differentiated itself from others and earned the Herculean title: the virus encapsulated the chemical mixture inside its membrane, rendering the infected unable to metabolize the compounds. Reduced hepatic function intensified the virus's effects. The combination proved fatal. Those plagued by the virus and the replicating chemicals suffered a complete mental and physical deterioration. The breakdown was swift, with patients dying within six to eight days after exposure."

One of her colleagues raised his hand and said, "I'm not following. Please rephrase." His request didn't surprise her. Dr. Schmidt often asked for clarification to make sure he missed nothing.

"A spike protein on the virus attached to a foreign substance, in this outbreak, a mixture of toxic chemicals," Madeline said. "The virus replicated its own genetic material…and the chemicals."

She scanned faces for their reactions.

"That's impossible," someone murmured.

Rather than ignore the comment, Madeline smiled. "We thought so as well until we had the proof. Further controlled studies prove the virus can replicate organic and inorganic substances within its host's cells." She took a sip of water, letting her colleagues ponder the implications. "The possibilities may be endless."

Madeline crossed the stage and stared out at the audience of scientists.

Dr. Sun raised his arm. "Were you able to control the virus? Or did it have a hundred percent mortality rate?"

"We got lucky in finding its kryptonite…so to speak."

"What was it?" Dr. Sun asked.

"A familiar substance." She took another sip of water, allowing them to speculate before answering. She couldn't help drawing out the drama. The information she presented was groundbreaking. It deserved to be showcased grandly. She smiled before telling them. "Nicotine."

Murmurs rose from the group.

"Nicotine is already being used in clinical research trials for treatment of Parkinson's disease, ADHD, dementia, depression and sarcoma. The N-1 Herculean Virus patients were first given cigarettes and snuff tobacco, then controlled levels of nicotine through dermal patches and nasal sprays. All forms of nicotine replacement therapies were effective at killing the viruses. All forms of nicotine replacement therapies were effective at killing the viruses. After a short period of withdrawal type symptoms, hepatic functions returned to normal, and the patients fully recovered." Madeline couldn't help but smile. "We do not know the limits of the virus' capabilities. From here on out, we'll be testing scenarios for which replication creates a positive effect for its host." Finished with her notes, she tapped the side of her papers to align them. "With that, I'd like to welcome any of you to join a new Herculean Virus Task Force I'll be heading up. Are there any questions?"

Everyone's hand went up.

Madeline pointed to one of her colleagues in the front row.

"Where did this occur?" the research doctor asked.

"An isolated community. I'm not at liberty to be more specific." Madeline registered her colleague's undisguised disappointment and quickly took another question.

"Which chemicals did the virus replicate?" a woman asked.

"Again, I'm not able to disclose that specific information. It's classified. But I can send all of you my research which includes a list of substances the virus has successfully replicated in our laboratory studies."

The woman frowned, as did those around her, their curiosity unsatisfied.

Wishing she wasn't bound by nondisclosure agreements, Madeline signaled to another person with his hand raised.

"I'm stunned by what you've told us," he said. "So many thoughts here. For one, if the virus encounters the wrong mix of chemicals or compounds, it could produce catastrophic results in a natural environment. How transmissible was the infection?"

CHAPTER THIRTY-ONE

Russian military base in Siberia

Nikolai kicked the snow off his boots and entered the shack. Inside, Aleksandr stood with his hands on his hips over his thick parka. Head bobbing, he exuded a youthful energy Nikolai rarely felt anymore.

"You're late," Aleksandr said. "What's the matter? Not up to another exciting day of guarding Putin's weapons?"

"I'm barely late and these aren't Putin's weapons." Nikolai laughed as he gestured toward the window. It was so coated with film he could barely see the bunkers outside. "Those weapons are over eighty years old. They're Stalin's. You don't know a lick of history, do you?"

The younger soldier shrugged. "I know enough. At least it's not as cold today. I could see the ice melting. Perhaps a woolly mammoth will emerge from the prehistoric ice. That would bust your boredom in a big way."

Nikolai laughed. "Don't hold your breath for a woolly mammoth. Anything in that ice is microbial. Although, if we were to find something, even a small bone I suppose…that could make our fortunes." The ice rumbled and cracked as he placed his book and a package on the table, then tossed his gloves down after them. "My wife made sweet buns. Have one before you go."

"Thanks, but I'm going to pass. Haven't had any appetite all day." Aleksandr headed to the door. "Tell your wife I loved them. Tell her I ate two and they're the best sweet buns I've ever had." He grinned. "I'm out of here. Start of my vacation travels, you know? With my brother."

"That's right. You enjoy yourself, Aleksandr. Don't you or your brother cause too much trouble."

Aleksandr rocked on his feet, head still bobbing. "I have a good feeling something exciting will happen to us. Just a feeling." As he put on his gloves, the young man burst into song, putting his words to a mismatched tune. "I'm leaving, da-do-do, on a trans-Siberian train for Moscow." He laughed. "Midnight train to Georgia. You've heard it?"

"Wish I had your energy," Nikolai said.

"Less of your wife's cooking and stop smoking," Aleksandr said with his rakish grin. "I do feel invincible today. Must be all the fresh air from shoveling slush away from the bunkers." Aleksandr waved and left. From outside, he turned and saluted Nikolai through the window before jogging, almost skipping, through the melting sludge.

Only yards away, inside a bunker, old chemicals leaked from rusting canisters with skulls and crossbones. The chemicals mingled with the melting permafrost and the prehistoric viruses it contained...searching for another viable host.

The End

NOTE FROM THE AUTHOR

If this is your first FBI & CDC Thriller, you might not know it's part of a series. I wrote the books so readers could read them alone without confusion. Each features a unique epidemiology or terrorist investigation which resolves at the end. Madeline and Quinn's personal stories continue from novel to novel.

ONLY WRONG ONCE

Two mysterious deaths: one in LA, one in Boston, each with the same horrific symptoms.

In Los Angeles, FBI Counterterrorism Agent Quinn Traynor receives an urgent call from CDC Agent, Madeline Hamilton. She's discovered the first victim of a lethal, unfamiliar virus. Their joint investigation uncovers an imminent bio-terror attack, and their only hope is to identify the terrorists carrying the disease. With just two days remaining before it's too late, the FBI and the CDC race to prevent a pandemic. The ensuing nightmare will hit closer to home than they ever expected, and one of them will pay an unimaginable price for protecting the country.

PRAISE FOR ONLY WRONG ONCE:

"ABSOLUTELY. POSITIVELY. FABULOUS."

"From the moment I read the first page I was captivated. I recommend this story if you enjoy Tom Clancy like suspense."-International Bestselling Author Kelly Abell

"Stunning, terrifying, and unforgettable."- Dennis Carrigan, Author of *Memphis 1873*

"*Only Wrong Once* seizes the reader's attention from page one and holds on until the very end . . .This thrilling and horrifying tale is a must read."- Karen D. Scioscia, Journalist and Author of *Kidnapped by the Cartel*

"Jenifer Ruff has done a magnificent job of intertwining heart-pounding international intrigue with the personal triumphs and tragedies faced by the men and women of Homeland Security." - James Charles Boatner, Author of *Red Pawn*

"The story is riveting, the characters are well drawn, and the plot moves at break-neck speed. Be prepared to be mesmerized." - Reita Pendry, Author of *China White*.

"Jenifer Ruff does an outstanding job of weaving personal stories in the lives of the characters amidst the action. This book will keep you glued to the pages from the beginning to end, wondering what will happen next." - Susan Mills Wilson, Author of *Hunt for Redemption*

ONLY ONE CURE

The President's only child is dying. Terrorists claim to have the cure.

When a private plane whisks CDC epidemiologist Madeline Hamilton to Washington D.C. for an urgent medical symposium, she knows something significant is underway—but she doesn't expect to face the most disturbing medical mystery of her career. A debilitating neurological toxin has stricken the children of several political families, and one of them is the son of U.S. President Anna Moreland.

With the lives of children on the line, Madeline assembles a team of medical experts. The investigation takes a horrifying turn when she receives communications from the terrorists, who want to engage in a deadly political game.

Desperate to find the perpetrators and a cure, the White House recruits FBI antiterror specialist Quinn Traynor to run a parallel investigation. As the teenagers start dying and the answers seem no closer, Madeline and Quinn fight to prevail before President Moreland is forced to make an impossible choice: give in to the terrorists' demands or let her only child succumb to an agonizing death.

PRAISE FOR ONLY ONE CURE:

"Dark and intense, filled with twists and suspense. *Only One Cure* will grab you on page one and not let go. Another winner from Jenifer Ruff!" – USA Today Bestselling Author, Dan Alatorre

"In *Only One Cure*, Jenifer Ruff weaves another suspenseful tale featuring the expertise of her relatable characters. As the stakes are raised, we're taken on an incredible journey. Ruff's narrative demands we read on!" - Author, Allison Maruska

Reviewers:

"OMG! Love it! And did it scare the heck out of me. "
"Loved it! Super engaging, I could hardly stop reading."
"A brilliant read!"
"This book is outstanding!!"
"A true page turner…maintaining suspense until the very end."

BOOKS BY JENIFER RUFF

The Agent Victoria Heslin Series
The Numbers Killer
Pretty Little Girls
When They Find Us
Ripple of Doubt
The Groom Went Missing

The FBI & CDC Thriller Series
Only Wrong Once
Only One Cure
Only One Wave: The Tsunami Effect

The Brooke Walton Series
Everett
Rothaker
The Intern

Suspense
Lauren's Secret

ABOUT THE AUTHOR

USA Today bestselling author Jenifer Ruff writes mysteries and medical thrillers in three series: The Agent Victoria Heslin Series, The Brooke Walton Series, and The FBI & CDC Thriller Series.

Jenifer grew up in Massachusetts, has a biology degree from Mount Holyoke College and a Master's in Public Health and Epidemiology from Yale University. Before discovering her love of writing, she worked in management consulting for PriceWaterhouseCoopers and IBM Business Consulting.

Jenifer lives in Charlotte, NC with her family and a pack of greyhounds. If she's not writing, she's probably out exploring trails with her dogs.

Sign up for her Reader's Newsletter at Jenruff.com and never miss a new release or promotion.

Made in the USA
Coppell, TX
11 March 2022

74844812R00166